THE DINOSAUR BITE

THE
DINOSAUR
BITE

a novel by
Ruth Moore

WILLIAM MORROW AND COMPANY, INC.
NEW YORK   1976

Printed in the United States of America.

1 2 3 4 5   80 79 78 77 76

Library of Congress Cataloging in Publication Data

Moore, Ruth.
   The dinosaur bite.

   I. Title.
PZ3.M7867Di [PS3525.05666]   813'.5'2   75-37831
ISBN 0-688-03021-1

BOOK DESIGN: H. ROBERTS

"The way to be safe from dinosaur bites is to be little, fast, furry, warm-blooded and smart."

—STEWART BRAND, in
The Last Whole Earth Catalog

THE DINOSAUR BITE

PART ONE

A field mouse, beguiled by moonlight and the mild May night, had come out to forage on the edge of Bess Bowden's corn patch, and was caught and eaten by an old one-eyed raccoon. The coon, who had raided the corn patch last fall, found it now a muddy waste into which a hefty animal like herself might sink to her belly. It had been a fine place last September, but the unholy mess of smashed-down stalks and half-eaten ears had been tilled in long ago—not even a kernel or two, pumped up by the frost, had come out of the ground, not a smell of corn about it now. She waddled along to the grass verge of the patch, where the mouse moved a split second too late.

The larger of her two kittens, seeing his mother crunching something, charged in to see if there might be enough for two. He was a lordly male, half again as big as his brother, used to twice his share of anything, and big enough now not to have to worry about competition from his brother. The other, born runty and small, stayed well back out of reach. He was skittish and skinny but experienced in survival, having been slapped down too many times not to be. He squatted and watched to see what next. What next was his mother took a sideways swipe at his fat brother and knocked him tail over tip.

The old coon was worn out and desperate for food herself. She had been a devoted mother to many litters over her span of years, defending them from dogs and hunters and other dangers to small young, knowledgeable about ledge crevices and hollow trees where they could be hidden away, but she had had bad trouble with this latest batch. Two had been born dead; she had not been able to feed the remaining two and had had to bring them out foraging earlier in the season than was safe. A week ago she had had a knock-down-drag-out with a big coon dog who had tried to kill them. She had lost an eye then and was still stiff and sore from the battle. It might be said that she had had it with motherhood, but she wasn't giving up. Not yet. She knew one more place she could try.

A hundred yards away across the mown hayfield, between a house and barn, were two chickadee feeders full of sunflower seeds. Long ago she had figured out how to get into bird feeders at the top of poles. Climb the pole, ease over the baffle—which was for squirrels anyway—work at the feeder until it came loose from its fastenings and fell to the ground. Nine times out of ten it had a glass front which smashed.

She moved to the edge of the field and stared across the dark stubble, turning her head this way and that as she studied what, if anything, might be loose tonight to hurt coons. There seemed to be nothing.

The little coon lagged his usual safe distance behind as the other two started toward the house. He sniffed at a vague taint in the air, sour and mean, but his mother was going, so it must be all right. The moon rolled overhead, in and out of puffy clouds. His shadow played now-you-see-me-now-you-don't. He followed along sedately and arrived at the bird feeders just in time to see his brother take off in a flying leap and land two feet up one of the poles. The small coon couldn't do that. He'd have to wait and see what came down. There might be a few mouthfuls of something.

What came down was his brother, who slid down faster than he had gone up. He landed on his chin with a cracking thump, lay there for a moment; then he sat back and stared at the pole in amazement. His mother hadn't jumped, but she had got two paws on the pole before she'd smelt the axle grease. This was new; she'd never run into a greased pole before. She gave up at once, went over to the birds' watering pan and washed her paws, scrubbing them together in the water.

Over in the woods behind the corn patch, Leafy Piper took his hand off the collar of his big coon dog and said, "Okay, Willie, go git'em!" Leafy had been watching the coons from the time they had come into the field; he could have let Willie loose then, if he had wanted to. But what was the fun of a coon hunt over too soon? Let the critters get a head start, give the dog a chance to use his smeller. Willie had a dandy—he was the best coon dog in the whole damn state, and he needed exercise, a good long hoot'n' holler through the underbrush. Let him run'em till they treed, then he himself could follow along with his gun, have his fun, too.

Willie took off with a leap that landed him ten feet out from the thicket. Moved like a flash of black lightning, so he done. Leafy came along, his shotgun in the crook of his arm.

The two coons under the bird feeders melted like shadows into the bushes at the edge of the yard. The little coon started to follow, but he couldn't tell which way they'd gone and the dog was close. An empty bucket lay on its side by the doorstep. He dived headlong into it, huddled there, shivering.

Willie took the scent from under the bird feeders and went on by. He crashed into the underbrush with a noise like a falling tree. Leafy, hustling now, didn't notice the bucket. He planted a foot on it and it rolled, sending him sprawling. The bucket clanked against the house doorstep, dumping out the little coon, who, too crazy-scared now to do anything but run in any direction, fled up the step, managed to jump to the windowsill, and clawed his way up the screen.

Bess Bowden, already waked up by the racket, snapped on the outside light in time to see him silhouetted against it, with Leafy Piper climbing the steps. She yanked open the back door.

"Now, look here, Leafy," she said. "You know I've asked you not to hunt on my land. You round up that black hound and hustle him off the premises."

"Ask away," Leafy said. "Just let me haul that little varmint down off'n your screen."

"You come a step nearer and I'll call Martin."

"Oh, shove it," Leafy said. He stopped, cocked an ear in the direction of the woods, where Willie's raving hysteria was telling him that the coons had treed and the sooner he got there the better. "You better git that feller out of sight before we come back through here or Willie'll make short work of him. Take him to bed with ya, at least you'd have something." He made off fast across the yard, picked his way through the bushes, and vanished in the underbrush.

Bess's brother, Martin, standing inside the door, said, "You want me to go out and put a tin ear on him?"

Bess laughed. "Lord, no. I've been a widow too long to mind that kind of foolishness."

"I take it he's in his spring flood," Martin said.

"Oh, yes. His sap always rises with the sap in the maple trees. I don't think he can help it."

"Well, he'll get some of it tapped if I catch him around here nights again," Martin said. "What was he up to, anyway?"

Bess indicated the small dark shape at the top of the

window screen. "Hunting coon on our back doorstep," she said.

"I'll be darned." Martin came out on the step, his bare toes curling a little against the dew-damp doormat. "Look what we've got here. Hi, fella. Come on down. You're among friends."

With his long arms and his six feet of height, he had no trouble reaching the coon, but it took a moment to pry loose the small claws hooked desperately into the screen.

"Come on, unlax," Martin said. "I don't want to break your toenails off. Hah, here we are."

The coon flapped its legs feebly, making running motions against Martin's hands. Then it lay still.

"It looks dead," Bess said, peering.

"Might as well be. Poor little duffer's nothing but skin over bones." He turned the creature over on its back, ran his fingers through the soft fur of its belly. "Half-starved, he is."

Off in the woods, not far away, two blasts of a shotgun, one closely following the other, announced the end of Leafy's hunt. The coon twitched and made an openmouthed grab at Martin's fingers.

Martin snatched his hand away just in time. "Well, he's far from dead. Seems it takes a sixty-pound dog and a double-barreled shotgun to clobber one of these."

"Bring him into the kitchen, where it's warm. I'm going to warm up some bread and milk."

"Un-hunh. No way. Account of fleas. He's probably loaded. You'd better let me put him out of his misery, hadn't you?"

"No, I hadn't." Bess started for the door. "We'll feed him and fix a bed in the workshop. I'll be out with a dish of stuff in a minute."

"Chuck me my slippers, then. I'm not about to stagger out there barefooted." He grinned down at the coon while he waited for his footgear, which presently came flying through the doorway. "Likely you'll survive to bust up a number of corn patches," he said. "Doesn't really make sense to start you going again, bud."

He did, though. When he and Bess left the workshop, the coon, fed full, was curled up in the woodbox on an old fleece-lined jacket.

As they neared the house, Leafy loomed up in the moonlight. The two dead coons, held by their hind legs, dangled from his hand. Willie, stepping high, followed at his heels.

"I want t'other one," he announced. "Where is it?"

"Where you won't find it," Bess said.

"Won't, hey? You let me turn Willie loose, he'll find it."

"You bug off," Martin said. "You've done enough killing for one night."

"You object to killing? Seems as if being in the Marines would've learnt you different. Or didn't you git to do any in Veet Nam?"

"Could be," Martin said quietly.

Leafy backed a little away from him. "Never meant that mean," he said. "Far as I know, you done good in the war. Bess, I'll be riding up to the Harbor on your mail trip tomorrow. Thought I'd let you know."

Bess said, "Why don't you ride Willie? He looks big enough." She went into the house and shut the door.

"What ails her? She runs a public carrier, don't she? If she won't take me, she'll be outside the law."

"Leafy," Martin said cheerfully, "how would you like to be bounced up and down a couple times?"

Leafy backed still farther away. "Don't you touch me! You better not. I got Willie here. He'll show you a trick or two."

"Trick or treat," Martin said. "Tell him to play the trick and see what I'll do."

Martin Hadley had never been a man to fool with, and no knowing what devilment he'd learnt in the Marines. Leafy made off hastily, telling himself that them Hadleys had always been high-diddles, from Old Man Hadley on down, and that took in Bess, too. You'd think a widder woman would look on it as a favor if a man wanted to take a ride with her in that logy old Friendship sloop. But did she? No. Likely she'd charge him a quarter for it and treat him like dirt. Well, he had a few rights left. He'd walk straight across their goddamn hayfield and take the shortcut home, instead of going around by the road.

Martin went into the house, chuckling to himself. Poor old Leafy, he'd run a mile if you so much as blew your breath at him.

"You take a poke at him?" Bess asked.

"Lord, no. He'd come apart like a mess of jackstraws."

"You wouldn't want to take chances with Willie, though. He's pure poison. Most people don't dare to go near Leafy's cove, down there, on account of Willie. What are you going to do, take a bath?"

He was looking over the week's laundry, hung on a wall rack to air. "Didn't I see some clean pajamas on here? Yes, I did. I don't want to tack a mess of fleabites onto what Mary's already got to contend with. She's one uncomfortable gal right now. I almost wonder if it's all right for her to go with you tomorrow. What if it blows? Ring around the moon tonight might mean a change in the weather."

Bess laughed. "I'll hit the tide rip on slack tide, both ways. Mary ain't due for a month yet. She's a good strong girl and she's not likely to lose her stopper ahead of time. Besides, if the weather changes, she'll know enough not to go, so don't be a fussbudget."

"I wish you'd get something besides that old sloop to haul mail and freight in, if you're going to keep on with it," he grumbled. "Now I'm home, you know you don't have to."

"What would I do? Haul up the old *Daisy* and get me a powerboat?"

"I know. You wouldn't know how to handle one. So *you* say."

"The *Daisy* and me make out all right. We took you back and forth to high school in town in worse winter weather than anything we'll see tomorrow, remember. You've been away too long, Marty."

"I wasn't any eight months along," Martin said, grinning at her. "You're just as stubborn as you were when I left. Haven't changed a particle."

"No reason to. You have a notion of when Otis Baker'll be back in the town office? I've got my tax bill, but I'm not going to pay any money over to Florence."

"No? You're a hard woman. You think Flo fritzes up the town books? I guess she could, she's Town Treasurer, but she'd have to be in cahoots with someone, wouldn't she?"

"I've got no proof of anything whatever," Bess said. "I just make a practice of paying the tax money to Otis. You may find it sensible to when you begin paying taxes on your own house."

"I spoke to Oat out on the Shoals today," Martin said. He went on soberly. "He said he'd be back in the office tomorrow. Told me the Coast Guard man said we might as well quit looking. I guess he's right. Don't see what more we can do. Whatever's left of McCarren's outfit has got to be washed out to sea by now."

For a week, Otis Baker, who was Town Constable as well as Tax Collector, had had crews out helping the Coast Guard scour coves and beaches of offshore islands for bodies or survivors from a boating accident, in which a man and four of his five children had been lost. Since the first day, when a Cove fisherman had come on McCarren's boat adrift on Cross Island Shoals with one child, a little girl, washing around in it unconscious, nothing had been found. The coast people were still in a state of shock, and shock, Bess guessed, was what ailed Martin, started him fussing about her and the *Daisy*. The Friendship sloop was a part of his childhood, as familiar to him as an old shoe and safe as a church—at least, in any weather that might show up tomorrow morning, the way the barometer was now.

"We'll be well ballasted down," she said, hoping to comfort him. "There'll be the mail, and I've got lists as long as my arm. Folks are low on hen and cowfeed for one thing. Fifty- and hundred-pound bags. They'll help. But I doubt if Mary'll go, if you ask her not to."

Martin had started for the bathroom, but he turned now and came back. "It's not just Mary," he said. He put a hand on her shoulder, gave it a gentle squeeze. She looked up at him, surprised. People who loved each other didn't need to let on about it, but it was nice when somebody did.

He said, "I don't ever want to have to scrape you out of the rockweed is all." He went off, and the way the water started to thunder into the bathtub, he'd turned on both faucets so that he wouldn't hear any reply she made to that.

He's thinking about Joe, she thought. And he knows I liked Will McCarren.

Joe Bowden, her husband, had had to be scraped out of the rockweed. He had been the mail carrier from the Cove up to Wentworth Harbor, the nearest town six miles away, running the same kind of public convenience then as she was doing now. Joe had been drowned out of a powerboat, not out of a Friendship sloop. His boat had swamped—at least, you had to guess it had. No sign of her had ever been found. It had happened on a December day when flood tide was meeting head on with a roaring northeast gale, out in the tide rip. That tide rip—Packer's Pasture, it was called—

was nothing to fool with, ever. What it took, it seldom gave back, but Joe's body had been found the next March, washed up on one of the outer islands.

Bess had never taken chances with Packer's Pasture—not to her way of thinking. She knew what the *Daisy* could, and could not, do, having sailed her for years. Her grandfather, Jonas Hadley, who had built the sloop, had been unable in his last years to handle her alone. He had taken Bess with him to help and, before he had died, taught her everything he knew. Left at her father's death with an ailing mother and with Martin a youngster of eight, Bess, at seventeen, had started to use the sloop in ways she had learned from her grandfather. She had gone handlining and trawling for groundfish; she had run a string of lobster traps in season. In any weather fit to go out in, she had always bundled up Martin and taken him along, so that he said now he had been brought up part lobster and part fish. Through the years, until he had grown big enough to help, she had supported him, seen to his schooling and even managed to put a little money by.

They had been tough years. From the first, she had had to contend with the Cove fishermen's inborn prejudice against a woman's working on salt water. No place for her, they said. What the hell, she'd drown herself out of that sloop, be a nuisance to every fisherman in the area. They'd have to look after her, make sure she got that rotten old hulk back into the Harbor, once she got out of it. After they had stuck a few well-meaning noses into her business, they found out that none of them really wanted to tangle with Bess. She was pleasant company and good-tempered when let alone, but she had a tongue which could take skin off if she had reason to use it.

The thing was, the *Daisy* was not a rotten hulk. She had been kept seaworthy for years, overhauled every spring. Bess had seen to that. The sloop was the only way she knew to make a living for herself and Martin—a matter of necessity. After a while, when nothing terrible happened to her, the buzzing stopped, but everyone had to admit that it was one big load off their minds when she married Joe Bowden and used the *Daisy* only for outings and picnics.

Bess's life with Joe had lasted only two years before she had lost him. And then she was back on the water again, working much as she had before, only now she had, in addition, Joe's mail contract. Three times a week, rain or shine—and weather had to be wilder than ordinary to prevent her—she sailed up to town with the mail, taking along anybody who wanted to go, shopping for neighbors at a moderate fee for each errand. She did own a ramshackle pickup truck, supposedly the mail truck, but in name only, which she disliked and used only when she had to. She wasn't about to pound her liver pin out, she told people, riding potholes on the so-called (and sometimes worse-called) road to town.

The road, built originally of gravel, had never been blacktopped and was mostly impassable for two seasons of the year—blocked with snow in winter, hub-deep in mud in spring, as it was now after an unusually wet April. In summer, the town fathers in Wentworth Harbor might send down a road scraper if they happened to think of it, but the Cove was tail-end Charley—only eighteen families lived there and paid taxes, and Cove traffic was mostly boat traffic anyway.

The Friendship was a splendid load hauler, broad of beam and steady. The more freight that was piled aboard her, the better she sailed. The same might almost be said of Bess. She was thirty-six, a tall woman, big-boned and handsome, with a cloud of bright brown curls which she wore cut short. She owned Joe Bowden's house, which she lived in, but after Martin had left for the war, she had made the *Daisy* almost a second home. Everything aboard was kept clean and shining, the bunks in the cuddy made up with sheets and many-colored patchwork quilts, the brightwork on the inboard engine polished to a silky sheen. The *Daisy*, bustling down the coast with a bone in her teeth, was a beautiful sight and one seldom seen elsewhere, now that powerboats filled most harbor moorings.

"Wacky or not," Bess would say, "the *Daisy* and me, we manage."

Martin, slipping carefully back into bed beside his wife, hoped he hadn't disturbed her, but she turned over and sniffed of him.

"My, you smell lovely," she said. "Like a sweet pea. But what was the idea, taking a bath in the middle of the night?"

Martin told her. The usual worry slid back into his head. She hadn't been sleeping well lately, was she all right? "You okay?" he asked.

"Oh, sure," she said. "It's the way I'm built now, like a balloon with arms, legs, and a head. When I stretch out, I teeter, sort of. It's to be expected. Don't worry, it won't be long now."

"You suppose it's all right, you going with Bess tomorrow?"

"If it's decent weather, I'd like to. I need a change, somewhat."

"I'd think so." It must be double hell, what she was going through. At the thought, he leaned over and gave her a long, thorough kiss.

"Wow!" she said. "You do that again, neither of us'll want to go anywhere."

"Why don't we just stay here till the baby comes?"

"All right. In a way, though, I would like to totter around town tomorrow and do some shopping. But I won't go if it'll worry you."

"Let's see what the weather is. If you do go, you tell Bess to start back by half-past twelve."

"You tell her." Mary chuckled. "I'm not going to be the one to tell Bess something she already knows."

After Martin had gone to bed, Bess sat where she was. She knew she ought to go to bed too—tomorrow would be busy, starting at daylight. She had got her shopping lists in order earlier in the evening and they were long. None of the Cove fishermen had taken time off from the islands search to tend gear or to make a trip up to the Harbor to buy necessary supplies. Lobster traps had gone unhauled; nobody had had a day's work. Now they were all plugging hard to make up for a whole week's loss of the spring fishing. The result was most of the neighbors had brought their shopping lists to Bess.

So go to bed, she told herself. Get some rest.

But she didn't feel sleepy. Thinking of Joe, then of Will McCarren and his children, wasn't anything to go to bed and rest easy with.

Joe, well and truly sorrowed for, had been dead for fourteen years. She had loved him and had not forgotten him, but the scar had healed. The years of grief had passed into time; his quiet ghost had never walked. But Will Mc-Carren, newly and mysteriously dead, had left a restless shade that haunted people's minds—particularly hers, because she had known him well and he had been neither a reckless nor a foolish man. Of his dying, only a single definite fact was known. He had loaded his family into his boat and had taken off for somewhere in a roaring south-easterly gale.

To local fishermen who knew Cross Island Shoals, McCarren's act had seemed suicidal. Or, some said, he was a plain damn fool—what could you expect, them out-of-staters was all crazy as coots. Who but a man out of his mind would take a batch of young kids to live on Cross Island, anyway? A place so lonesome that even the gulls wouldn't light there, and if they did, they didn't stay long.

Will McCarren, a stranger, had moved to Cross Island a little under a year ago. Since he and his children had been the only people on the island, there had been no neighbors to know what he had done on the day of one of the worst gales of the year.

Warren Petersen, a young fisherman who had given up trying to haul traps on the Shoals in the heavy seas, had pulled one child out of McCarren's drifting boat and had managed to get the boat in tow. He had looked around, but it was useless to try to spot any swimmer. Nobody could possibly have lived long in the icy water. The child had been unconscious, in bad shape. He had headed for town and a doctor.

Later that day, a Coast Guard boat, with a party of local men as well to help search, had gone out to the island, finding it abandoned.

Bess didn't go along with local opinion—that Will had been a landlubber, who hadn't any respect for wind and weather, hadn't known how to handle his boat. She knew better.

The first time she had met him, she had been handlining, with the *Daisy* anchored off the southern point of Cross Island. He had come alongside in his boat.

"I can't stand it any longer," he'd said. "I've seen you go past Cross Island Cove a number of times and I've hardly been able to believe my eyes. One Friendship sloop left in the world, by gum! I thought you wouldn't mind if I came out and got a closer look at her." He grinned. "I'm Will Mc-Carren. If you look behind this bush, you can see me."

He did have a remarkable bush—black, curly hair down to his shoulders; black, curly beard spread across his shirt-front. His eyes were black, too, and what could be seen of his forehead and cheeks was deeply tanned.

Quite a dark man, Bess thought. Aloud, she said, "Pleased to meet you, Mr. McCarren. I'm Bess Bowden. I take it you like the old *Daisy*."

"Case of love at first sight. Oh, she's a sweetheart! All the Friendships were. You see one nowadays, you think if I'd had her I could sail around the world in her. Which is more than I'd care to do in some of the crazy designs they're building now which can't outrun a healthy following sea."

Mildly surprised, because people who had met McCarren had said he was standoffish, unfriendly, Bess found herself liking him. She said, "I can't take you around the world, Mr. McCarren, but if you'd like to go for a sail, there's a fine breeze for it."

He anchored his boat where she was and jumped aboard, a slim fellow, medium tall, light as a cat on his feet. Anyone who thought, now, that McCarren hadn't known anything about boats should've been along that afternoon. At first, he'd sat, polite like company, but after a while Bess couldn't help but see that his fingers were itching, and she'd handed over the tiller. She could keep an eye on him, she'd thought, just in case.

It hadn't taken him long to show her that that wasn't necessary. He'd known well what he was doing. There was a good, brisk breeze blowing, and he'd done something that she often did, more by feeling than by knowing. As if you reached for and found the best that the *Daisy* could do and brought it out with her helping.

"You've made quite a hand," she told him as she left him back aboard his anchored boat. "I don't know when I've seen a man have a better time."

"I've had a ball! It's been great. I've always loved boats and sailing. I've even designed a few."

"Did you design that one?"

His boat was a stout craft, something between a lifeboat and a whaleboat, with a canvas sprayhood, a mast and sail which could be stepped, and an inboard engine. It was broad of beam, safe, you'd think, for a boatload of kids. Only, in the end, it hadn't been.

"Not entirely," he'd said. "This is a modified version of

an Outward Bound Survival School craft. I fooled with the design a little is all."

There had been other afternoons. She'd got in the way of stopping by Cross Island Cove, times when she'd had a free one. The McCarrens had always been delighted to see her. They'd always said come again and she had. But though she'd got to know them well, she'd never found out very much about them. She guessed from their accents that they had come from out of state, and Will had once mentioned that his wife was dead. They didn't volunteer further information. Once Bess caught sight of a tall boy who vanished around the corner of the house and did not appear again. He looked so much like Sarah, the oldest McCarren girl, that Bess suspected they might be twins—that Will probably had six children instead of five, one lying low for some reason. She hadn't asked any questions. Their business was their own. If they'd wanted to tell her any of it, they would have.

One thing she did know, for sure. Will McCarren would never have taken his children out in that storm without some desperate reason.

She thought, No one'll ever know now.

She missed them sadly. Cross Island had been a light-hearted place, full of gaiety, kids buzzing in and out of the house like bees around a nest; and now only one little girl left. That would be Rosie, the ten-year-old.

Bess had asked Justin Bradley in Wentworth Harbor about Rosie and he'd said she'd been in the Waterford Hospital for a day or so, and then a nice family up in the northern part of the state had taken her in. "Pleasant people. Own a big farm. She's all right," he'd said.

How could she be all right? Bess asked herself. As soon as she could get somebody to run the mail for a few days, Bess meant to go and see.

More than anyone, she found herself missing Will. Since

Joe's death, she had been too busy scrabbling after a living to remember how nice it had been to be a woman. She'd had Martin to bring up, his schooling, a living to make, taxes on the property—a dozen ways to pay out money that had come hard. She supposed now that the way she'd had to work for it, she didn't even look like a woman to the men she saw every day—too much like one of them, maybe. But to Will she had. She remembered the day he'd told off the drunk in the cabin cruiser which had come alongside the *Daisy* out on the Shoals. Will had been with her that day, helping her haul traps. Because he'd liked to, he'd said, and besides, he'd get a chance to sail the *Daisy*. She'd supposed that had been why, hadn't thought of anything else.

But when the drunk had started to unload a mouthful about how she'd looked in oil pants—"Get a load of the lady lobster-chaser! Build 'em rugged in these parts, don't they?" —that was as far as he'd got. Will had said pleasantly, "This lady is beautiful, smart-ass. But if she were as ugly as an old warthog with blisters, she'd rather have her looks than your manners."

Gone now. Like Joe. She'd have to do the best she could with what she had. As soon as she'd been able to, she had put the good times with Joe out of her mind. It didn't do to let your grief for the dead last too long. Now, she knew, she'd have to do that all over again.

The sun was just beginning to brighten the trees on the Hill Road behind the village as Martin and Mary started along the footpath which was a shortcut from Bess's house to the dock. Bess had gone down earlier. Ordinarily Martin would have preceded her by a couple of hours—four o'clock was his usual time. This morning he had waited for Mary, and she was glad he had. The footpath, not long, but worn slick by generations of use, was muddy, slippery with frost patches. She was grateful for his hand, steady and warm, under her elbow.

It was six o'clock of a fine day by anybody's standards. Water ran with a quiet bubbling sound along a small ditch beside the footpath. The big cleared field that spread between the foot of the hill and the houses on the Shore Road had no snow left—only a network of grooved ice curves where snowmobiles had cavorted all winter, going round and round. The roofs of the big old houses on the Hill Road ridge sparkled with frost. Most of them were closed now—unlived in since the old families had died out or their young people had gone away—but one of them, the Hadley house, which Martin had inherited from his father, showed up new cedar shingles and white freshly painted clapboards. Martin was having it remodeled and repaired. He and Mary would move into it when it was finished and after the baby came.

The Cove was quiet as a pond. A few cat's-paws ruffled it here and there, and the *Daisy* was tied up at the village float. Bess had had to use the engine to bring her in from the mooring. There was no wind for sailing, that was for sure. And that, Mary thought, ought to cheer up Marty.

This morning, all the Cove harbor moorings were empty except for Martin's big dragger. He looked at them and snorted. "Hell! Every boat out, two hours ago, and here I am all frigged up—"

Mary thought it best not to say anything. He was a dear and he was worried and worry always got him down.

Bess, on the float, tossed aboard a mailbag and glanced around. "Hi," she said. "Couldn't ask for a nicer day."

"Nice now," Martin said. "Could come on to blow, later on. Today could be a weather breeder."

"Could," Bess agreed. "Turns out to be one, you look after yourself out on the Shoals this afternoon. We'll be back before that. Shove that mailbag over, Mary, if it's in your way." She steadied the *Daisy* for Mary to climb aboard. "Oh, blast! There's Leafy."

"You don't have to take him along if you don't want to," Martin said.

"All right with me if he goes, but I'm not about to wait for him. Look at him; he's keeping me waiting because he thinks he can. Cast off for us, will you, Marty?"

Leafy had been standing still at the foot of the path, peering at something in the top of a tree.

Martin grinned. "He's watching birds and maple buds. You girls better look out today. His spring has come."

"Don't doubt it has," Bess said. "Wouldn't be the month of May if Leafy's juices didn't start to run."

Seeing Martin casting off lines, Leafy took off in a series of leaps, his coattails flapping. His last leap landed him aboard the *Daisy,* across a six-foot strip of water. "Tried to git gone without me, didn't ya?" he said.

"I don't hold up the United States mail even for you," Bess said. "Now you're here, if you've got any strength left, you can start the engine. We're going to have to hunt for a breeze."

"If I'm going to work my way, I ain't going to pay you no quarter."

"Suit yourself," Bess said. "No tickee, no washee. You'll walk back."

As the *Daisy* put-putted sedately out of the Cove, Martin's big dragger shot past, its bow wave sending the old sloop pounding up and down. Bess eased off the tiller until the big wake had gone by. "Men," she said mildly, "is sometimes inclined to be a little bit thoughtless, speaking of joggling you."

"He's worried," Mary said. "But it's a lovely morning, not a breath of wind."

"Prob'ly wants his wimmen to stay on land, where they belong to be," Leafy said. "All the more so, when one of 'em's in the shape you're in." He swiveled his eyes at Mary, apparently enjoying the way she looked now. "Gal in a hatching-jacket ain't got no call to go stramming around aboard of boats, anyway. Nobody has, don't know nothing about'em. Like that crazy hooglum out on Cross Island. Look what happened to him. I don't blame Mart one damn bit." With this pompous pronouncement, Leafy paused to see what effect it would have. It had none. Nobody answered him.

"I warn't one bit surprised when Quack McCarren come to grief. Man was out of his mind. Crazy's a loon. I know it for a fact."

"You do?" Bess said. "You knew him well, I expect." Bess's voice was quiet, but Mary glanced at her quickly, and then back at Leafy, who winked.

He's trying to make her mad, Mary thought. He'll be sorry. Bess didn't often get mad. When she did, she made it known.

"I wasn't buddy-buddy with him. Not like some," Leafy said. "Me, I only visited him but once. He told me to git the hell out or he'd blow my head off with his shotgun. Assault 'n' batt'ry, that is, threaten a man with a shotgun."

"What did *you* do to make him talk like that to you?" Bess asked.

"That oldest girl of his was awful pretty. Had the best-built pair of knockers I ever—"

"You keep on, you'll find yourself swimming," Bess said.

"What'd I say? Who'd run of an idea that a bum like that, all them dirty long hair and whiskers, would give a damn what anybody said to his girl? Lived like ducks in a pond out there, tackiest bunch I ever see."

"Which was why you and a few other clamheads nicknamed him 'Quack,' I take it. Too bad you didn't have a looking glass along to see yourself in," Bess said. "If you'd looked and wiffled then the way you do today, likely you'd

28

have shot your own head off. That capful of wind's going to touch us. Take the tiller, Mary, whilst I h'ist sail."

She's held onto her temper, Mary thought, and was glad. Also, she's let him know that his filthy talk isn't worth listening to, and now he's the one that's huffy.

Apparently in some kind of a sulk, Leafy sat where he was in the cockpit, not saying anything. He didn't offer to help Bess with the sails, and she didn't ask him.

Mary sat watching with pleasure the snowy sails go up. The breeze from the northwest was hardly enough to fill them, but the *Daisy* knew how to use what there was of it. She made it from one light puff to the next, and Bess came back to the cockpit to cut the engine. Leafy, still in drear silence, climbed to the top of the cuddy and sat down back to.

He's a very strange man, Mary thought, the way he doesn't add up to sense.

A local girl, brought up at the Cove until she had gone away to school to train for a teacher, Mary had known Leafy as long as she could remember. He lived in a run-down shack on the ocean side of the Point, just back from the sand beach of a small tidal cove, where he kept a skiff for fishing. For three seasons of the year, he was a loner, living by himself with only the company of his black dog, Willie. But in the springtime, he changed into a different kind of man. In the spring, he had a liquor problem. In the spring, he liked to see, be around, and compliment ladies. While he had never been known to harm anyone, his remarks were nature's own, likely to sound crude to sensitive ears.

Teachers in the grade school at the Cove, of whom Mary had been one during the years she had waited for Martin to come home from the war, had always been asked to keep an eye on Leafy if he were seen hanging around the school building. Glancing at him now—his dirty jeans, ragged jacket, shapeless cap pulled low above his sharp-nosed brown profile—Mary thought it might not be surprising if mothers had worried sometimes.

A stronger puff of wind reached the *Daisy*. She heeled a little as the sails snapped full. The rest of the ride up the Harbor was glorious, long reaches against the wind and the first of the ebbing tide. Bess grumbled because she said there was hardly enough breeze yet to give the *Daisy* way, but Mary could find no fault. Of all the times she had sailed with Bess, this seemed one of the best, and she really had needed this trip to town.

Leafy remained in his dignified isolation while Bess got the sails down. As they came alongside the Wentworth Harbor town dock, he jumped to the float and stood with his hands in his pockets, ignoring the stern line which Mary tossed to him.

"I'll do it," Bess said. She got out, bent to pick up the line, and found he was standing on it. "Move!" She stared up at him and Leafy moved, but as he did his thin rump bumped quite hard into hers.

Bess whirled on him, and seeing her face, he started to back away. He backed one step too far. His heel hit the raised edge of the float and he toppled over it. He struck the water with a mighty splash.

"Oh, Lord!" Bess said. "Oh, Lord!" She reached down as his head came out of water and got him by the collar of his jacket, helped him scrabble back onto the float. "Well, I must say you're a pitiful sight," she said. "But you ought to know better than to try your natural capers on me. Go on up to Cousin's dry goods and get some dry clothes to put on before you catch pneumonia. Tell Floyd to put them on my bill."

Leafy went. He legged it up the gangway without looking back.

A lanky young fellow coming down flattened himself against the railing to let him by. "What'd he do—fall overboard?" he asked.

"I guess likely," Bess said. "How's with you, Charley?"

This was Charley Franklin, who owned the wharf buildings and ran a fish- and lobster-buying business there. He said, "Good's I'll ever be, I guess. Hi, Mary. Stranger in town. Here, gi'me that. I'll make it fast."

Mary, who had been holding the bowline to keep the *Daisy* from drifting off, handed it over to him. "Nice to see you, Charley."

"Nice to see you. Weather report says we're in for a gale northwest, Bess."

"Won't breeze on till after the flood tide makes," Bess said.

"Well, you'll want to get back as early as you can, I guess. Gi'me your grain orders. I'll phone them up to the feedstore, and the boys can haul down and load whilst you do your grocery shopping." He shouldered the mailbags. "Mail truck's up there now."

"Thanks," Bess said. "Appreciate it, Charley, be a big help." She handed him a list and followed Mary up the gangway.

"I ought to be ashamed getting mad at Leafy," she said.

"I don't blame you," Mary said. "That was a real sexy rub he gave you."

"That didn't amount to anything. It couldn't. Poor soul couldn't *do* anything even if he ever got the chance to. Most people know what's the matter with him and they make fun, so he has to get back his own by being a know-it-all and a loudmouth. That trashy claptrap of his is hard to take sometimes, and when he got going on Will McCarren's youngster, I guess I stripped my gears. I didn't push him overboard on purpose, but I could have."

"He'll be pretty sore at you, won't he? I shouldn't think he'd make a very pleasant enemy."

Bess laughed. "I'll see the day I'm scared of Leafy Piper," she said.

Their shopping lists were long, but they finished in good

time. After the grocery store truck, loaded with bags and bundles, started for the town dock, they walked along the street to the town office, finding it open but empty.

"As usual," Bess said. "Oat Baker ain't here. Well, we can wait awhile. We've got time if your grampop's clock is right."

The town office clock was a grandfather, a tall, aged timepiece, whose voice was "Tick," and then, after a deliberate pause as if to say all time had come to an end, went on to say "Tock." Years ago it had had more to say—clear, sweet chimes marking the quarter and half hours, and on the hour, a series of deep, dignified "Bongs." Now, every fifteen minutes, it gave out a creaky whirr, like an old person with stopped-up lungs. Mary wondered if it still struck the hour. She was very familiar with this clock.

Her grandfather, Moses Gwinn, had had this office, a Selectman from as far back as she could remember to the day of his death. In his time, a good many of the town's well-to-do and solid citizens had lived down at the Cove. The Cove's Hill Road had been status. The owners of shipping, of lumber mills, the elected town officials, rode leisurely to business in buggies with flashing gilded wheels, drawn by the best horses money could buy. The road had been kept up then. Hard-based, it had been regraveled each spring; in winter, ox teams drawing heavy rollers had packed down the snow for the passage of smart sleighs.

Wentworth Harbor had changed with the changing times. Moses Gwinn, a Cove man, had held his office for years, being known as honest and the best man for the job, while any status the Hill Road had had slowly eroded. The citizens of Wentworth Harbor now considered the Cove as hind end. Even though a few Cove men sturdily ran for office for some years after Moses Gwinn's death, he had been the last one of them elected.

The grandfather clock had belonged to him—his grandfather had brought it from Scotland, where most of its works had been carved from choice woods by a craftsman who had known how to carve wooden works for grandfather clocks. Moses had valued it; he had taken care of it and kept it ticking through the years. Skillful with his hands, he had even carved and replaced some of its inner works as they wore down, duplicating the parts as best he could in whatever suitable woods he could find. His will had bequeathed it to the town, provided the town officers took care of it, to his son, Mary's father, if they didn't.

Mary's father had wanted it.

"It had better stay where it is," Moses had told him. "It's rung the town's time, honest and steady, for a good many years. That clock's watched a mint of money in and out of the town office. Don't know what it would do if somebody got light-fingered with the tax funds. Bet you it'd start striking, keep it up till the cash found its way back to the till."

The clock, its hands now marking the hour, stirred inside. "Bong," it said flatly. "Bong . . . bong . . ." and whirred to silence. Three strokes for eleven o'clock.

"I don't guess it would strike and go on striking, whatever it might see here now," Mary said sadly.

"Well, there's been talk about what goes on," Bess said.

"I've never heard Otis Baker was dishonest," Mary said. She got up and crossed the room for a closer look at the clock.

"Neither have I. But there'd be pickings, here and there, if somebody was. What'd you see inside there?"

The door of the clock had been ajar. It squawked as Mary pushed it open. The inside of the case was rank with dust and cobwebs. In one corner, a malevolent black spider hung motionless above the dried-up bodies of three houseflies.

"Humph!" Bess craned to look. "Nobody's bothered to

clean it for years, looks like. That nice old clock, it's a wicked shame! I'd give a pretty to own it myself."

"I guess I do, now," Mary said. "It was left to my father under Grandfather Moses's will, with the condition that it go to him if the town didn't take care of it."

"If that's how it is, we'll take it right out of here when we go." Bess stared speculatively at the clock. "I believe I could lug Old Grampop myself without too much ado."

"I expect I'd better speak to the Selectmen about it first," Mary said.

"What's that you want to speak to the Selectmen about?" Justin Bradley, a member of the Board, had come quietly through the office door. They hadn't heard him and they both jumped.

Justin twinkled at them. He twinkled well. He was a tremendously stout man, not tall, with plump rosy cheeks and bright blue eyes, clear and innocent as a baby's. His abundant snow-white hair, which curled handsomely over his ears and down the back of his neck, gave him a fatherly air, and his manners, too, were lavish, particularly with ladies. In spite of his size, he moved limberly on his small feet—too small, it almost seemed, to hold him up, but he was known as one of the best dancers in town. "Didn't mean to take a jump out of you," he said. "Ought to have stamped my feet, let myself be known. What can the Selectmen do for you, Mrs. Hadley? The Board's always available to pretty girls."

"Oh," Mary said, a little taken aback. "The clock. Aren't you using it now?"

"That old ruin? Lord, no. Some old-time politician willed that to the town years ago, and it's cluttered up the office ever since. I'm just waiting for the woods to dry up so the road crew can take it out somewhere and dump it."

"Yes," Mary said. "My grandfather. He willed it to my father, when the town got through with it."

"Oh . . . uh . . ." Justin said. He recovered quickly. "Might as well let us dump it for you. No good to anybody now."

Bess said. "I'm headed down-harbor right away soon. I'll be glad to take Old Grampop, there, and dump him off in the tide rip."

"Couldn't let you do that. Much too heavy for you to handle. The road crew'll winkle it out of here in no time."

"Not a bit of it. Glad to save their time and gas and some of the town's money," Bess said blandly.

"Well, it certainly does my heart good to hear someone interested in saving the town's money," Justin said. He went over to the safe, opened it, rooted around for a moment, and came up with a folded paper, which he thrust in his pocket. "I'm all of a bustle today. Got to get back to business. Customer coming in. Don't see too many of those these days."

"Real estate business not good?" Bess asked.

"Gone to h . . . down the shoot, like everything else. Sorry to have to blow through here like the wind. Call again, ladies, do. But you leave that clock where it is. I'll take care of it myself, and it won't cost the town a cent." He vanished through the doorway as silently as he had come in.

"Now, what was that about?" Mary said. "He doesn't seem to want to let the clock go. Old ruin, cluttering up the place?"

Bess chuckled. "Old antique, worth quite a lot, wouldn't you say? That boy's skun the feathers off of Uncle Sam's eagle on every quarter he ever saw. *What* in the world is that racket? Don't tell me he fell down the steps."

There had been quite a flurry and stamping of feet outside the office. The door crashed open. Through it spun a smallish child, as if propelled by some violent force. After her, Florence Baker, Otis's wife, strode and stood glaring. "Mr. Baker and I ain't going to have you in the house one minute longer!" she said. "Not the poison way you act! You heard me say this morning and I'll say again, if anybody had told me I'd ever harbor a nasty little hippie in my nice clean house, there wouldn't be a Bible holy enough to make me believe it!"

The child, who had spun halfway across the room and then skidded on her hands and knees, got to her feet and glared back. She was a thin child, oddly dressed in a faded gingham overall, a type once known as a "tier," not seen for years now, shapeless and drear, with one button at the back of the neck. The light through the town office windows, cobwebby and fogged with the grayish-brown film filtered through the building from the furnace all winter, was dusky, but enough could be seen to show that the "tier" had been haggled off above the hem, apparently by a dull blade. It hung in raveled scallops over black wool stockings, scuffed out at the knees. The child's kneecaps showed through, skinned and bleeding from her skid across the worn wooden floor. The skinned places undoubtedly hurt, but the youngster wasn't crying. She stood backed against the wall, her eyes a smoldering glitter under the mop of stringy hair which nearly covered all of her face.

"You seddown!" Florence said. "Or you'll get whacked again the way you did this morning when you broke my sugar bowl."

Florence jumped. Apparently, in her fury, she hadn't noticed that there was anyone else in the office. "Who's that there?" she demanded.

"Flo!" Bess said. "What in the ever-living world do you think you're doing?"

Florence dropped into a chair. She turned glazed eyes on Bess and struggled to speak. After a gasp or two, she got up, moved back between the child and the door. "For heaven's sake! No reason to scare a body to death, is there?"

"Not that anyone can see. You appear to be trying to."

Florence stiffened. "I am trying to keep from going out

of my mind. And me with this rotten cold." She sneezed, blew her nose long and juicily. "I've been drove so far that I'm—"

The child, seeing Florence's face buried in her handkerchief, moved like light. She shot across the floor, ducked under Florence's ineffectual grab, and vanished through the doorway.

" 'N there!" Florence said. "That has done it. I am *finished!*"

"Where's her shoes?" Bess said. "That kid's in her stocking feet. She hasn't got a coat on, and it's chilly out."

"She's got good shoes, which are in my apern pockets." Florence stalked across the room, dropped heavily into the swivel chair behind the desk.

The chair, limp from holding up generations of town officials, tipped and nearly tossed her over backwards. She recovered by grabbing at the edge of the desk. "If she ain't got no wearable clothes, it's her own mizzable actions. That tier! A perfectly good tier, belonged to my girl, Isabel, when she was little."

"Seems it's been a long time since Isabel was little, by the looks of things."

"I ain't like some, I don't throw away, I put aside for future use. I rummaged them things out of the trunk in the attic, where I laid them away when my kids outgrowed them. It wasn't up to Oat and me to buy new, that's up to the town. I *give* her a whole new outfit. And you know what she done? She chopped them up with Oat's hatchet."

"I can see you've taken quite a loss in dry goods," Bess said. "Did you walk her here through the mud and slush with her shoes in your apron pocket?"

Flo's cheeks reddened. "If you are a-mingling into this that ain't any of your business, Oat and me has took her in out of the goodness of our hearts, and you can put that in your pipe and smoke it."

"I am," Bess said. "And I'm putting out quite a cloud. What little girl is she? She looks colored."

"She prob'ly is. Them ab-origins out on Cross Island all was."

Bess stiffened. "Oh, my God!" she said under her breath. She got up and strode over to the desk, seeming as she went to swell a little. "Let me have her shoes."

"Now, you look! That yow'un's kicked my whole shins into lumps big as a egg, the yelk . . ." Florence's voice wavered and faded. She began to tug at her apron pockets.

"Bess," Mary said, "is that the little McCarren girl?"

"Yes," Bess said in a frozen voice. "The Lord only knows what this old she-loucifee has done to her. Nobody would know her—God forgive me, I didn't. Hand me the shoes, Flo, before I come after them."

The shoes turned out to be a pair of ancient basketball sneakers, scuffed and worn through at the toes and big enough for a boy of sixteen.

"Sweet godalmighty!" Bess said. She lifted the objects between a thumb and forefinger and went out of the office, slamming the door so hard the glass rattled.

"She better be careful how she busts the glass in that door," Flo said. "She'll be sued to pay for it, and I could sue her myself for swearing and slandering me in the town office. What call's she got, nosing into the town business? I don't know what she thinks she can do, where Oat and me's had a complete failure."

"But, Flo, she's so little," Mary said. "And after what happened to her——"

"That yow'un ain't much more'n a animal. You ask Justin Bradley. He's took all that time, been all over the County to find someone to take her in, and couldn't. He come in this morning to tell us, and that little devil grabbed my gra'-mother Willameen's sugar bowl off'n the table and hove it at his head. Missed him by a inch and come near as could be to smashing a window. You ask me, that crack on the head she got left her crazy."

"Is that dark on her face black and blue—where she got hurt?"

"Dirt. She won't wash herself and won't let me. And dark blood, you can't mistake it. Right straight down from old Amadee Courvette, used to live down Bullet Bay, where I come from. My uncle Nails Potter, down there, knew them McCarrens. Hooglums and renegades, he told me. Them black hair and eyes and tougher'n old tilly-tripe. No doubt in the world old Amadee was their gre-grandfather." Florence snuffled her cold and blearily regarded her past. "Why, that old man when he was ninety fell off'n a mowing machine, slap into the moving blades. Never even got a cut." She paused and went on with relish. "Hoss got bit by a hornet."

I had better get out of here before I throw up, Mary thought. If Bess caught up with the little girl, she surely wouldn't bring her back here. It would be better to go down to the dock and wait, where the air was clean. She said aloud, "Well, I expect we won't have time to wait any longer for Otis."

"If you come in to pay your taxes, I c'lect when Oat ain't here. The Lord knows where he's got to by now. He was helping me clean broken glass and sugar off'n the kitchen floor when the telephone rung, and it was the schoolteacher, scairt to death and howling because Leafy Piper'd come at her when she was walking up to the school'ouse."

"Oh, my goodness!" Mary said, jolted. "Leafy? Oh, dear. I guess we shouldn't have brought him along with us this morning."

Florence stared. "Well, I must say! You folks down to the Cove don't help much, do you! Here we are, working our very hearts to the bone to keep the criminal el'mint off'n the streets, and you bring that sex maniac up from down there, knowing full and well how he is in the spring of the year. I suppose you two women sailed up here alone with him." Her nose suddenly seemed to point. "He try anything on with you?"

"Don't be silly. There's no real harm in Leafy. All anyone has to do is say 'Boo' and he runs."

"No harm! That poor girl, just passing by, minding her own business, and here's this whiskered-out bum winks at her and says can't she come over and let him feel of her leg. Let me tell you, Oat took off after him. He catches up with him, he's going to sock the filthy critter into jail for a good long time."

"Oh, stop it, Flo! Leafy might rate a fine, but a long jail sentence, that's nonsense."

"You down to the Cove got a peculiar way of thinking. Morals is morals and the law's the law. When I think of what that Cove used to be, the very best and highest-minded! Some of them good old men lived down there years ago must be spinning in their graves."

"Not about Leafy. There might be some other things going on that would cause a few vibrations."

"Let me tell you, Otis Baker and my aim in life is to rid this town of the lowest of the low, and what a struggle! Not many has even heard of how he and Justin tried to scoot Quack McCarren's tribe off'n Cross Island. 'Go back where you come from,' Justin told that feller, 'you're breaking the law, trespassing and not sending your kids to school.' Told him the next time they come, Otis would have a warrant, Quack to go to jail and them wild kids spread out to whatever orphans' home would take them. If so be there's any that would."

"What!" Mary said. She felt a sudden chill of horror. Was that why? Could it have been why Will McCarren had done that crazy thing?

"Justin said he never see such a mess in his life, that

house. Stink, you wouldn't believe! There was one girl, six-teen-seventeen; anyway, old enough to sleep with her father——"

"That's not true! Bess knew that family——"

"I don't see that Justin had any reason for lying. That girl come parading through in a towel. A *Turkish* towel, in front of them men, if you please!"

"Did Otis tell you that?"

"Oat never says much about a nasty case, he's too nice-minded. But Justin's helpful, he lets people know. He even told what that feller said to him, and it's so filthy I can hardly bear to repeat it." She had to stop and blow her nose. "This cold has got me crazy. I can't help but think it ain't a cold but some disease I've picked up from that child. Touch filth. Aspirin, Golden Oil won't touch it. That feller told Oat 'n' Justin to clear out of there or they'd go home ballocky bare-assed, with their pants shot off. Where you going?"

Mary closed the door quietly behind her.

Flo, of course, was known to be a vicious gossip. Any tale she got hold of was bound to branch out and flower. This one had produced some deadly blooms.

Sickened, Mary walked down the street that led to the wharf. She walked slowly, keeping an eye out for Bess.

If Bess can only find her, she thought, we'll take her home with us. A child—any child—would be better off with a rattlesnake. She recalled how both of the Baker children, Isabel and Bud, whom she had known in school, had run away from home as soon as their legs had got long enough, and had never been back.

Bess wasn't at the dock. The freight for the Cove—bags of grain, groceries, mail sacks, all carefully covered with tarred canvas tarps to protect against flying spray—took up most of the *Daisy's* cockpit, but the boys who had loaded it had left a narrow passage down the middle. Mary sat down, leaning her back against what felt like a bag of corn.

41

"Ouch!" she told a sudden disturbance inside herself. "This is no time for you to start banging your heels around, you little fireball!"

She waited. Time went by.

Presently she became aware of a sound as if someone were driving an iron spike with a maul somewhere along the waterfront. It sounded almost like— It was. Bess was heading down the street, strolling along as if she had no worry in the wide world. Balanced on one shoulder was the Town Hall's grandfather clock, which was striking steadily. "Bong . . . bong . . . bong . . ." and going on striking. Behind her, a half-grown youth, bright red in the face, stalked, keeping his distance and carrying a big dress box and a bulging shopping bag. Behind him, some six or eight other youths of his age, massed in a group, hooting and yelling.

Bess came down the wharf, slid out from under the clock, lowered one end of it, and backed down the gangway. The other end bumped along as gently as might be. As she upended it on the float, the clock hiccuped, whirred, and stopped striking. "Hope I haven't killed him," she said. "He's been doing that all the way down through town."

Charley Franklin came down the gangway, his helper, Fred Folsom, clattering along behind him. "Bess," Charley said, "one of these days you'll bust a gusset. Where you want that put?"

"Stretch him out down the middle of the platform. And tuck that tarp end over him good and solid, will you?"

"Bess, did you find——" Mary began.

Bess flapped a hand, which in anybody's language said shut up. She waved a dollar bill at the red-faced boy, who dumped his load at the top of the gangway and fled, without looking at her.

"He turned out to be bashful," Bess said. "I had to stop at the dry goods store, so I left Old Grampop here, braced against the outside entry. He stood there clanging like a fire truck. I suppose those kids thought it was the fire truck and were disappointed, because when I came back quite a mealley of them had gathered round with rocks. Seems there's no school today, teacher's upset. You know the young ranicks used to holler, 'Quack, quack,' at Will McCarren?"

Fred Folsom colored slightly. "God, yes. One of them was mine. That was him, brought your bundles. Uh . . . Finney Wilson put him up to that hollering. I'm sorry for it."

"Wasn't you, was it?" Bess said. She went on without waiting for an answer. "I said, 'You little devils put the rocks down. One of you muckle onto the aft end of this clock and help me down to the wharf with it.' So one of them did. Turned out Old Grampop clangety-clanging and folks looking and the rest of the kids hooting was too much for him. I see his ears were about to scald off, so I handed him my bundles and took over Old Grampop myself."

"That's my kid Joey, all right," Fred said. "He's hoss's-ass age, but he ain't a bad kid, Bess. Finney Wilson runs that whole gang of teen-agers, being older'n them. Some says he's on dope. I don't know. I worry some about Joey. I'll get them bundles for ya." He fetched the things down and handed them over.

"Much obliged," Bess said. "Here's Joey's dollar. Tell him thanks."

Fred looked at her uneasily. "Thing is, somebody hauled half my string of traps out on the Shoals. Now I'm sorry the poor duffer's dead, it's an awful thing, but McCarren had the name of that, down around Bullet Bay."

"According to whose tell?" Bess said. "Cast off for us, will you, Charley?"

"Flood tide's made," Charley said. "It's going to come over green in the tide rip, Bess."

Oh, dear, Mary thought. And after we promised Marty!

Far down, past the Harbor mouth, she could make out the line of whitecaps as the flood tide in Packer's Pasture began its war with the northwest wind.

"Wind hasn't picked up much yet," Bess said. "It won't be too bad a chance back."

"Might even be fun," Mary said. If Bess wasn't worried why should she be? Coiling down the stern line, she wondered if Bess had heard about Leafy's disaster.

Whether or not she had, Bess said nothing until she was settled at the tiller, with the sails drawing well and the *Daisy* taking the head tide in her stride. Then she said, "That little girl's name is Rosie."

"You found her! Oh, Bess, where is she? Surely you didn't take her back to Flo!"

"Well, now. You must be wondering how I pried Old Grampop out of Flo. It's a long story, and everything'll come out in good time. I hunted that building over, down in the cellar first amongst the ruins of old gear and road machines, and the mess down there you'd have to see to believe. If the Selectmen were to sell that curiosity shop to a junkman, none of us would have to pay taxes for a year. Rosie wasn't down there, but Leafy was. I saw his foot sticking out from under an old upside-down snow-plow blade and I could tell it was him by the boot on it." Bess chuckled. "Seems when he bought his dry outfit up at Floyd's, he preferred his own boots, even if wet. His old cap, too. But the rest of it—oh, my! I hauled him out by the foot, and I said, 'Wow, Leafy, I ought to've told you I wouldn't pay for anything fancy,' but he was beyond listening. He was drunk and scared to death, and he began to puke. So I hustled him into the chem toilet and held his head. When he got rid of his load and felt better, he told me what he was into with Oat Baker. Said he thought when I grabbed his foot I was Oat himself. Said he'd tried to think of the last place Oat would look for him, and what made him sick wasn't liquor but the thought that he'd been so dumb he hadn't been able to outthink even Oat Baker. So I looked at him, bright orange sport jacket and black-and-white checked pants and a red bow tie, and I thought, I may have an old rauncher of a bill up to Floyd's, but it's been worth it. Went girling, poor soul, and spoke courting words to the first pretty lady he saw. God knows what he said to the teacher.

"I says, 'Leafy, you may be the world's worst loving fool, but right now you're the gift of God to me. You come along, and if Oat touches you, I'll yank his nose down into his upper plate.' And up we went to the third floor to hunt up Rosie."

Bess peered ahead at the whitecaps on the bar, some way away yet, but coming closer. "That doesn't look too bad. Not wind enough to be worth reefing down for."

"Looks bumpy."

"Well, you pinch. That little bit of a four-foot chop, shoot, you 'n' I have taken her through there when it was a ten-foot one. Let's see, where was I? We sneaked by the office door and hunted all over the third floor, turned out closets and cubbyholes. Leafy finally ran across Rosie on the second floor, wedged in under that throne with the drapery and gold tossles in the Lodge room. I started in, but he stopped me, both arms held out across the door. 'You can't come in here, Bess,' he says. 'This is the Lodge room. No woman is allowed to set foot.' Oh, he was getting his zing back fast, Leafy was.

"I took one look and I says, 'No woman would want to, I shouldn't think.' My Lord, the paraphernalia! I suppose it means something to menfolks, gold tossles, and like mystery, or a wet dream. Anyway, there was I and there was Rosie. 'Two females' footprints,' I says. 'Across this holy floor, and how they'll ever resanctify it you and I'll never know.' And Leafy turned a funny color, but he let me by.

" 'Don't you go pulling and hauling on her like you

done me,' he says. 'You let me.' And down he goes on his hands and knees.

" 'Don't you be scared, sweetheart,' he says. 'You come out to Leafy,' and he kept on, like to a dog or a cat or any scared-to-death thing, but little good it did. Rosie was under there and she wasn't coming out for anybody. And not to be blamed, either. I said, 'It's all right, Rosie. This is Bess; we've come to take you away from here,' but not a sound or a movement. Then Leafy said, and I could have killed him dead for saying it, 'We've come to take you back to your daddy, Rosie.' And she began scrabbling and out she came. I took her on my lap and wiped her nose and face. A lot of that black stuff came off, coal dust it looked like, and she smelt not only of dirty kid but of tar and paregoric. The tar was on her hair.'"

"Dear God, Bess. Is Florence Baker crazy? Paregoric?"

"I don't doubt she rummaged a bottle of something out of that old trunk. Used to dose her own kids with it, or maybe she drinks it herself. Rosie had had something or whatever, because it was beginning to take. Her eyes looked funny, and I hoped she was woolly-headed enough not to remember what Leafy'd said. He was coursing around, all chirked up. 'Bess, this little girl is in her stockin' feet. Where's your shoes, honey?' And he looked at me as if he was trying to make out I'd stolen them. In a way, I guess I had, because when I went to haul him out from under the snow-plow blade, I'd dropped those god-awful sneaks on the floor and there they are still. Let Flo Baker make what she will of that the next time she goes to the chem.

"I said, 'Leafy, you're in a bind, and any more foolish-ness out of you, I'll go get Oat Baker and tell him where you are. You do as I tell you and I'll get you back home.' And I shoved up the window onto the fire escape. 'You carry her down and into the woods behind the Town Hall and don't let anyone see you. And when you get Rosie out of sight, you wait for me.'

"He says, 'Ain't nobody sees me, if I don't want 'im to.'

"I knew that well enough. He can move like a shadow in the woods. He spotted a deer in the trees out back of my house one time, and he bet me a cent he could sneak up on it and touch it before it ran, and he did. Only trouble was, the critter took off like a skyrocket, went twenty feet in the air. Knocked him galley-west and tore the pocket off his coat. He was cut up some and lame, and I set him down in the house till he got his wind back. Paid him the cent and stitched the pocket back on his jacket. All I got for my trouble was that cussed Willie tried to tear my leg off. Where was I?"

"Coming down the fire escape," Mary said. "Or weren't you?"

"Well, I was. It didn't look to me as if the Selectmen had taken any better care of that fire escape than they had of your grandfather's clock, and I'd figured that if it was going to cave in on anyone, it had better be me alone, not lugging Rosie. That was one reason why I wanted Leafy to take her, and the other one was that if we'd all gone together, someone might have come nosing around to see where the parade was headed. Hold your hat, Mary. Here we go."

The *Daisy* slammed into the tide rip. Her bowsprit went almost, but not quite, under. Salt water cascaded along her washboards, spray blew in ribbons and rainbows. Then she rose, magnificently stood on her tail, and did it again. Obviously she liked it. So did Bess. Watching the high white bow waves spanked out on either side, Mary thought, And so do I.

It took ten minutes to cross the tide rip. On the sea side, the chop was quieter. If it had been more than a four-foot one throughout the crossing, Mary wasn't about to complain.

"You know, that wind's beginning to come on strong," Bess said. "Another hour or so, and you'd really have had to pinch. You about to miscarry?"

"I'm a good solid-built girl," Mary said. "You ought to know."

"If I didn't know, I would by no means have put you through it. Leafy made it to the trees with Rosie eeled up under his chin like his necktie. Coming along behind him, I couldn't even see he had her. He went like a bullet, and I didn't even catch up till I got down to the woods back of Cousins's wharf, and then it wasn't him I caught up with. There behind a tree stood Rosie, her feet on his jacket and Leafy nowheres to be seen. Through the underbrush I could see Old Man Cousins taking a nap in the sun, his back leaned against the wharf building. And then off the wharf comes flying a boulder as big as a bucket, hit the water with a splash like the end of time.

"Old Man Cousins leapt up, batted his eyes this way and that. 'What hell?' he says. 'Who done that? Billy, you heave something off the wharf?' His boy, Billy, ran out of the building, and in off the wharf comes Leafy, hollering his head off. 'Call the police! Git Oat Baker down here! Somebody phone the Coast Guard! That was a little bit of a girl jumped off of there, I see her do it!' And here he scoots, up the bank, grinning like a punkin devil.

" 'When it comes out that a crazy kid's been running wild around here, them Cousinses is going to have a story about it,' he says, and scoops up Rosie and made off with her."

"Bess, for heaven's sake, where is she? This is wild. Like . . . savages."

Bess nodded. "I'd stood there looking at Rosie McCarren, the way she is now, and my heart broke. She's a real pretty little girl and bright's a dime. I think Flo Baker the great do-gooder's kept her in the coalbin. Her hair's not black, it's a real dark chestnut. I tried to wrap her up in my coat. She wouldn't let me near her, started to run into the woods, so I had to stop." Tears came into Bess's eyes and she dashed them away.

"Why was she left with Flo in the first place? There are people in Wentworth Harbor who'd have taken her in, used her decently, if they'd known. We would have. If we'd known."

"I think I know why. I asked Justin Bradley where she was, and he told me a whopping fib. They'd farmed her out upcountry with some pleasant people, he said. Well, the Health and Welfare pay board for . . . for orphans. I don't know how much—probably be peanuts divided in two. But peanuts and other pickings are partly what's got Justin where he is, and he certainly had an interest in Rosie's whereabouts or he wouldn't have lied to me. I think he and Flo are splitting whatever cash there is in Rosie's board."

The *Daisy* was heading up into the Cove. Her main boom rattled over as Bess jibed, the sails snapped full on the new tack. Bess smiled, seeing Mary's appalled face. "Not much farther to go," she said. "And I'm nigh to the end of my story. I went back to the Town Hall, and there sat Flo eyeballing me like a female buffalo at Dan'l Boone.

"She says, 'Where is that yow'un's shoes?'

" 'Where you can find them if you want to look,' I says. 'It doesn't seem to me that youngster's in the building now. I guess you'll have to skurry around and hunt.' So I went over to Old Grampop and tipped him across my shoulder.

"She jumped up with a squawk. 'What you doing? You gone crazy?'

" 'Yes, I have,' I said. 'Stark, staring crazy and boiling mad. Don't get in my way. I might use Old Grampop here as a batt'ring ram.' She ducked behind the desk and I walked out. I never uttered the word *antique*. And that's the story of how I pried your clock out of Flo."

"Bess, come on! You couldn't have left Rosie with Leafy."

"If anybody should ask you, you don't know where she is. I expect Leafy sneaked through the woods till he came to the wharves along the waterfront. Wouldn't surprise me if he went under some wharves—he could have, where the tide's still fairly low. And the time of day it is, most everybody's taking their nooning, gone home to eat. If he waited till Charley and Fred went, he could have popped himself and Rosie aboard here unbeknownst to anybody."

"But I was here—"

"If he did that, he got here first. You walk pretty slow, and Leafy doesn't." Bess grinned. "You didn't see a soul come aboard here, did you?"

Taken with a sudden fit of the giggles, Mary said, "Not a soul."

"Leafy's trick with the rock might work. I don't know. They might not come after Rosie. But Otis'll be down here after Leafy, fossicking around, seeing Flo's got the cussed fool all set up for a jail term."

"We're going to keep Rosie."

"We are. But we're going to lie low for a while and see if a brushfire starts. That cuddy hatch is cracked open a mite to let the air in there. Slide it to, will you, and then nobody'll accidentally peek down. Including you. You've never been a very good liar. Not like me."

"All right. I won't look." She did, though, in spite of herself. As she secured the hatch, she couldn't help but make out that both bunks were occupied. In the cuddy's dim light, no one could have told who the two sleepers were, dead to the world.

Quite a number of people had come to the dock to take home their grocery orders. The Post Office truck was there, and another pickup for hauling and delivering heavy freight. Their drivers, as was the custom, made fast bow and stern lines, came aboard to unload. The tarpaulin-wrapped clock gave them pause.

"What's that, Bess? Somebody's casket? Who's dead?"

"That's an aged veteran sent for burial at sea," Bess said. She stood leaning against the closed hatch, checking off orders on her tallyboard.

The truck driver stooped and jerked off the tarp, and the clock, jolted, said resonantly, "Bong!"

"Don't seem to be quite dead yet. Hey, ain't that the Town Hall clock?"

"It was. Belongs to Mary now." She made another check and absently waved at Mary, who waved back and started up the path for home to make up the spare room bed with warm blankets for Rosie McCarren.

Martin Hadley had been hauling traps off Lantern Island when he first spotted Warren Petersen's boat heading out across the Shoals. He wondered briefly—but only briefly—why Warren was heading for outside at this time of day and in such a hurry. He had his throttle wide open, and the boat was staving into the chop, sending out wide fans of spray.

Probably for fun, Martin thought. Warren was a young fellow, eighteen or so, who enjoyed driving his boat fast in any weather, and this weather now ought to be rough enough to satisfy him. The wind, as Martin had guessed it would, had come up with the tide and was blowing a half-gale northwest already, with, apparently, more to come.

Burn out a bearing if he keeps that up for long. Not that his business is any of mine.

He himself couldn't see the point of wearing out an engine when you didn't have to. He had been trained to take care of good machinery. That engine of Warren's was a dandy, brand-new, and Warren was proud of it. Its thunderous roar was music to his ears; he liked it, and he thought other people ought to like it, too. Summer people complained when he hauled traps in the early morning a few hundred feet from the front windows of their shore cottages. A doctor had told Warren that he'd be stone deaf before he was forty if he kept on working in that din all day. So far Warren hadn't noticed anything wrong with his hearing; that was a lot of bull. As for the summer people, it did them good to hear the sounds a workingman made at four-thirty in the morning. So said Warren.

The boat was new, too, a gift from his grandfather, Calvin Petersen, who had brought him up after the death of Warren's father. Calvin was well off. As a young man, he had inherited some money; for years, he had owned the fish wharf in Wentworth Harbor, which he had sold to Charley Franklin's father. From that he had gone into politics and, for several terms, had represented the area in the State Legislature. Because he had had little formal education and had been inclined to pursue debate in strong, rather than parliamentary, language, he had been known to certain colleagues as the King of the Wild Frontier. "Well," Calvin had said, "wild I may be, but able, boys, able. Don't forget that."

Now, at eighty, he was running a fish and lobster buying wharf at the Cove. Warren's new dragger, equipped with all the electronic devices money could buy—depth-finder, ship-to-shore radiotelephone, and other up-to-date marine gadgets—was to show the world that Warren was the apple of his grandfather's eye. It was also to indicate how tickled Calvin had been when Warren had finished Vocational School and decided to live at home and go fishing.

Calvin, at his age, was probably a little childish about some things, notably Warren, Martin thought. But, shoot, if the old man was a little soft on his grandson who could blame him? Warren was a likable young cuss, outside of being brash and sometimes foolish; but he had learned to handle his big boat very well and was a terrific worker—outside in all weathers and in his spare time helping around the fish wharf.

Seeing the mountainous bow waves he was creating across the Shoals, Martin grinned. He'll learn, he thought, and turned back to the trap he was hauling. This is going to be the last one, he told himself. No sense hanging'er tough out here any longer, with the wind blowing on, getting worse every minute.

He had got the trap aboard and rebaited when he glanced up and saw that the oncoming boat was headed straight for him. Warren was frantically waving something—his windbreaker, looked like. Something was up. Martin's heart did a double thump. Mary—gone to town in that damned old sloop. Bess could say all she wanted to that it was safe as a bathtub, but he'd known her to take some godalmighty chances in it in his time. He flipped the switch on his own radiotelephone. "What's eating you, Warren? Over."

Warren's voice at Martin's elbow said, "Mart . . . I spotted one of those bodies . . . one of McCarren's kids, it's got to be, washing around on Cross Island Beach. Couldn't do anything alone . . . I saw you out here and I thought the two of us might . . ."

Martin didn't wait to hear any more. He shoved his throttle ahead, circled to dump the trap overboard, and swung his boat to follow Warren's.

How in the hell are we going to land on Cross Island Beach in this tommycane? he thought. That was going to be a tough one, with the wind blowing head on there.

What they'd need would be a tender of some kind. Thing to do would be to go back to the Cove and get one— a big skiff, maybe, or better, a dory. Still, by the time they got back to Cross Island, the way the wind was breezing on, nobody'd be able to land there in anything. Call the Coast Guard? Well, the same thing. Take them a while to get here, too. If they waited for ebb tide, chances were that the body, what was left of it—and there couldn't be very much left after pounding around in the water for a week—would be gone. Be dark then, too, or damn nigh. Best thing, get in to Cross Island and take it from there.

My boat draws less water than Warren's does. Maybe we can get her in close enough for one of us to wade ashore.

Martin didn't at the moment see how. His training with the Marines had included landing craft, though. Might not be much worse than North Carolina surf.

Cross Island Beach was small as beaches go—thirty feet or so of pebbles halfway down, then clamflats studded with barnacled rocks ranging from the size of a cup to a washtub. It faced the whole sweep of the western bay, and nobody in his right mind would try to land there in a northwest gale unless he had good reason to. It was, also, the only landing place on the island. To the north and south of it, ledges began, and the whole eastern shore was high granite cliffs.

The place was beautiful on any day. Tall spruces and hardwoods grew close to the shore, with a wall of under-brush hiding whatever secret might be behind them. Today, in the spring sunlight and against the rich blue of the sky, the spruces were so dark green that they seemed almost black. Birches and shadbush were in pale new bud. Wind poured over everything, shaking out the hardwood buds in a wild dance, sending some of them flying, rocking the tops of the trees.

A pretty place and not one to fool with, Martin thought,

eyeing the sparkling green rollers driving spray halfway up the beach. He had laid his boat bow on to the wind, the engine ticking over just enough to hold her off the shore. Whatever Warren had seen must be somewhere in that mess of froth and stirred-up rockweed, but Martin couldn't see anything that looked like a body.

Must be buried up under something, he thought. There's a pile of cultch flopping around in there.

Somebody would have to get ashore and see. Nobody decent could leave a dead body to be mangled up in that mishmash unless the job of getting it turned out to be impossible.

Martin had definite feelings about that. He had seen dead bodies washing around in water. You didn't leave them there. You might have to for a while, but as soon as you could you took care of them and put up markers. Death in war was bad, it had to be. You could see reason in it, though. It was done to you by a thinking enemy, by human beings. But to die in the ocean and be left to drift while the mindless damn thing clawed you to pieces, that was the final insult that took away the last shred of dignity a man had. And this body wasn't even a man's. It was a little kid's.

He opened his throttle and jogged out to where Warren's boat was lagging off and on. "You anchor," he said into his radiophone. "Come aboard. I think we can do something."

He heard Warren's anchor splash overboard, saw him paying out anchor rode. Then he watched his chance until he could slide near enough, without slamming the two boats together, for Warren to jump aboard.

"It was right there." Warren pointed a finger, but the finger shook and an outsized roller stood the boat on end, so that he might have been pointing anywhere. "I don't see it now."

"South end of the beach by now, likely. You sure you saw something, Warren?"

Warren turned slightly green. "Oh, Christ, yes. No doubt of it."

Together they stared at the beach while the boat jogged off and on. They could see the beginning of the beaten-down path Will McCarren and his kids had made, which led from the top of the beach to the old farmhouse they'd lived in, and the rough spruce cradle equipped with a winch which he had built for a place to haul up his boat. On the cradle, a roughly built, obviously homemade punkin-seed punt had been left upside down. It didn't, Martin thought, look like anything he could use, but he'd have a look at it when he got ashore—if he could figure out how to get ashore. Under a young swamp maple, braced against its trunk and moving as the tree moved, was a crude drift-wood shelter—some kind of children's playhouse.

"Kids," Warren burst out. "Bring kids to live in a god-forsaken hole like this! What ailed the man? Goddamn the crazy fool to hell!"

"All right," Martin said. He guessed that since Will McCarren was dead, whatever hell he had coming to him was probably tended to by now. No need to talk about it.

Warren leaned his hands on the cheeserind and stared at the shore. "I'm sorry. He was a nice guy, McCarren. I never could see very much wrong with him. One of his kids wasn't too bright, retarded, I guess. Cute little duffer, though. I used to run into them around the wharf or up-town at the supermarket. That oldest girl, she was one of the prettiest girls I ever saw. Sarah, her name was." Warren's voice thickened in his throat. He wasn't crying, but Martin wondered if he might not be going to.

Probably got the horrors. He's got reason, he's already hauled one of McCarren's youngsters out of the water. And seems he'd known the oldest girl quite well. Thing like that was tougher on a youngster, somebody near to his own age being dead. Warren wasn't nineteen. Kids that age always felt immortal. I know I did. But not after the war.

Martin went on putting a loop in the end of a coil of nylon line, hauling on the knot with all his strength. Cussed stuff was likely to slip, but he guessed he'd handled enough of it to know how to make a bowline tight.

"There was a lot of bull talked around," Warren said. "Fred Folsom. Johnny Wilson. Said that whole family lived like ducks in a pond. Put kids up to hollering, 'Quack, quack,' at them. Put it out and around that McCarren hauled their traps, stole their lobsters. You believe that?"

Martin had taken off his jacket and heavy rubber boots. He thrust his head and arms through the loop he had tied and made fast the other end of the line to the barrel of his winch. "I don't know as I do," he said.

Warren, turning, stared at him, appalled. "You going to try it? Geezus, Marty, why don't we call the Coast Guard?" He eyed the rollers ripping up the beach and flinched. "We better leave it. It may not even be there now. That water's colder'n hell."

"If you saw it, it's there somewhere. No place else for it to go."

"Can you swim?"

"I've seen worse and waded through it. Let her sag in as close as you can without knocking her propeller guard to hell against the boulders. If you can't haul me back and handle the boat at the same time, use the winch."

He waited until he could see sand show dimly tan under the froth and sea mess and then went over the side. The icy water hit his body like a blow from a falling barn door. He thought for an instant his heart had stopped beating. An oncoming roller went over him; its undertow pulled him backwards, wallowing. The next one, bigger, carried him in toward the beach, and his feet found bottom. Squatting, he clung to a jutting boulder until the undertow sucked away; then he ran, skidding and sliding over barnacle-crusted rocks to the smoother pebbles halfway up the beach.

It's like those times from the landing craft, he thought a little crazily. No heavy pack this time, though. Only this cussed rope.

The rope dragged at his shoulders, slack and taut, slack and taut, as the rollers worried at it. It would dump him, sure, if he tried to navigate beach rocks in wet socks with it yanking at him. He signaled to Warren for more slack. At the top of the beach near him was a big drift log, once a tree, now nothing more than a silver-gray stub with scraggly roots at one end. He hauled in slack, slid out of the loop, and dropped it over one of the roots that was substantial enough to hold it. He glanced off at Warren to make sure Warren had seen what he'd done, and Warren signaled that he had—that he'd let out slack when needed, make sure the boat's heft didn't tear the rope loose.

Warren was all right. He might be reckless as a fool, but he sure could handle a boat. Lose that rope, and brother! Here I'd be.

Martin started for the south end of the beach, keeping as close as he could to the tide line. He checked the sea drift as he went along. It was rough going. Once he planted a foot solidly on something rubbery and soft which slid sideways and dropped him flat on his face. He rolled over, sickened, and stared groggily at an outsized sea cucumber, churned up from the bottom and trundled ashore by the gale. He swore and got up limping.

God, he thought, at least in the Marines, I had boots on.

At the south end of the beach, the flood tide had already

piled a three-foot mess of wrack—kelp and rockweed mixed with lengths of old lobster warp, driftwood sticks, cast-off beer cans. The rollers were running under it, heaving it up and down. Martin tore it apart, finding nothing.

The ledges began here, rugged granite outposts, their bases set in patches of fine sand. Between them and a solitary high rock, which had been split off the main ledge as cleanly as if by a stonecutter's plug and feathers, was a tide pool three feet wide, its surface covered with foam blown from the spray along the beach. Humped up in yellowish mats a foot thick, the stuff looked almost solid enough to walk on, but was no more than bubbles light as down. In this sheltered place out of the wind, the mats circled sluggishly, but as Martin watched, a wave broke against the rock and overflowed the pool. Washed out where the wind could get at it, the foam streamed away high in the air or splattered in scurrying dabs along the tops of the ledges. Then the undertow sucked back and he caught a glimpse of something that might be what he was hunting for.

He thought at first that the thing had been the kind of sponge called mermaid's fingers. The handlike object which had floated briefly to the surface of the pool hadn't looked like anything that could possibly be human. He stood, peering, as the next roller swept in. Then he stepped down into the pool.

Alive, the child had been very small, not more than two or three years old. It was not like a child now, except for one hand and a streaming tuft of black hair. The bleached cloth floating above it could not be called a child's shirt, but only rags shredded from some unidentifiable material. Martin tried not to look as he took off his soaked shirt and wrapped it around the tiny thing.

It was light to carry. He set off toward the place where he had hooked his lifeline, going along the top of the beach where the pebbles were smooth but still lumpy enough to make his lacerated feet wince. The wind cut through his wet clothes. He could hear his teeth clacking together.

Warren was standing off and on. He had had the sense, Martin saw, to build a fire in the cabin stove. Smoke was blowing raggedly out of the stovepipe. God, was that fire going to feel good!

The boat was not as close inshore as he'd thought it would be. Warren had had to bend on another coil of line to keep a safe length of slack. The tide was higher now, rollers breaking above the strip of boulders. Warren wouldn't be able to see the rocks now; he couldn't come in as close as they had the first time. The wind was stronger, too. A wild gust that tore past Martin almost knocked him off his feet.

He took a look at McCarren's punkinseed punt on the cradle a few feet away. Lord, that rig would sink like a clamshell—cracks in its bottom a quarter of an inch wide. You couldn't row it even if McCarren had left any oars around. You couldn't tow it—there was nothing in it to hitch a line to, no ringbolt in the bow, no thwarts. Hell with it. Warren would have to tow him through the surf.

He'd need both hands on the line, hauling to keep his head above water. Even then he'd have to swallow suds. The body would have to be rope-wrapped and lashed to his belt. He hauled in slack, sliced off a generous piece of line with his jackknife. He knotted another loop and got it securely on over his shoulders before he knelt and tied up the shirt with the piece he had cut off, cursing under his breath at the slippery nylon.

Cussed stuff. Be easier to tie knots in an angleworm. But it was the toughest rope there was, a blessing to fishermen. You couldn't break it.

When he finished, the bundle—it was just a bundle done

up in a shirt now, a damnsight easier to look at—hung snug against his back. He stepped down into the water.

Warren had come inshore as far as he'd dared to. He went out slowly, but faster than was comfortable for a man towed through surf at the end of a rope. The slack tightened around Martin's chest. He pitched forward and plowed underwater past the first line of rollers. Safely clear, Warren hove to, used the winch, and wound him in fast. Martin came up alongside the boat, grabbed at Warren's reaching hands, and was hauled, gurgling and spluttering, in over the gunnel.

"Geezus!" he said as soon as he could speak. "What'd you think you had on there—a goddamn water skier?"

Warren at the moment was too busy to answer. He had barely got Martin aboard before he had had to jump for the gearshift and the wheel. The engine roared as he opened the throttle and put distance between the boat and the wicked line of breakers. When he judged there was enough, he slowed down, looked over his shoulder with a white-faced grin. "You all right, Marty? I did yank you out of there pretty fast, but I didn't see how else . . . I was good and damn scared, if you want to know."

"You did fine," Martin said through his chattering teeth.

"Whack that line off you and get below, where it's warm. Here." He reached for the work knife which Martin carried in a sheath fastened to the wall of his pilot shelter and skidded it along the platform.

Martin fielded the knife with his foot, but he didn't use it. No sense to cut good nylon rope, the stuff was expensive, and he'd already had to cut it once. He stood up and wriggled out of the loops.

"I saw you fall down ashore there," Warren said. "Thought sure you'd busted something. You get hurt? I saw you got up limping." He didn't say what he'd gone through, wondering what he'd be able to do if Martin had, say, broken an ankle.

"Slipped on a cussed great sea cucumber didn't want to be there any more than I did. Picked up some barnacle cuts."

"Looks as though you troddled on every barnacle on the goddamned beach." Warren eyed the bloody footprints on the platform. "You got anything to put on the cuts?"

"Got a first-aid kit in the cuddy." He hadn't, but no sense to frig around with cuts now. He undressed quickly, down to his hide, grateful for the fire in the cuddy stove. When he was dry and as warm as he thought he was going to be, he dressed in what he had aboard the boat—a pair of old jeans, his jacket, and on top of that a suit of oilskins to keep out the wind. He hadn't anything handy that would keep his feet from bleeding into his rubber boots.

That would be a sticky mess. They were new boots, but he probably wouldn't wear them again unless he thought of something to soak up the blood. He hated blood—had, ever since the war. He finally took out his knife and slashed a couple of thick pads out of the quilt on his bunk. Inside the boots, they felt good, warm and soft, and the cuts didn't sting quite so much now.

Warren grinned at him as he poked his head out of the cuddy. "I've been trying to call ashore," he said, "but I can't get anybody on the CB except Edie Bickford singing hymns."

"We'd better light out, then. Folks'll worry, where we're so late. Try it again on the way in. Maybe somebody'll shut her up."

"Gramp likely will. He'll be having a nippershin." Warren jumped a little, staring at the shore. "Hey, you ever hear of any deer on Cross Island?"

"Could be. Why? You see something?"

"Some kind of a tan-colored patch, moving. Could've been a big owl, I guess."

"Anybody landed there now, there'd have to be a boat," Martin chattered.

"That's right. Damn spooky place. I wouldn't land there now if we did have a tender. Come on, let's go before you freeze to death."

It was late; the sun had set half an hour ago, leaving an orange slash across the western sky. Behind them, Cross Island answered no questions, its trees already beginning to darken in the windy dusk.

PART TWO

Will McCarren, lying flat behind the drift log where Martin Hadley had hooked his lifeline, watched the two boats go out of sight behind the spray on Cross Island Head. After they had gone, he still lay there, crumpled, his hands clenched in the soft sand collected behind the log, while slow tears trickled down his face.

He hadn't noticed the boats lying to off the beach until he had almost walked out of the path entrance into plain sight. He had ducked fast. At first he hadn't been concerned about their landing. They didn't have a tender with them, and even if they had, they'd have had a wild time getting one through the surf. From what he knew about the Cove fishermen, they were handy fellows with their boats, careful; they wouldn't risk one in a stunt which, today, only a fool would try.

Besides, nobody'd have a reason to land here now, he thought with bitterness. They think we're all dead. Nobody left to shove around.

Then, with growing amazement, he had watched Martin Hadley coming ashore on the end of a rope. He had seen Martin pull the body out of the tide pool, had been within ten feet of him when he had wrapped it up and tied it in his shirt.

That had been Hal, too little for Rosie. Hal, his son, his youngest, dearly loved. Not that it made a difference. He had loved Rosie and she was gone, too.

I ought to have taken Hal away from him.

Why hadn't he? It was too late now. He had lain there in a kind of paralysis, watching a stranger go off with the body of his son. Then, when the man was safely back aboard and the boat seemed ready to leave, he had jumped up—to yell, to make himself known, realizing at once the futility of that. Nobody could possibly get ashore again; there were reasons why he had to stay hidden.

I suppose I'm still half-crazy, he thought.

For a week, he had felt this numbness, this shock, whatever it was, which had kept him from even trying to decide what to do. Would it be better to knuckle under, take the remaining children back, face up to what he had run away from? He could hail some passing fisherman, get ferried to the mainland, and do that. And that would be the end of his son Bill.

Should he tough it out here? Get ashore somehow, locate his boat? There'd be no living here without a boat. Fight back at what was here to fight against? That would take doing, too. Staring out at the darkening waters of the wide bay, at the bleak ledges splattered with foam, he felt a vast, icy loneliness.

Civilization, it seemed, came after you with bloodhounds until you were dead. Then the whole clout of it went into action, gave you everything it had. Like this man Hadley, who'd risked drowning, not for a living body but for a dead one. Somebody dead, show respect. Do whatever possible against the disaster of death, which had made a lifeless body what it was. Kid yourself that there was something human about it still. Bury it gently with prayers and decency.

But I and my kids, still living, aren't we human?

He got stiffly to his feet, shaking the sand off his fingers. A dried beach-rosebush stalk clung to one hand, its thorns driven deep into his palm. He pulled it away, realizing he hadn't even felt the pain.

The afternoon a week ago, the day of the southeasterly storm, when the Coast Guard search party had arrived at the island, Will had not yet known that his boat, with two of his children, was missing. At lunchtime the kids had been milling around the kitchen—the custom was for everyone to get his own meal at noon—and in the commotion Will hadn't noticed that Rosie and Hal weren't there. Or, if he had, he'd have thought they were still down on the beach. They played all over the place, came in to eat when they were hungry.

Earlier in the day, before the wind had breezed up and made fishing impossible, they had been out in the boat with him, handlining. Rosie hadn't wanted to come in—she loved to fish. She'd sulked a little, and then, ashore, she'd asked if she and Hal could stay and play in the boat. Will hadn't seen any reason why not, provided she kept an eye on Hal. Not that he'd been worried about that. All of the kids knew how important it was to look after Hal.

Hal, going on three, was not retarded—at least, not from his birth. For his first year, he had been a sunny little boy, bright as a button; but he had never got over a dose of dope given him by a baby-sitter. The baby-sitter, a high school freshman, had said when found out that the kid was driving her crazy, fussing, and she'd tried a little acid to shut him up.

It had been nip and tuck with Hal. He had had a very serious reaction, an allergy, which resulted in brain damage. Doctors had given Will a forlorn hope that Hal might get better as he grew older. "Keep him quiet," they'd told Will and his wife, Amy. "Don't let him get too upset or scared, if you can help it."

For the past months on the island, it had seemed to Will that the baby had been better. He had started to take an interest in things—which was the main reason why he had had to be watched, because his interest took the form of a blind, aimless poking into things, touching a hot stove, or reaching for the handle of a steaming kettle. He would carry something—an oar, perhaps, down to the water's edge and set it adrift, as he would one of his shoes or his jacket. But this kind of interest, Will had told himself, was better than none at all, and recently Hal had spoken a couple of words, something he hadn't done since before his illness.

His brothers, Julian and Hank, scouting around the mud-flats in the cove, had discovered a hen clam bed. Hal had been delighted with the big six-inch shells. He had brought one to his father and had said, not plainly, but plainly enough, "Hin clam."

In a southeasterly, Cross Island Beach was in the lee, only ripples washing up and down its edge as the tide went out—a safe, quiet place for kids to play. Will had carried the boat's anchor halfway up the beach and had bedded it firmly behind a big rock. He had fastened it to a trip-line, so that he could haul the boat up when the tide came in. He had been on his way down the path to do that when he had seen the Coast Guard boat making into the cove with quite a crowd of men aboard. Among them, he had spotted Otis Baker.

Ever since the town officers had warned him, Will had been expecting another visit from them. He had prepared for it, so that when they did come with a warrant, they weren't going to find anybody to haul off the island. He had drilled the kids to climb into the loft over the kitchen, pull up the ladder, and close the access hatch. The loft, actually not much more than a crawl space, was a dark, airless place with no windows. The hatch had been sawed out of the ceiling boards so that cracks matched. When it was closed, you had to look twice to see that it was there.

The children had been scared to death the day Will had had the run-in with Baker and the other man who had come with him, who had turned out to be a Town Selectman. The two had come tramping in without so much as a knock, threatening jail and the orphanage and a warrant for Will's arrest, and he, after his first astonishment, had lost his temper. He had been bewildered to hear that he had been stealing lobsters out of traps set around Cross Island; that he'd committed a crime not sending his kids to school; that he was trespassing on private property.

What had upset him at first was not the charges, since all three of them were certainly without foundation, but Hal, terrified by the loud, angry voices, had suddenly begun to scream.

Sarah had got Hal out of there fast. She had been taking a bath in the back room at the time. She had raced in, scooped up the baby, and hustled him behind a closed door, where he couldn't hear the racket. Sarah had been in too much of a hurry to put on more than a minimum of clothing, which had given Baker's friend the chance to remark that it was sights like that that made a man think McCarren had better give his kids an education.

Bill, Sarah's twin, had ducked out of sight, as he had to when anyone came, but Julian, Will's second son, had started for the man. Will had got between them. He hadn't taken his shotgun from the brackets where it hung on the wall, but he had glanced at it. He'd said, "Gentlemen, these charges are a made-up mess of lies. You get out of here. You're scaring my children."

Today, seeing the boat off the beach with Baker aboard, Will went back up the path fast. "Here they come, kids!

Bill, get the crowd up the ladder, and don't any of you so much as breathe."

He himself hadn't planned to hide in the loft. With all the kids up there, there wasn't room for him. Besides, he wanted to be somewhere within hearing to find out what was going on. Handy to the house was a big spruce, easy to climb and thick with branches at the bottom. He jumped, forced his slim, lithe body between two of the lower limbs, and lay out of sight, comfortably braced, ten feet above the path while the party of men went heavy-footed in single file below him.

Why the Coast Guard? And why so many men? A regular gang. They must have expected a fight. They would have had one if he hadn't seen them first.

But I'm no giant, he thought. One of them, possibly two, could get handcuffs onto me.

The hefty Coast Guard boat undoubtedly had been called out because of the rough weather. But why had they come at all in the middle of a roaring gale? It didn't make sense.

He thought uneasily of his boat, triplined off down at the beach. What if they decided to tow that off with them? Down at Bullet Bay, where he'd stopped for a while at an island in the harbor on his way north, he'd had a small skiff which he'd used for a tender, stolen off the beach. Here, he'd taken no chances. His boat, hauled to the beach at night, or in bad weather, winched up on the cradle, was kept secured by a steel chain, padlocked at both ends. To get the boat free, a man would need either the keys or a bolt cutter. But not today.

The men were gone for quite a while. Occasionally, above the roar of the wind, he could hear them nearby crackling through the underbrush. Apparently they were searching the island. Will hoped Bill and Sarah weren't having too tough a time keeping the kids quiet. As long as Sarah cuddled Hal, he wouldn't be any problem, and Hank and Julian were old enough to know better than to make a sound. The joker in the pack was Rosie. She was ten, with ideas of her own. Like as not, if she took it into her head, she might spit down on somebody through a knothole.

Presently two of the searchers came back and stood waiting on the path below Will's tree. Peering down through the twigs, he could make out Otis Baker's potbelly. The other man he couldn't see at all, but he could hear him. He said, "Christ, this is an awful thing, Oat!"

Otis said, "It's a turrible thing, Alby."

"All them kids in that tub of a boat in this tommycane. Man must've been crazy."

Otis said, "That boat ain't no tub, Alby. She's a good stiddy craft. Like a lifeboat. Justin and I looked her over after Warren towed her in."

What the hell? Will froze in his tree. His boat? His boat was down in the cove right now, hitched to a stout anchor and a tripline.

"Flo was telling the womenfolks at the Ladies' Aid that you and Justin scared the bejeezus out of him."

There was a short silence. A gust of wind roared through the tree, and Will momentarily lost the voices. When he could hear them again, Otis was saying, ". . . madder than he was scared, I took him to be."

"What'd you say to him made him take off like that?"

"What we had to." Otis spoke out, loud and clear. "Justin says, 'You're trespassing here on private property,' and he says, 'I've got permission from the owner. I plan to stay here, buy the island, if I like it.' Well, now, Alby, I knowed that was a lie. It ain't likely a man in McCarren's shape and condition could rake up enough cash to buy Cross Island."

"Took it on yourself to know that, I guess."

"Jerry Cross, my girl's husband lives in Oregon, owns

it. Pays the taxes on it. I'd be likely to know what it's worth. Then Justin told him the law about sending kids to school. 'Go back to where you come from. Put your kids to school where you b'long to.' That's what he told him. 'You been seen hauling people's traps. They is a witness to it.'"

"Who? Who see him?"

"Johnny Wilson . . ."

"Johnny Wilson, for godsake! Him and his kid Finney been doing that for years. You crazy?"

"I will be if folks keep on blaming me for what happened to them McCarrens. I d'know what Flo could've said . . ." Otis paused, went on. "We did give him a chance to clear out."

"You sure did. Took care of the problem for you, didn't he? Goddammit, Otis, let me tell you, I don't think much of the way you and Justin done. Makes me good and damn ashamed of the whole town. I met McCarren once, and I see his kids. You wouldn't ask for a nicer bunch of people. No call to talk that rough to a man like him. What was behind it? Sounds to me as though something was."

"I'm an officer of the law, and what I got to do, I do. If someone takes off from me doing it, I ain't righteously to blame—"

"Oh, bullshit!" Alby said. He called loudly, "You boys find anyone?"

The voices died away along the path.

My boat, Will thought. She's gone adrift. Somebody's found her and towed her in.

He wormed his way down the tree. Hidden in the underbrush above the shore, he could see the whole curve of the beach. Baker's party was getting into a tender at the edge of tide. The Coast Guard boat was anchored in the cove. And no other boat in sight. Will could make out his trip-line washing around in the ripples like a watersnake. Someone had untied it, put the anchor aboard. Flood tide, southeasterly wind. The boat had floated off by itself.

Old Hal, the potterer. Futzing around into everything, not a rational thought in his head. Why hadn't Rosie stopped him? She knew better than to let him fool with the boat's anchor. She couldn't have seen him, didn't know he'd done it, or she'd have said.

He turned back up the path, thinking with a kind of wry amusement, So we're all dead. That's one way to get rid of us.

From up by the house, the kids were talking. Bill came running down the path. "Dad, where are Hal and Rosie? Were they with you?"

Will McCarren's fighting war with civilization dated from the loss of his wife, Amy. On the day of her death, she said to him, "Will, get the children away. Get them out of it, somehow, somewhere, whatever way you can."

Sarah and Bill, the twins; Hank and Julian; Rosie. What, Will asked himself in bewilderment, was happening to them? They were good kids, or should have been, with a decent upbringing, and so were the kids in the gangs they ran with —eleven- to fourteen-year-olds, mostly. The kids of birthday parties and games along the shady streets in summertime; the icebox raiders; the bicycle riders. The kids; the dearly loved. Who had changed almost overnight into a secret and furtive nation of their own.

Amy, at first, had refused to believe it. But Bill and Sarah were arrested, along with a gang of other youngsters, for breaking into a store and wrecking it. At the hearing in Juvenile Court, she heard the judge talk of drugs handed around on school grounds, of unsuccessful attempts to stop the traffic, of effects on the children.

"Nevertheless," he said grimly, "the laws are written for the protection of society and for the punishment of crime; and crime is crime, no matter how young the criminal may be. The charge in this case, breaking and entering and larceny in the nighttime, could be malicious mischief if cigarettes and candy hadn't been stolen. This is a first offense, however. A second offense will have more serious results."

He paroled the children to the custody of their parents, provided damage was paid for.

Fathers got together and paid damages—two thousand dollars to the owner of the store, whose reaction was that if they didn't want their damned brats shot, they'd better keep them away from him.

Sarah seemed sobered by the hearing, but if Bill was, he didn't show it. "So we got busted," Will overheard him tell Sarah. "If we hadn't, there wouldn't have been any hooha, would there?"

Ethics? Will thought. So anything goes, just so you don't get caught at it? How does he get to think that way?

Throughout the hearing, he had watched his children. They had listened politely, if not respectfully. Something about the closed and shuttered young faces wrenched at his heart.

He tried to comfort Amy. "Kids are a tribe, they all run together. It's all of a piece with everybody taking to white socks instead of colored ones. It won't last. It can't."

Amy's reply surprised him. "If what civilization offers school children is dope, hell-raising, and lawbreaking," she said crisply, "what's to prevent concerned parents from seceding from it, creating a little circle of decency of their own?"

Will stared at her. "I don't get you."

"We ourselves could teach our kids to read, write, and figure, give them a solid base to start out on. The schools aren't doing it. Look at Bill and Sarah. They can't even read a newspaper."

"They don't feel it's worth their while to try," Will said.

He didn't believe the kids were entirely to blame. He took a long, hard look at the world they had to live in. He didn't know that he himself cared very much for the mishmash he had to put up with every day. The morning battle with traffic to get to his business in the city; the same battle at night, driving home to the suburb where he lived. Violence; muggings; people not safe on the streets or in the parks they paid taxes to maintain. Steel doors and shutters a must on stores and businesses like his own. And for all you wanted to, you didn't dare, these days, to pick up a hitchhiker.

"We're planning to send the kids to college," Amy said. "We've got quite a nest egg put by for that. But what use is college to youngsters who can't read? The university people say that most entering freshmen are illiterate. It's not just our own kids, Will, that this outrage is happening to."

Seeing him so downcast, she smiled at him. "Times are changing. They're leaving us behind. I would like to leave the times behind for a while; it would be one way to fight. I'm not taking this lying down."

She didn't. She fought back as best she could, with good humor and, at times, exasperation. "They're so kindly," she told Will. "They treat me the way you'd treat a doddering old great-aunt who's nosing around into plans and projects she doesn't know a thing about or understand. Just do anything, say anything, that'll shut her up, so they can go their ways in peace. How do I handle that? It's quite a psychological technique, let me tell you. Leaves me without a leg to stand on."

"Bat their silly heads together," Will said.

"That wouldn't change their world."

She was a rock—a rock for Will and a great steadiness throughout the continuing horror of what had happened to Hal. A fighter who couldn't win the battle of her own illness. She died of cancer the year Hal was two years old.

If he hadn't lost her, Will might have tried to tough it out. But he had his business in the city; commuting took a big bite of his time. With Amy gone, he had to hire housekeepers. None of them stayed long. Five kids, all of them hellions, plus that crazy baby who had to be watched all the time, they complained. Housekeepers streamed through Will's house like a migration of birds.

One of them, leaving, reported on Rosie. "I asked her to help do dishes, and you know what she said? She said she wasn't anybody's little mother and, praise God, she never would be, now that ladies had the pill. Ladies!" The housekeeper snorted. "Some of you rich people better take a look at the schools they go to. From the elementary on up, they're rotten with dope."

Will paid the woman without saying anything and watched her stamp off down the driveway, relieved to get her fury out of the house.

Rosie, he thought, and had to grin a little. That one. Rosie was smart; she was not yet ten. He couldn't see that information about the pill would do her much harm; she'd probably picked it up on TV. Or maybe she'd heard Sarah's crowd talking. But Sarah— Sarah was sixteen. She had calmed down somewhat after Hal's accident, and her mother's death had hit her hard; but he guessed that things being as they were now, it was a good idea if she did have the pill. The thought curdled his blood; they were all so damned *young.*

He sat down, a deeply worried man. Amy had told him what to do. When she had been so sick, he'd wondered if she'd been quite rational, but now he thought she'd been more rational than he was. She'd said again, "Get them away, Will. Get them out of it."

Will's business, these days, was a small chain of garages and service stations, which he owned in partnership with his brother, Frank. The business had done well; McCarren

Brothers had not made the partners rich, but it had made them well-to-do. There would be no question of money, Will knew, if he wanted to pull out and go somewhere else. Eventually, if he found a place to settle down—the "decent" place Amy had dreamed of—he could sell out to Frank, which he would be delighted to do. From the beginning, the business had been to him a desolate, dragging boredom.

As a young man, he had trained as a teacher, had taught science and mathematics, but as his family had increased, the salary hadn't been enough. Before his marriage, the love of his life had been boats—sailing, navigation. He had studied boat design, and been for several summers an instructor in a coast Survival School, heading up crews of high school boys, teaching them how to survive on offshore islands. He had never forgotten those summers; they had been among his happiest times. Sitting, thinking, Will made up his mind.

Quietly, without saying anything to anyone, he went about getting ready. From his files, he dug out the plans for a boat, designed after the craft used by the Outward Bound Schools, and had it built at the city boatyard. It was nothing elaborate. His project was simple and he meant to keep it so. The boat was sturdy, broad-beamed, big enough for him and his load of kids, with an inboard engine and a mast and sail which could be stepped in sailing weather. It had a removable canvas sprayhood which could be set up to fend off flying spray. He also bought a small skiff, equipped it with oars, mast, and spritsail. Rowed, it could be used as a tender; but one of the things he recalled with keen pleasure was sailing a small skiff, and he wanted to teach his children how to do it.

He brushed up on navigation, found he could pull out of his brain a good deal of past knowledge of the coast islands and of the Survival course he had used to teach.

He planned to start out in June after school closed, telling the kids it would be a summer outing. At the end of summer, it would be up to them whether they came back or not.

In April, his plans were knocked galley-west. Bill was again arrested, this time on the serious charge which the judge of the Juvenile Court had mentioned. This time it was the matter of a car, stolen and smashed up, the back seat loaded with loot; and this time the Judge didn't hesitate.

Will talked with Bill on the morning the boy was taken away to the Boys' Correctional School. He didn't say how he himself felt, or that anyone was heartbroken. He told Bill in detail of the project he had planned. "I wish I hadn't waited so long," he finished. "I wish we'd gone when I first made up my mind."

Bill stared at him. The boy was bitter, not saying much. He did say, "Uh-huh. You're telling me it's too late now."

"No. It is not. Listen. We'll be on an island off Bullet Bay for the summer. Here's a map showing where it is. I'll be in touch with the Bullet Bay Post Office, over in the town. Write me if you need me, or . . . need anything."

"Okay," Bill said.

God, Will thought. How do you talk to a stranger whom you love better than anyone in the world? He held out his hand. "Good-by, son. Take care, as best you can."

The next week, he put his affairs in order, listed his house with an agent for rental, turned his business over to Frank. He did not tell Frank where he was going. Then he bundled his astonished family shopping for warm, outdoor outfits, loaded them aboard his boat, and put to sea, with nothing much more than necessary supplies, camping equipment, and his own high hopes.

He had expected howls of protest. He had snatched the kids away without warning from their friends, their schools, from all their interests—whatever their interests might be. Will didn't know. How they'd take it, he couldn't say. Times before, on projects, he'd ask them what they'd like to do.

This time, he told himself, he wasn't giving an inch, whoever blew up a storm. He braced himself. To his surprise, there was no storm. The kids went from acute bewilderment to hilarious joy, and nobody regretted school.

They had been moping around the house for days, shocked and sobered by what had happened to Bill. Sarah had been particularly dispirited. As twins, she and Bill had always been close. It had seemed to Will that they could pass words without words—by osmosis, Amy had called it. How Sarah felt about Bill's disaster she didn't say, except only once when Will had tried to comfort her; a mistake. She had burst out in a fury, "He had it coming! Why did he act like such a fool?" And that was that.

As they sailed north in the big boat, with the small skiff towing behind, Will watched with vast relief the tension going out of everybody. He hadn't realized how strung-up-tight his children had been for a long time. There had been Amy's death; the housekeepers' nagging; the school year nearing an end—a bad time for all children; and then, Bill. The old routines, on and on, like forever.

He saw the springs unwinding with change, as his own springs were. The kids were fascinated by the boats, by the tents and camping supplies, by the idea of staying on an island. Will found his stock was higher than it had been for a long time. Everyone seemed to feel his plan was a nice surprise that Dad had dreamed up for them. He overheard Hank and Julian: "The old man hasn't gone bananas after all." "Yeah. Thank God."

The island in Bullet Bay was forty miles up the coast and two miles from the mainland town of the same name. Will had known it well in the days of his Survival course teaching. To come back was almost like coming home. It was a smallish island which had once been farmed and was now abandoned, with all its buildings rotting down. There had never been any trouble with its owners about the Survival School youngsters camping there, which was one reason why Will had chosen it. Except that the buildings had rotted flatter, he could see no change since he'd been there before.

They put up the tents and lived there for a month. Will produced everything he could remember from his Survival course. He taught everybody, down to Rosie, how to sail the small skiff, how to hook on the spreet—the slender pole that spread the triangular sail; how never to tie the sheet in a knot that couldn't be untied fast—say it was safe ever to tie the sheet at all. His star pupil, not much to his surprise, wasn't one of the boys, it was Rosie. She loved to sail and she loved to fish. She also had a mind of her own. Will had put his foot flat down about anyone's taking the skiff out alone. But Rosie did, when no one was looking. Will spanked her for it, not that it did any good. He told himself he had to recognize an obsession when he saw one.

"It's all right for the three of you to go sailing together as soon as you learn about the wind and tides here and what's sensible to do and what isn't. So you all buckle down and learn. Until you do, the mast and sail will be padlocked to a tree so that nobody can sneak it aboard the skiff." He wasn't about to coddle anybody.

He was delighted at how quickly they did learn, so that they could go by themselves. Fill them so full of things they like to do, he thought, that there won't be time for any hell-raising.

Puzzled one day by a drift of smoke coming from the far side of the island, he walked over there to investigate. Someone must have landed and built a beach fire, he thought. After a week of dry weather, outdoor fires weren't anything to fool with in the spring of the year, when leaves were still off the trees. He found the skiff drawn up on the beach of a small sandcove. Rosie, Hank, and Julian were boiling a pot of lobsters in a kettle swiped from the camp equipment. Their fire, he was pleased to see, had been built below high-water mark—a small blaze contained in a fireplace of piled rocks, exactly as he had taught them to make a cooking fire. The lobsters, however, were something else again. There was only one source they could have come from. So here was trouble, looking for a place to happen.

A look, something akin to an electric shock, passed between the three as they saw Will heave in sight.

"Hi, Poppa!" Hank greeted him. "Want some lobster, they're almost ready."

"We're practicing survival," Rosie said. "Living off the country when we're starving to death."

Julian said nothing.

Will sat down on a nearby ledge. "Are you starving to death?"

"Yes, we are," Rosie said. "We didn't catch any fish, and there's nothing to eat over at camp but bread and some rotten old canned stuff."

"I know. But we're going to town today. I thought we'd eat at a restaurant. Where'd you get the lobsters?"

Hank rolled his eyes at Rosie, but Julian spoke up. "We hauled some lobster traps."

Rosie said, "You told us. Make use of what there is, you said. So we did."

"Look," Will said, "I've never told you to make use of what belongs to somebody else. Those lobsters are some fellow's living he's worked hard to get. Come on, let's have it straight. You knew you were stealing or you'd have come ashore and cooked at the camp, not sneaked over here by yourselves. You had it in mind when you went sailing this morning—you took a cookpot along. Whose traps were they? I've got to find the fellow and pay him."

"We don't know."

"What color were the buoys?"

Seems they'd hauled quite a lot. The buoys had been different colors.

Julian said, "A man in a big white boat chased us. That's why we put in here. He couldn't come ashore because he didn't have any tender, but he hollered at us."

"Oh, great!" Will said. He got up, took a hefty kick at the kettle, scattering its contents. "Take the skiff back around the island," he said. "When you get there, you'll find me and Sarah and Hal gone to town. You jokers can stay home today. You can have bread and rotten old canned stuff for lunch."

He helped them launch the skiff and saw them well on their way. Then he threw the lobsters off into deep water, used the kettle to douse the fire. Heavyhearted, he walked back across the island, with it dangling from his hand.

Sarah always shopped better than Will did; she made the grocery money go further. After they had eaten lunch at the waterfront restaurant, she went off uptown to the supermarket with lists and duffel bags, taking along the letters to Bill, to mail at the Post Office. Each week, everyone except Hal wrote to Bill. So far, there had been no word from him. Surely, Will thought, if Sarah had had a letter, she'd have said so, knowing how we all feel. Strange, he hadn't written, even to her—she'd be the likely one. Perhaps there'd be something today.

He set Hal on his shoulder and began walking along the waterfront, making his inquiries. Had anyone complained about his kids hauling lobster traps? He met only noncommittal answers, unfriendly glances. Who had a big white boat? Half the fishermen in the Harbor. If he could find out who owned the traps, he said, he'd be glad to explain and to pay damages. Nobody knew anything about it.

After a while, Will gave up. He'd be in town next week, he could try again. Perhaps, in the meantime, some of the owners of the rifled traps would come to him. Sarah would have the duffel bags loaded by now. He'd better go see about getting them down to the boat. He had one more errand to do, at the lumberyard, to buy some lumber for tent platforms and see about getting it boated out to the island. But as he walked along, Sarah caught up with him.

"The duffel bags are loaded aboard, Dad," she said. "A . . . a fellow helped me. I spread the sprayhood over them so the sun . . . you know . . . keep it off the milk and meat." She seemed ruffled and breathless; she didn't say why, but went on unwrapping a Milky Way, which she handed up to Hal.

"Any letter from Bill?" Will asked.

She shook her head.

The young fellow at the lumberyard glanced at Will's list and put it down on the counter. He looked at Will and at Sarah, and he turned an embarrassed pink. "I only work here, Mister. The boss . . . I . . . uh . . . I got orders not to sell you anything."

Surprised, Will pulled out his wallet. "Matter of money, son?"

"Un-hunh."

"Then why?"

"Look, I'm sorry. But I've got my troubles, too. Old Nails Potter owns this lumberyard. I work for him. He's going on for ninety years old and he's a heller on wheels. Owns a lot of shore property around here and he's got bugs in his hat about the hippies camping out on his land. That includes the island you're camping on. He could make real trouble for you. If I was you, I'd go somewhere else."

"Why, thank you for telling me," Will said. "He wouldn't consider letting me pay him some rent?"

"Oh, gosh, no. He hates hippies. And anybody who's got a hair sticking out of a pimple on his chin is a hippie to him."

He glanced again at Sarah. He was obviously somewhat taken with Sarah.

She said, "My goodness, then. Who's that old hippie hanging on the wall there?"

The portrait, in a thick antique frame with some of the gilt chipped off, was of an aged codger with side-whiskers and a tremendous gray beard spread all over his front.

The boy glanced at it with a wide grin. "That," he said, "is a true copy of old Mr. Nails Potter's father. Raised a bush, didn't he?" He turned to Will. "Look, Mister, what did you want this lumber for—anything you need in a hurry, like repairs on your boat?"

"Oh, no. For tent platforms; we were getting a little damp on the bottom. But from what you tell me, I expect we won't need it now; we'll be moving on."

"Better if you do. I'd go soon if I was you. Them fishermen, they'd rather see their wife violated than one of their traps."

"Yes," Will said. "I've been trying all afternoon to find out who owned those traps. Three of my kids hauled some, took out the lobsters to cook. They're city kids, didn't know any better. I've batted their ears down about it. They won't do it again. Do you know who I ought to see to pay damages to?"

"No, not any one feller. There's five or six wouldn't welcome seeing you, money or no money. I'd skip it if I was you."

"If I leave some money with you, could you see it goes where it belongs?"

"Sure, glad to. Hey, how many lobsters did your kids steal?" The boy stared at the bills Will had put down on the counter.

Will grinned. "A camp cookpot full. The extra is to say I'm darned sorry. And if you see Mr. Potter, will you tell him that unless it blows a tommycane, we'll be moving off his land tomorrow?"

On the way home, at first, nobody said much. Hal, worn out, slept. Sarah was silent and, Will knew, upset. He didn't wonder. He himself felt as if he had been gone over by something with claws.

Is it because we're strangers and the way we look? The way we speak? Not slicked up and our hair too long?

He had never seen any reason to make the kids dress up for a trip to town. They'd always worn their camp clothes for a sail across the bay. Their everyday shirts and jeans showed plenty of rugged wear and weren't too clean, but not too dirty, either. They all needed haircuts, not that anybody wanted one. Most kids, nowadays, wore their hair long. His own hair was already bushy, and he was starting a thick black beard to be proud of. The twins and Rosie had inherited their mother's dark chestnut curls; the other three had got theirs from him, coal-black and also curly. Dammit, he liked the way they looked now—alive, tanned and husky, without the something-that-had-crawled-out-from-under-a-stump paleness they'd had at the fag end of the school year.

He glanced down at Hal, asleep in Sarah's lap. Hal had enjoyed his Milky Way; he was smeared with chocolate from his chin to his eyebrows.

"Old Hal," Will said, "does he look like a dangerous character to you, Sarah?"

"No, Dad." She managed a smile. "He looks like a chocolate-frosted leprechaun."

"So he does. Do you think he might be getting a little better?"

"Sometimes I think so."

The sail was drawing nicely; the boat spanked with gentle sounds over the small late-afternoon ripples on the bay. The island was closer. They could see the kids waiting on the shore.

"Dad . . ." Sarah began, and stopped.

"What's wrong, Sarah? I know something is."

"Nothing's wrong. Something's right. Something's gone terribly right at last. It's Bill. He's here. Aboard the boat. He's under the sprayhood with the duffel bags."

Will sat for a paralyzed moment, unable to move. He said in a half-whisper, "How . . .?"

"He ran away from a work gang. He's been on the road, hitchhiking for two weeks, trying to get to us. He's so thin . . . and hungry. I'm scared he's sick." She stared at Will, her lips tight. "Dad, you won't— What will you do?"

"I'll say thank God. Here, take the wheel, will you?" He made his way forward, past the engine box, to where he could see the boy's pale face peering out of the covered darkness. "Bill? Son?"

"I'm here," Bill said. "Who else?" He looked past his father at the two who sat in the stern. "Hi, Hal, old socks-o."

Hal, who had waked up, slid away from the shelter of Sarah's arm. He stared around anxiously, not sure where the voice had come from.

Bill wriggled past the duffel bags, came out to where he could be seen. He snapped his fingers. "See? Bill, Hal. What's left of him," and stretched his arms to catch the small figure lurching toward him. "Looks like he's glad to see me, almost like he knows me. Man, I never saw him do this before."

For Hal had snuggled his head into the front of Bill's shirt and was patting both hands on his shoulders.

"You better take him, Poppa," Bill said. "I'm filthy as a hog. He might catch something." He stared up at Will. "I'm not going back there."

"Who says you are? We're heading north tomorrow. You're one good reason why we're getting out of here fast."

"You're taking me along? Breaking the law?"

"I'm doing what I think is right. If I've got the guts to finish what I've started to do, I'll have to say I'm a lawless man. I might even say a man without a country. I'm glad to see you. I've never been so glad to see anyone in my life."

They packed that afternoon, leaving the tents to be dismantled in the morning. Sometime in the night, Will heard a powerboat in the cove, but there were numerous lobstering and dragging outfits around at all hours—he didn't think much about it. In the morning, they found that the small skiff, Rosie's pride and joy, had been stolen.

Will considered sailing over to Bullet Bay and making inquiries, decided that, with Bill here now, he wouldn't risk it. Trouble, he told himself wryly, had found the place to happen and there'd be more. The powerboat very likely had belonged to one owner of the rifled traps, paying back in kind. He'd let the skiff go and get out of here as soon as he could.

It was a lovely morning, sunny, with a brisk breeze for fine sailing. The island behind them looked beautiful, but abandoned now, and lonely. They had had fun there.

"You think anybody'll ever see our brush camp again?" Hank asked Julian.

"Nope. We hid it too good. Nobody'll ever find it."

Rosie said, "Nobody'll go fishing in the cove again. I wish we didn't have to go."

"We'll find another island," Will said. "With a sand cove and bigger flounders."

"We don't have any skiff to fish in," Rosie said mournfully.

"We'll buy some lumber and build one."

Will's spirits were high. He had Bill back; he meant to fight for him, tooth and claw. He told everybody about his plan, speaking into a stunned silence. For a moment, his hopes had sunk into his boots.

"You mean," Hank said, "no more school? Anywhere?"

"I don't know everything in the world," Will said. "But I can teach you basic stuff, along lines you're interested in."

"Learn what I want to? Not a mess of half-fried old crap? Do what I want to?"

"Could I learn how to build a windmill that would generate real electricity, pump water?" Julian asked.

"We could have a stab at it. Get a book, with directions."

Sarah drew a long breath. "No more competition," she said dreamily.

Bill grinned at her. "No more competition; who needs the pill? No more B-ball. No more roaring out to play for dear old Titmouse because you're big and pretty and have lovely muscles." He had slept all night and had eaten. He felt and looked better.

Thinking things over, Sarah had sobered a little. "How'll we keep warm in tents this winter, Dad?"

"Electric heat from the windmill, you goony bird," Julian said.

"I want to find an island with an old building on it," Will said. "One we can rent or buy and make livable. There are lots of abandoned farmhouses on offshore islands. If people lived in them once and got by, we can, too. We can try it. I want you to think this over pretty carefully, because it's going to be up to you whether we go back to live in a city again. Rosie?"

Rosie, far out on the pink cloud of a new skiff, said, "I speak first to name it. The *Goony Bird.*"

"Who wants ever to go back?" Hank suddenly let out a shrill yell. "EE-yow! How about that?"

A good day to start north, Will thought with content as the island diminished behind them. The prevailing wind, the southwest wind, was fair for the north. The boat was loaded deep, but she could take it. A survival boat—survival in more ways than one. He said silently to the small island, Thank you for what you've done for my family. And for me.

Bill said suddenly, "Hey, Poppa, look at that guy. He's really heading this way."

A big powerboat was overtaking fast, a bone in her teeth.

"Duck, Bill. Get down. Crawl in under the tents. Quick!" Will said. A big white boat. Hell, he thought. Not again!

The fellow was not trying to run them down, but he was coming close. Some of his bow wave splashed wetly aboard as he slowed alongside. A skinny old man leaned out and jammed a boathook into the gunnel of Will's boat.

"What the devil!" Will yelled. "Take it easy, you fool!" He had let the sheet go and dumped the wind out of his sail as quickly as he could, but not before the boat had heeled enough to ship some water.

"Thought you'd git away with it, did ya? Well, you ain't going to! Trespassing on my land, damn ya, you'll pay me damages."

"Look here," Will said. "We're not on your land, we're peacefully sailing here." He was roaring mad. He could feel the hackles rise on the back of his neck, but he checked himself. Hold it; not with a boatload of kids. Not with Bill here. Since this was the owner of the island and since the boy from the lumberyard was running the boat, he guessed that this must be Mr. Nails Potter.

Mr. Potter started to screech. His old man's treble rose higher, his Adam's apple jerked faster as he brought out his threats and sentiments, most of them obscene.

Hal began to whimper. He buried his face in Sarah's lap, and she put her hands over his ears.

"Take your gaff off my boat," Will said between his teeth.

"By the so-and-so and this-and-that, I'm towing you back to town to court." The old man lifted the bo hook, but not to let go. He ripped it through a flap of tent canvas which showed a little above the gunnel, leaving a long slash.

Will reached. He got both hands on the boathook, disentangled it, and gave it a stout shove. Mr. Potter went over backwards. His lank buttocks made a healthy thud as they landed on the platform of his boat. Apparently his wind had been knocked out, because he stopped screeching.

"If you bother me again," Will yelled at the empty space where he had been, "I'll make a citizen's arrest and take you ashore for damage to property and using filthy language in front of children. You'll have a lawsuit on your hands you won't forget."

The boats drifted apart. There was no sound from Mr. Potter.

Lord, Will thought, I hope I didn't kill him.

Mr. Potter's head, its hat still on, rose into sight above the cheeserind. It hung there motionless, looking as if it had been chopped off and stuck to the gunnel. Behind him, the boy from the lumberyard clasped his hands over his head and shook them, like a boxer's. He wiped the grin from his face just in time, as Potter turned to speak to him. The powerboat started up, circled, and headed back across the bay toward town.

Bill stuck his head out of his hiding place. "Right on, Poppa," he said, and began to roar with laughter.

Two hundred miles up the coast, the McCarrens began island-hopping, looking for a place to settle down. Many of the offshore islands had old houses, abandoned years ago, when owners had moved ashore for the sake of cars and movies. The best place they found was Cross Island, named on the map, four miles out to sea from the mainland. It had an aged farmhouse which could be made livable, a freshwater pond, and a long meadow, once under cultivation and now not too overgrown with puckerbush for another garden to be spaded there.

Will was determined not to take any more chances with an outraged owner of wild land. He made a trip to the County Court House, in the mainland city of Waterford, and hunted up Cross Island's title of record. The owner was a single heir, long moved away from the district, now living in Oregon. His name was Jeremy Cross. Written to, he wrote back, and Will sensed from a kind of regretful nostalgia between the lines of his letter that Jeremy Cross had loved the place.

> The island's no good to me now. I haven't been back there for years and I doubt if I ever will be. If you'll pay the taxes on it, you're welcome to stay there as long as you want to. Or you can buy it, all the same to me.

He named a price and added some details which he thought might be of interest. The house was old, built by his great-grandfather in 1816.

> There're three generations of my folks buried there. You'll see their stones out back of the pond, if the clearing hasn't grown up by now. I used to keep it mowed, went there every Memorial Day. Folks never went there much, on account of word got around somehow that old Jeremy hants the place. I don't think he'll bother you, he never did me, and I used to spend a lot of time there when I was a boy growing up in Wentworth Harbor. There's a cistern in the cellar that's really built. Old Jeremy was a stonemason out of Scotland. He cut the granite blocks and fitted them together so tight they didn't need cement. I don't know if that cistern will hold water now. It did once.

A craftsman, old Jeremy Cross, Will thought. I wouldn't mind shaking hands with his ghost, if it's still around.

Will took an option on the island, but for the present, he chose the tax deal. He wanted nothing permanent until he made sure that no insurmountable difficulties would arise. He sent young Jeremy the required sum of tax money and hoped he'd found the right place. As the months went by, he became more and more convinced that he had.

The kids thrived. They were healthy and busy, and Will was proud of the way they took to his teaching. Through the summer, they lived in tents until the needed repairs to the old farmhouse could be made. Basically, it had been a fine house, built by craftsmen who had known what winters were in this sea-surrounded place, when the bleak easterlies began to whistle snow around the gables. They had set the house on granite blocks, hand-quarried from the island's own tough rock, fitted along the sides of two deep-dug frostproof cellars. In one cellar, most of the room was taken up by old Jeremy's cistern, which, Will eventually found, was indeed watertight. The wooden eaves gutters which had collected rain were rotten, and the hand pump in the kitchen was clogged with rust; but, Will thought, I can buy metal gutters and a new pump, and we can have an inside supply of water, so long as we get rain.

Most of the summer was taken up making the house livable. Will didn't rush things. He planned, at first, only to stop leaks and stuff cracks to keep out the wind. The kids thought otherwise.

"Why can't we shingle the roofs?" Hank asked. "It's going to be our house."

"We might not want to stay," Will said. "What if you get fed up with living like this? Think you'd want to go back and live in town?"

Sarah spoke for herself. For everybody, as Will soon found out. She said, "After this summer, I'd rather die."

Julian said, "I have to build my windmill. I'm only starting to read the directions." He had sent for a technical book on windmills and, Will had noticed with silent delight, had had no trouble reading it.

Bill had taken apart the aged hand pump in the kitchen. He was "fooling" with it, trying to make it work. "Don't ask me. I don't have a vote. But how about that skiff you said we might build? I wouldn't mind taking a crack at that."

"The *Goony Bird*," Rosie said. "I'll help you, Bill."

"Not much you won't," Bill said. "You goony bird."

Will looked around at his children. They had bumps and lumps and pounded thumbs from learning to use tools. Their shirts and jeans were stiff with paint and putty. He wished Amy could have been there to see them. Amy, with her gaiety and laughter, her courage, who would have taken on windmills and backed him up to take them on, too.

They shingled the house. They helped him rummage through secondhand and antique stores in town for wood-burning stoves and came up with two—a cookstove and an airtight. On his next trip to town, Will bought lumber for *Goony Bird* and turned it over to Bill, together with a design for a punkinseed punt.

Under the circumstances, Bill couldn't go to town. He didn't seem to want to. Staying out of sight wasn't so bad, he said, he liked it that way. After he got hold of the lumber, he spent his time building *Goony Bird,* and finished her late in the fall. Nobody could say she was a success, but punkin-seeds, being homemade, seldom were. This one, flat-bottomed as a raft, low-sided and low-bowed, could be used only in the cove on a calm day. She had a tendency to put her bow under even a moderate ripple, and she leaked enthusias-tically, because the only available lumber had been green. No amount of soaking would swell tight the cracks in her bottom planks. Bill did his best with caulking oakum, but somehow *Goony Bird* always found a way to open up a seam.

Disgusted, Bill turned her bottom up on the bank. "That freak spits out oakum on purpose," he told Will. "Let her dry up wide open. I'll have another try with tar and battens. Next time, I'll know enough to season the lumber first."

"By next time, we'll have a steam box rigged up so we can shape the timbers for a skiff," Will told him. "It was a darned good first try, Bill."

He had given Bill the project with no strings tied on and no instructions. No nagging from Poppa . . . Poppa was learning something, too. Everyone, young or not, had a right to privacy.

Ought to be written into the Bill of Rights, Will thought. Maybe it is—what else is the Pursuit of Happiness? Could be we're one up on civilization for the masses.

Bad luck, when it arrived, stemmed from coincidence and old Mr. Nails Potter from Bullet Bay. Florence Baker, born a Potter, had grown up in Bullet Bay. Nails was her uncle, and he, visiting his niece on a short stay, spotted the McCarrens in the supermarket. Being as scared of a lawsuit as of the devil himself, old Nails had from the first decided not to carry his pursuit further; but he certainly remembered the dirty hippie who had knocked him down, and there were other methods of pursuit.

"Squatted on my prop'ty," he told Flo. "When I called him on it, he committed assault 'n' batt'ry on me. That bunch of outlaws stole everything they could get their hands on, hauled other people's traps, and no knowing what-all damage they done before I and the law caught up with'em, chased'em outa town. That feller's the spit'n' image of old Amadee Courvette. Related to him, I don't doubt. You recall what a hooglum he was."

Flo did indeed remember Amadee's reputation, which had been a talked-over part of her childhood. An old aborigin, if there ever was one.

"I tell you, Flo, you folks here better git rid of him. The town'll not only have to support him, you'll have that en-tire ragtag 'n' bobtail in your school, along with decent people's kids."

Good, juicy venom of this kind was meat and drink to Flo. "You know full and well," she told her friends, some other ladies, "I speak no evil of anybody, but the only livable, nameable thing in my mind always and forever is the good of this town. *But . . .*" She repeated Uncle Nails's story with additions of her own to make it interesting telling, and trailed the red rag of her gossip all over the town.

"'Ere's a strynger, let's 'eave 'alf a brick at 'im," was a saying which she might never have heard, but she lived up to its gospel with all her pious might.

PART THREE

On the afternoon of the northwest gale, after the kidnapping of Rosie McCarren from town, Bess didn't come home to lunch, as was her usual custom. Mary waited awhile, puzzling over what was best to do. If Bess meant to keep Rosie hidden away here at the Cove, she would hardly care to bring her up to the house in full daylight, or have Leafy carry her. Word of Bess and Leafy parading a small child up the path in full sight of neighbors' windows would be all over town and up to Wentworth Harbor before morning.

If I were doing it, I'd let it be known. I'd tell the world how the poor mite had been abused, Mary thought. I don't know what Bess can be thinking about. Maybe she knows something about the situation that I don't.

Mary glanced out of the window to see whether the *Daisy* was off on the mooring or still tied up at the float. She could see the stubby mast still showing above the wharf building. Bess had moved around to the lee side of the wharf. And no wonder. That wind had certainly picked up fast.

The bay was already curdled with whitecaps. On Western Point, at the windward side of the Cove, breakers were curling far up the ledges. Most of the lobster fishermen had given up trying to haul traps and had come in. Their boats were already at the moorings, yawing and tossing in the wind. Martin's mooring was still empty, and so was Warren Petersen's.

She felt a small twist of worry and laughed at herself because of the way the weather had turned the tables—now she was the one to worry. But it was early yet, and there were two of them still out. If one had a breakdown, the other would be around to tow him in. The fishermen all looked out for one another. Besides, both Martin and Warren had ship-to-shore telephones. They could call for help if anything went wrong, or if they wanted to let families know that they'd be late. Just about everybody in town was on the Citizens' Band. The CB was a great comfort to fishermen's wives waiting for their men to get in.

Maybe I can pick up one of them, if they're sending, Mary thought.

She flipped the switch, and a blast of sound poured in over the air—a high soprano singing, "There's a Home for Little Children Above the Bright Blue Sky."

Oh, Lord. Edie Bickford, practicing her solo for Sunday. Edie sang in the choir and took great interest in choosing hymns timely with regard to current events. Quite often she broadcast her choices on the CB, for the edification of her neighbors.

Well, that's no use. Bess'll be starving, and I'd better take her down something. Besides, I've got to have groceries for supper. Martin'll roll in ravening hungry, and he's not going to appreciate warmed-over stew, which is all I've got.

She filled a thermos with the steaming-hot stew, which she had warmed up for her own lunch, and added another thermos of coffee.

Bess's pickup truck had been backed into the barn— Bess said to get the cussed thing out of sight, she hated it. Mary decided to take it instead of the car. There'd be a lot of stuff to haul home, including, oh, Lord, the Town Hall clock.

In the workshop adjoining the barn, something too big for a rat was making a scratching and whimpering sound—in the woodbox, it sounded like. Mary walked past the pickup and looked in. Now what? The small coon, seeing her, backed into a corner, glared at her balefully, and made a sound like grating a nutmeg.

"For heaven's sake! Where did you come from?" Mary said to him. One of Bess's waifs—she was always picking up refugees, seemed.

The coon still had some water in a dish, but the tin pie plate which had held food was empty.

"Okay," Mary said. "Bess always says, enough for one enough for two." She reached in for the pie plate and snatched it out, just in time to avoid the coon's charge and his tiny, snapping teeth. "Mean, aren't you? Don't know what's for your own good." She tipped stew from the lunch bottle into the pie plate, blew on it to make sure the hot stuff wouldn't burn the little creature's tongue.

The coon apparently smelled it, for he stopped grating and stood on his hind legs, watching her. She was careful putting the plate back, but this time he went for the food instead of her fingers.

"Stomach first," she told him. "Bet you're a boy coon."

The *Daisy*, even on the lee side of the wharf, was pitching with the rollers which the wind and flood tide swept under the pilings. Bess was nowhere to be seen, but as Mary backed the truck down, she appeared out of the *Daisy's* cuddy and came up the wharf ladder.

"Good girl," she said. "I thought you'd have the sense to bring the truck down. Rosie's still asleep, poor mite."

"Is she all right?"

"She's worn out, of course, but it doesn't seem natural.

It's probably that dose of whatever Flo poked into her. Drop the tailgate, will you, honey?"

The supplies for the house were piled up against the wharf building, under a tarp. Bess stripped the tarp off, revealing, flat on his back at the top of the heap, Old Grampop. "We'd better get him out of here on account of dampness," Bess said. She lifted the clock and slid it carefully into the truck, cushioning it with bags of flour and grain.

"Bess, you shouldn't lift those heavy bags. Can't they wait for Marty?"

"They could, but there's already some spray flying up here, and if the wind keeps on the way it looks like it's going to, this whole place'll be awash, come high tide." Bess puffed a little, heaving in the last bag. "There! Those two ducks we bought today'll go awful good, if you feel like cooking that elaborate."

"Roast duck with fixings," Mary said promptly. "Marty'll love it. I wish he'd get home, Bess."

"He'll be along. Warren's out, too. We'll hear on the CB if they're going to be much later." Bess tossed into the truck the dress box and shopping bag from the dry goods store. "Clothes for Rosie," she said. "Some real pretty little girl's blue pajamas in there. I'll get her."

She climbed back down the wharf ladder and presently appeared with Rosie, who was buttoned inside an old sheepskin coat. Mary marveled at the way Bess came one-handed up the ladder, but then, Bess had a way with wharf ladders. She had been known to ascend this one no hands at all.

"Still sleeping," she said as she climbed into the front seat of the truck and settled with the child across her lap. "I can still smell that stuff. Leafy said it smelt like booze to him, but the shape he was in I guess most anything would. Thank God I got rid of him at last. I asked him to help lug groceries up off the float, and he vanished like a snake under a rock."

"He'd better, hadn't he? Before Otis comes after him?"

"I expect so. I'm going to cover Rosie's tracks, too. There'll be a quick rat smelt when it gets around that I bought a whole set of little girl's duds in to Cousins's. I may have to let on that our cousin Hattie's little girl down in Dover's got a birthday coming up."

"Why? There are certainly laws against the misuse of a child. They don't change just because Flo Baker wants her board paid."

"Um," Bess said. "You have to remember that Justin Bradley carries considerable clout, and Rosie's the town's business till she's settled somewhere legally. That trick of Leafy's with the rock may work, but I don't count too much on it. Back up as close as you can to the doorstep, Mary."

Inside the house, she laid Rosie gently on the couch in the kitchen. Rosie still slept, but she moved a little and turned her small smeared face away from the light.

"Oh, Bess, look at her, the poor little thing!"

"We'll keep her," Bess said grimly. "Don't you worry." She moved over to the CB and turned it on. This time the shrill soprano was rendering, "When the Saints Go Marching In."

"Edie," Bess said. "You'd think she'd have to catch her breath once in a while." She went to the telephone and rang the Bickford number. The singing stopped with a strangled squawk as Edie got up to answer the phone. "Edie," Bess began, "could you—"

She was cut off by a bull-like roar which rattled her eardrum.

"Edie, for Chrissake, will you shut up? Warren and Mart ain't in yet, and we're listening for word."

The Cove was all on one telephone line, and it was neighborly. Sometimes receivers clicked all along the line as people wondered who was calling whom and what for. Bess realized that Calvin Petersen had been about to call Edie at the same time she had.

"All right, but I'll thank you to say please," Edie said.

"Please, hell! The CB is to use, not to squawk hymns over. Once a week, stuck hearing you in the church choir is bygod enough!"

"Don't you dare swear at me, Cal Petersen! The CB is for everybody, not just for you. I'll sing over it if I want to."

"You take that screeching out to your hens, it'll bust the eggs in their bowels. If all the damn fools in the world was laid end to end it would—" What it would do would never be known because Calvin hung up with a crash.

Bess caught back a chuckle. She said into the phone, "Never mind, Edie. There're people who'd go a long ways to hear 'When the Saints Go Marching In' sung right. Calvin's always on a short string, and today he's worried. We all want to listen hard, right now."

"*I* never knew nothing about it." Unmollified, Edie hung up.

"Whoo! There's a gal Josie Petersen's going to have to send a cake to," Bess said.

Josie Petersen, Warren's mother, made cake. If Edie Bickford sang for her soul's satisfaction, in the same way, Josie made cake. She made lovely ones, layers high, decorated with many-colored patterns squeezed from frosting guns. Anyone who was sick, unhappy or bereft, or made an enemy by Calvin's hair-trigger temper, could be sure of a magnificent gift cake from Josie, and that was nice and it often helped.

"I'll leave the CB on," Bess said. "Likely we'll hear from the boys anytime now. I've got to go back down and put the *Daisy* off on her mooring before she chafes her planking to splinters on the wharf pilings. If Rosie wakes up and you can get near enough to her, wash her. I'll be home as soon as I can."

Nothing was coming over the CB except an occasional buzz-and-hum of static. Everybody in the Cove would be listening now. The phone rang, and she flew to answer it, hoping someone had word, but it was only Albemarle Spicer, who said, "This is a wild one, Mary. You think it'd be an idea to call the Coast Guard?" Alby was known to be a calamity howler, but that wasn't any comfort.

She didn't need to be told how wild the gale was. The wind was roaring around the house, whistling at corners. The Cove, now whitecapped, was feeling it in the lee as it was. Over on Western Point, spray was hurtling up into the trees.

Get busy, she told herself. Stuff those ducks and get them in the oven or there won't be any supper and everybody starving. She remembered suddenly that she'd completely forgotten to give Bess the thermoses of lunch. They were still in the truck.

She went first to check on Rosie. Under the blanket Bess had put over her, Rosie still slept.

Mary stuffed the ducks—plain bread stuffing, the kind Marty and Bess both liked; she peeled vegetables, brought an apple pie from the freezer, put it in the oven to defrost. That, she told herself, is the stuff to feed the troops.

The CB was still silent except for static. "Crackle and hum," Mary said to it. "Say something, blast you!" But it didn't.

She went back to Rosie, and as she leaned closer, she was aware of a pair of bright, intelligent-looking eyes staring at her through the wild mop of sticky hair.

"Why, you're awake, Rosie. You've slept a long time. It's time you woke up and had a bath and something to eat, isn't it?"

Rosie said nothing. She continued to stare. After a moment, she said, "In a bathtub?"

"Of course. Let's get those awful clothes off; how about that?"

Rosie sat up. "I can do it." She put her feet down on

the floor and stood, wavering a little. "My hair's awful. I have to wash that, too."

Mary put a hand down to feel of Rosie's hair. "What on earth did you get on it, Rosie?"

Rosie ducked away from the hand, but she didn't panic. "It's *stuff*. To kill nits, that ugly old woman said."

"Mercy, did you have nits?"

"Of course I didn't. I fought her and spilled the stuff all over her clean floor. She put me down-cellar in a black, dirty place." Rosie blinked and rubbed her eyes with her knuckles. "I feel funny."

"Come along. The bathroom's this way. A bath'll help."

She's still fuzzy, Mary thought. If a bath doesn't help, we'll have to get Dr. Fletcher down. Maybe we ought to anyway.

Half an hour later, Mary stood up from leaning over the tub, to ease her aching back and to calm down Martin's heir, who obviously hadn't liked the position. "Rosie, I've run you through three waters and worn out the soap. Everything else has come off, but I can't get that stuff out of your hair. Most of it will have to be cut off, so I can get at the rest of it with lard. I think I can give you quite a pretty hairdo, though. All right with you?"

Rosie nodded. "Oh, yes. I wouldn't want Dad and the kids to see me with stuff on my hair for nits. Hank and Julian'd laugh their heads off at me."

Mary froze. Oh, my God, she doesn't remember. She thinks they're all alive. What do I say now? Or do?

But Rosie remembered something. Her eyes suddenly shone; she sat up straight in the tub. "There was a funny-looking man who said he'd take me home. Why didn't he? Why did he leave me here?"

I can't tell her. It's too soon . . . later, when she's better . . . Aloud, Mary said, "You hear the wind blowing, Rosie? There's a terrible storm."

Rosie listened. "Yes. I hear the wind. It's northwest. No one could land on the beach now. I'll have to go tomorrow."

With hands that she tried to keep from shaking, Mary trimmed Rosie's hair. As the filthy mess fell away, she saw what might be the reason for Rosie's not remembering what had happened. On the child's head was a lumpy bruise, which, judging from the size of it now, must have been a big one a week ago, and might have caused concussion.

"Is that sore, Rosie? Am I hurting you?"

"No. Only a little now. It hurt awful when I woke up in the orphans' home. My head ached and ached."

"The orphans' home? Did anyone tell you that's where you were?"

"No, but I guessed. The mean men who hollered at Dad said we'd all got to go there. I guess I was the only one they caught. Hal . . ." Rosie's small confident voice faltered. "I can't remember . . . but they must've caught me. I waited and waited for Dad to come. I knew he would. Then Bess and the funny-looking man . . . I was scared of the funny-looking man—he was the one Dad made go away from the island because he made kiss-kiss noises at Sarah. But I went with him because he said he knew where Dad was. And then I felt all dopey and sleepy. I do now, some. Do you know where Dad is?"

"Yes," Mary said.

God forgive me for a coward. But I can't. Not now. She's still worn out. Soon enough she'll have to know.

"There," Mary said, putting down her scissors. "Now some lard rubbed on and washed off with shampoo."

Rosie appeared at the end of the operation with a close-cut thatch of dark chestnut curls.

"My, you look elegant," Mary said. "Want to see? Here's a looking glass; you can see how it looks in the back."

"That's nice," Rosie said. "Makes me look like a boy. Wasn't I a mess! I'll never tell Hank and Julian."

Mary heard, thankfully, the back door open and close. That would be Bess or Martin. Somebody else around, so I can go off by myself and howl to high heaven, she thought. Maybe it's Marty. Oh, I hope so!

But it was Bess who came to the bathroom door. "Why," she said cheerfully, "it's Rosie McCarren, looking like a dreamboat. I must say, I hardly know you."

And it was true—anyone who had seen her before her bath would have had trouble now recognizing the pink and clean child, with her haircut and new blue pajamas.

"I had to have three baths," Rosie said with some pride. "And look at my awful hair, it's got to be scraped up off the floor."

She wasn't very hungry. She drank a glass of orange juice and got halfway through a poached egg on toast before she drooped over her plate, and Bess carried her upstairs to bed.

"I'm sure she's all right. Just tired," Bess said, coming back. "I took her temperature and it's normal, and her pulse is good and strong. We'll see how she is in the morning."

The CB suddenly broke its static sounds with a hoot and what sounded like a long-drawn breath. "Calling Calvin Petersen. Calling Calvin Petersen. You there, Gramp? Over."

"I've been here all the afternoon. Goddammit, where you been?" Calvin's roar choked off. He added, after a moment, "Over."

"Cross Island. Martin and I. Heading home now. We're all right. Repeat, all right. Over."

Limp with relief, Mary let herself drop into a chair. She heard Calvin's bellow, "Josie, ring up Mary on the phone, tell her Mart's all right." But why, if Martin's all right, didn't he call me before?

The phone almost at once began to ring. Bess answered it. "Yes, we heard, Josie. We're listening."

Calvin was going on. "Why in the long-johned, pink-dimpled hell couldn't you have let us know before? Over."

"Cool it, Gramp, I'm trying to say. We spotted a body, one of McCarren's kids, little tiny kid, on Cross Island Beach. We got it off of there. We're bringing it in. Over and out."

Calvin hadn't even heard Warren's "out." "You cussed fools landed on Cross Island Beach, the wind blowing on there the way it is? Why didn't you call the Coast Guard? You crazy? Wonder you ain't both washed to hell an' gone out with the tide, smashed your boats to kindling. Over."

A voice said, "The CB's to use, not to holler cusswords over, Calvin." Edie Bickford had grabbed the chance to flip her own switch to "Send" and get some of her own back.

Albemarle Spicer phoned again. He lived in the last house on the Point Road, his windows overlooked the ocean toward Cross Island. Telephone receivers clicked as people waiting for any possible news listened in.

"I can make out them two boats, Mary, their running lights off 'n' on. They appear to be making heavy weather of it."

John Pray, up the road, said, "Shoot, Alby, no use to get the womenfolks all haired-up. If you can see running lights, the boys are all right."

Josie Petersen said, "Nobody can scare me now any worse'n I was. I been on tentacles all the afternoon. The way that boy slams around in that great washtub of a boat . . . 'Tis, too, a washtub, Calvin; don't you holler at me. I tell you I never know. And oh, you just think of it, that poor little child!"

A new voice chimed in. "I wouldn't want to be Oat Baker when this gets around. Nor Justin Bradley, neither. If they'd let Quack McCarren be, that whole family'd be alive, you know it?"

Albemarle said, "Scared the poor duffer to death, that was what it was. Oat told me what Justin said to him, and it was about as rough talk as a man could hear. In front of his young ones, too."

"None of our boys ever caught Quack hauling traps . . ."

". . . took it he was too smart to get caught . . ."

". . . heard that feller from Bullet Bay said he was known to be a hoodlum . . ."

Mary turned away from the phone. "Bess, how would Flo Baker or her scurrilous old uncle, or anybody, know for a fact that Will McCarren slept with his own daughter?"

Bess turned away from the window where she had been watching for lights in the Harbor. "I guess we know what's been merrily done," she said. "You'd better put your biscuits in, Mary. I can see Marty's running lights."

Martin didn't come directly into the kitchen. He went in at the shed door and turned on the light out there.

Mary flew to meet him. "Oh, darling, am I glad to see—" She gasped, seeing the wet clothes he had dropped on the floor—his underwear, the work pants he had worn this morning, his gray wool socks, shredded and stained red. "Marty! Have you been overboard?"

"You could call it that. Have we got any rum left? Where's Bess? Hey, Bess, fix me a hot buttered rum."

"Coming up," Bess said.

He hobbled into the kitchen and sat down at the table. Bess put a steaming mug in front of him. "You watch that; the rum's cooled it some, but it's still blazing."

He seemed not to hear, but downed the scalding brew in a couple of gulps. "God, that's good. Fix me another one."

"Mary will. Let's get your boots and oilskins off. Stick out your foot. Start a hot bath running first, Mary. That'll warm him up quicker."

Mary started the bath; she brought out fresh underwear, shirt and pants and a big bath towel, hung everything to warm on the rack by the kitchen stove. Bess had got Martin out of his oil jacket; she was struggling, without much effect, at one of his rubber boots.

"Here, can't I help? Let me—" Mary began. She gasped, as the boot came off, at the sight of his lacerated foot.

"Well, don't look at it. Stay away from it," Martin said. "Fix the rum, will you? I need a good dollop, too, so don't skimp."

He's been overboard . . . in that water . . . like ice! she thought. She felt herself turn cold, almost as cold as he looked. She didn't skimp. She handed him the second mugful as Bess, with a great heave, pried off the second boot. "Marty! How on earth. . . ?"

"Barnacles. I walked on some."

"Barefooted?" Bess said. "That was smart." She got up, headed for the bathroom.

"I had socks on," Martin bellowed after her. "Godsake, you expect me to wade ashore in rubber boots?"

Bess didn't answer. She could be heard turning off faucets, clinking bottles in the medicine cabinet.

"Look, I'm all right," Martin said. "Just cold, that's all, and a few cuts don't amount to anything. So don't get all tore out about it." He set the mug down and managed a grin. "Whee-oo! That was no dollop, that was a slug. You feel all right?"

"Of course." She followed him into the bathroom, wincing as she realized how those cuts were hurting. Some of them were deep. They'd have to be disinfected and dressed. Bess had put out gauze pads, cotton swabs, and tapes. There'd be iodine in the medicine cabinet. Mary looked for it and couldn't find it. Surely the bottle was somewhere on the shelves.

Martin, relaxed in the tub, let out a roar. "Ow! Goddammit, Bess, what'd you put in this water?"

"Epsom salts," Bess said tranquilly from the kitchen.

"What the hell! That's *physic!*"

"You soak your feet in it," Bess said.

She always kept a package of Epsom salts handy—she was old-fashioned about a laxative. Apparently she had dumped in plenty. The empty package was in the wastebasket.

"Where's the iodine?" Martin's feet had been numb when he'd got into the tub. Now the hot water had soaked open the cuts, which had begun to sting and burn. "Dammit, you womenfolks and your notions! Go on out and get supper on the table. I'll doctor my own cuts."

"Supper'll be ready when you are," Mary said. He was tired to death and hurting like blazes, but no need to bite heads off. She left him growling and mumbling and went back to the kitchen, where Bess was halfway through her meal.

"I had to eat," she said. "I was knocking together."

"I should think you might be. I see you rescued the biscuits. I forgot them. Right now I wouldn't care if they burnt black."

"Right now they're a work of art," Bess said. Placidly she buttered one, poured over it a lavish spoonful of gravy. "He'll simmer down soon as his feet let up a little and he eats. He's had a rugged day."

"Anybody would know he has. He might give us the credit of knowing it instead of roaring around like a mad bull."

"That's just noise, don't mean anything. He's worried now over how much he can tell us without hassling up you and the baby."

"It would have saved us considerable hassling up if he'd called earlier on the CB, let us know he was all right."

"Edie was on, remember? Anyway, he is all right. And you aren't hassled up, are you?"

"Oh, dear, I know I'm being childish. But it does rankle, in a way."

"The big knuckleheads, they don't ever tell their wives anything but what they think a woman ought to hear. It's nice of them to take care, but they ought to get it through their thick noggins that it's better to know about horrors than to imagine them."

In the bathroom, Martin let out a yelp and swore resoundingly.

"Uh-huh," Bess said. "I hid that iodine in the empty salts package, hoping he wouldn't find it, but he has and he's slopped it all over his cuts. You put iodine on a raw cut, takes it longer to heal. That's another thing he can't get through his thick head." Bess pushed herself back from the table. "I don't have room for pie, Mary, too many biscuits. I'm going out and feed my coon and put a flea collar on him."

Mary took Martin's towel and warmed clothes from the rack, hung them on the bathroom door within his easy reach. He was out of the tub and in the middle of a fine mess. He had hauled towels down from the linen closet. Bloody bath mat, ripped-open packages of pads, and tape surrounded his feet. He didn't look up.

"Want help?" she asked.

He didn't.

He dressed, put on the soft slippers she held out to him, and limped out of the bathroom. In a moment, she heard him at the telephone and gathered that he was talking to Otis Baker. She moved to the bathroom door and unashamedly listened—and learned details she never would have wanted to know.

What was left of the child, wrapped in Martin's shirt and an old oil jacket, locked in the cuddy of his boat, where nothing could get at it. Boy or girl? Hell, no. Not enough left of it to tell. Oat could pick it up tomorrow.

Mary went back into the bathroom and closed the door. She didn't try to hold back the tears, but moved blindly, clearing up Martin's mess. It took quite a while before she got the tears dried and the bathroom floor mopped up.

When she got back to the kitchen, Martin had dished

up his own supper. He sat before a heaped plate, a moun-
tain of biscuits on a platter beside it. He said through a
mouthful, "God, this is good. Bring some more butter, will
you, Bess's used it all. D'j you eat?"

She hadn't, but now she didn't feel hungry.

"You and Bess must've had a high old time in town
today," he said. "What'd you do, all go with Leafy and get
zonked together?"

"No. Why?"

"Seems Bess stole the Town Hall clock and Oat's out
after Leafy for attempted rape on the schoolteacher."

"Leafy told the schoolteacher that she had pretty legs.
And Justin Bradley told me that Dad's old clock was no
good, he was going to take it out in the woods and dump
it. So Bess offered to save him the trouble. It's out in the
pickup now."

"So you'll have to go to jail, along with Bess and Leafy.
Come on, eat some supper, kid. This is great."

"I will, later."

"Oat'll never catch up with Leafy. He's likely taken
Willie and hopped it for the tall timber, the way he always
does when his spring flood starts to ebb." He glanced at her
and went on eating. After a short silence, he said, "Some
ladies feel they have to fly off the roost if a man comes right
out and says he likes their looks. Shoot, I don't doubt for a
minute that's all Leafy did. The way to handle that is for
somebody to go to the teacher and explain, get her to drop
the charge. Might be me." He grinned. "I'd like to. I could
be arrested myself for thinking what I think when I look at
that gal's legs." His grin grew as he looked at her. "Epsom
salts! Hell of a thing. Wasn't you I yelled at, it was my feet
felt like red-hot stove lids. Still do, or I'd rise up and dish
you some supper."

"Give me time. I'm trying to get Will McCarren and
his children out of my mind."

Martin sobered instantly. "So am I."

"You don't sound as if—"

"Look, Mary. I'm in my home with my girl, whose tracks across the carpet I could kiss every day of my life and not get enough. If I've been kidding around, it isn't because I . . . My God, talking with Oat, I damn nigh puked. You know what Flo's up to now? She's setting up a memorial service for the McCarrens, inviting people, asking them to have flowers sent down from the city. Well, now she'll have a real honest-to-God body for a centerpiece. Two if the Coast Guard finds the other one." He choked a little. "The one who jumped off Cousins's wharf today. The little girl."

Mary started to speak, but he went on. "Beat it, they told the poor devil. Go back where you came from. Put your kids to school there, we don't want them here. What Alby found out, the whole town's in a state of shock. It'll be a fine funeral, and everybody'll go. Send flowers!" he snorted. "Send us a couple of town officers who don't carry their decency in their pocketbooks."

"Martin, listen. Rosie McCarren didn't jump off any wharf. She's upstairs in our spare room, sleeping. Bess and I brought her home."

Martin stared, stupefied. "You did? How did . . . she is?"

"She is." Mary went on to tell him about the scene in the town office and what followed on the way home.

"You and Bess, huh? I might've known. What was that splash Old Man Cousins heard? Bess jump off the wharf herself to make it?"

"Leafy threw in a big rock."

Martin roared. He sagged back in his chair; she could see the tension go out of him. "You three outlaws!" he choked. "Outdiddled poor old Oat. Made off with Flo's runaway. Stole the Town Hall clock. Thunderation, you *will* all end up in jail."

"I didn't do much. I was only backup crew."

He smiled at her in a way she knew. "Go get yourself some supper," he said. "And on your way make some tracks on the linoleum."

When Bess came back into the kitchen, she was pleased to find that Martin and Mary had gone to bed. They'd needed to be by themselves, get a chance to work off steam without anyone looking over their shoulders. They needed to have their own place, and would as soon as their house was finished. She'd be lonesome as a dog when they moved, but it would be better for all of them. She'd got used to being by herself while Martin had been away.

I need to sprawl out, she told herself. And, let's face it, times, I butt in. Not meaning to, but I do.

She had built a fire in the workshop stove and had spent some time making friends with the coon. She'd fetched the thermos from the pickup and fed him small portions piece-meal—not enough to fill him up all at once, so that he kept coming back for more. He'd been snappish at first, but he'd got the point that she was the place where the food was coming from. After a while, he would take bits of cooked meat from her fingers. Coons tamed easily, she knew that—she'd done it before. Most small wild animals did if you didn't pull and haul on them. She'd never tamed one except to save it or heal it, and once you rescued a hurt thing, you didn't keep it. It wasn't fair.

"You needn't think you're going to be a fixture around here," she told the coon. "You get eats a-plenty till you're big enough to take care of yourself in the woods, where you belong."

When he was full and curled up asleep, she'd slipped the flea collar gently over his head and replaced the slatted screen over the woodbox.

In the kitchen, she sat down to rest for a while by the cooling kitchen fire.

That's a real plucky little youngster. Anybody with that much innards I'd be happy to have around here for good. She doesn't appear to be grieving overmuch about her family, probably too dopey to realize it yet, or doesn't remember anything. Warren did say she was out cold when he pulled her out of the boat. They say kids forget easier than grown folks do. I don't know if that's so. I can remember how I felt when Gramp and Ma and Pa died, but I was a lot older than Rosie is. If she could find somebody to take the place of what's gone, be sure she was loved . . .

Martin and I turned to each other. We had a good life after we were over grieving. We could be the salvation of each other, Rosie and me. I get dog-lonesome sometimes, alone or not alone, might as well face it.

Lord, I'd better go to bed. I won't be fit to tie my shoes tomorrow.

She was halfway across the room when the phone rang.

Now who? What lump at this hour of the night?

"Bess? Bess Bowden? Is that you, Bess?"

Flo Baker. No one could mistake that nosehole-stopped-up squawk.

"Yes, this is Bess."

"I just want you to know what your criminal actions today has led to."

"You do? Keep till tomorrow, won't it?"

"No, it won't. Maybe you can sleep, I can't. You've killed a little child, that's what you've done. Chased that poor baby around the Town Hall, scairt her to her death." Flo could be heard wheezing hard, waiting for Bess's reply. When there wasn't one, she went on, her voice a portent. "She run down to the shore and flang herself off'n Cousins's wharf."

"Did?" Bess said. "Did you see her do it? Why didn't you jump in and pull her out?"

"Joshway Cousins heard the splash when she went in and—"

"How'd he know it was her? Might've been Leafy Piper. Leafy'd drown himself rather than go to jail. There're a lot of folks down here wondering what happened to him."

"Leafy Piper was *seen*, right there. Joshway Cousins see him, heard him holler that he seen what that poor baby done. And let me tell you, there's folks here in town wondering if 'twarn't that crazy Leafy done it to her."

"Well, then. He's likely taken off into the woods. This time of year he'll die of pneumonia. Talk about hounding someone to their death—"

There was a silence, preceded by a series of phlegmy honks.

"My Lord, Flo, your tubes sound terrible. If it's pneumonia, you'll never know what happened to Leafy, and think of the loss to the town!"

"You ain't going to get out of it by changing topics, Miss Bitch," Flo said. "The Coast Guard's been dragging that channel, and the whole town'll be informed of what you done."

"I don't doubt the whole town'll be informed of something. I shouldn't think the way the tide runs past Cousins's wharf that they'll drag up much more than somebody's old stove lid. Why don't they just let her go? Save the town burial expenses, and you could go ahead and forget all the trouble and money you put into taking care of her."

"You ain't human!"

"I ain't . . . uk . . . am I? By the way, tell Justin I didn't drown that old clock in the tide rip. I took it to Mary Hadley; it belongs to her. You and Justin check up on her grandfather's will. It's worth two-three thousand dollars as an antique. Did you two know that?"

Flo slammed down her receiver. Bess hung up, poked her little finger into her ear, and wiggled it to ease the echo of the crash.

I ought to be ashamed of myself, prodding up that old

tornado like that, she told herself. But my, my, she's certainly got a little something coming, I guess.

On her way to bed, Bess looked in on Rosie. All was well there.

And I guess the hoot 'n' holler after you'll ease up now, honey, she told the silent sleeper silently.

Rosie McCarren dreamed she was adrift in the boat, with the horrible old woman chasing her, running on top of the whitecaps. She woke up whimpering a little. It took a minute for her to realize she'd been dreaming. But where was she? Somewhere. In a nice warm bed. She was clean. The sticky stuff was gone out of her hair. Everything was dark. The wind was blowing. And suddenly she remembered.

The last time she had heard the wind blowing hard, she'd been in Dad's boat with Hal, drifting out of the cove, away from the beach. The bay had been awful rough. On the beach, she'd stopped watching Hal for a while. She'd been trying to poke up a little fish that had been swimming around in a pool on top of the ledges. All at once, she'd looked up and there was Hal in the boat and it drifting off. He'd untied the anchor from the tripline and had carried it aboard the boat. She had had to run through water up to her knees before she could crawl aboard herself, and then the water had got too deep for her to get out and haul the boat ashore. She'd hollered as loud as she could, but nobody'd heard. A way out from the beach, the wind had seemed to pick the holler out of her mouth and blow it away.

She remembered how she'd tried to start the engine. The boat drifted and drifted. The water came into it. Then she couldn't remember any more. The next thing had been the ugly old woman and the strange place, and some awful-tasting medicine out of a spoon and everything funny and fuzzy.

It was what that fat man had told Dad. They'd come

back and take everybody off to the orphans' home. They must've come and Hal and I were out in the boat, so they caught us. If that old woman's house was the orphans' home, it was no place everybody would want to be taken to. But where was Hal? He hadn't been there. Maybe there was a boys' side and a girls' side to an orphans' home. Maybe the funny-looking man had found Hal first and taken him back to Dad on the island. All the lies that old woman had told about Dad and the kids being drowned—Rosie hadn't even listened, because she hadn't believed it; and now she remembered, she knew the others hadn't been in the boat. Only Hal and her.

Rosie shivered. It was lonesome here and dark. Where was the side they had put Hal on?

She got out of bed and began to hunt through the house. It was dark on the stairs and cold in the kitchen. The wind was making a *duddera-duddera-duddera* sound rattling the windows.

Of course Hal wasn't here. What it was, she wished he were. Or if Dad were here, or Sarah, she could go and get into bed with one of them and get warm.

There was a sudden noise near her, a clinking sound. She froze, listening. Somebody else was here. She could hear whoever it was, moving. She said, "Who . . . ?" and couldn't go on.

A flashlight beam swept over her and went out. She couldn't see which way to run.

A voice said, "Don't you be scairt, sweetheart. Don't you holler now, you'll bring everybody down on us. This is only old Leafy, and he won't hurt a hair of your head."

"All right. I'm not s-scared. I won't holler."

"That's a good girl." He snapped the light on again, and she could see him, a dark shadow behind it. She could see what he was doing, too. He had a big pile of grocery packages on the table and he was packing them into a big bag. Why was he doing that?

She asked him, "Why are you stealing their things?"

"I'm fixing to take you home. And we gotta eat. When I was uptown, I didn't have any chance to buy stuff, I had to help you out. So I'm low on everything."

"But it's only out to the island, and Dad'll have plenty. We won't be hungry enough to eat all that stuff you're taking." She had almost said "stealing," but if he got mad he might not take her home.

He said, "You crazy? Hear that wind? I ain't taking you with me tonight, you'd blow away like a feather. But in the morning, real early, I'll be back. You look out your window, you'll see me on a ladder, and we'll go. You be sure to put on all the warm duds you got, see? It'll be cold where we're going." He closed the bag, shouldered it, and made for the door. The light in his hand made his shadow with the bag black and lumpy.

"But—" Rosie began.

"No but about it. You want to go home, don't you?"

"Yes, I do." He was trying to shut her up, not letting her say what she wanted, needed, to know. "Will we go tomorrow morning?"

"When the wind stops blowing, we'll go. Might take two-three days to calm down."

"Where will we stay for two or three days?"

"I got a nice place. You'll see. Where nobody can find us."

The door clicked behind him. He was gone, leaving her in the dark kitchen.

She groped back upstairs and stood at the top, not sure which way to turn to get back to her room. She began to shake. She didn't—she *didn't* want to go anywhere with him. He was awful-looking and he smelt awful. He was a thief.

He'd taken a lot more of these people's things than he needed to. If she went with him and helped eat the things, she'd be a thief, too. What she ought to do, she ought to go wake somebody up so he could be caught before he got too far away.

Someone, somewhere, was snoring—a soft, gargly sound, ending in a tooting noise, like a whistle. She tried to locate it. Maybe it was the nice lady who'd cut her hair.

Rosie felt along the wall, found an open door, and went in. The snoring sound wasn't here, but she could hear breathing. A few steps along and there was the foot of a bed. Two people in it—she could feel four lumps of feet sticking up. One of the persons turned over, said, "What?" and lay still again. A man. Rosie backed away. No more strange men for her. No knowing what this one might do.

Along the hall, she found the room with the gargly noise. This had got to be Bess. Rosie hesitated at the door and did not go in. Mrs. Bess Bowden. What did she know about Mrs. Bess Bowden? Out on the island, she'd been nice and lots of fun, but after all, Rosie thought, I don't know her at all well. Maybe she's one of them who want to keep me here. Maybe they all did. If they didn't, why hadn't they said something about taking her home to Dad? Why hadn't they said something like, "You're just staying here tonight"? Not even the lady who had cut her hair had said that—she'd just said she knew where Dad is.

I won't stay here. I'll go with the funny-looking man. And if they catch him and put him in jail, how can I ever get home?

Dad said only if you're starving, in dire need to help you live, is it ever right to take other people's things. For survival. And then, if you can, you pay for what you took.

I am in dire need to help me live, because I can't live if I don't get back to him. This is for survival.

So stop being a baby. Go find your own bed. You don't need anybody here to get warm by, Rosemary Chester McCarren.

Leafy planned to spend the night in the haymow over Martin Hadley's workshop. He wasn't about to try to make it home tonight, lugging that helmonious great bag of vittles through the woods. Rough going, even with a flashlight, along that shortcut, and the way the wind was tooling on now, he'd likely get drove into the ground like a spike by one of them big trees falling on him. Might as well make himself to home in the hay and spend the night there. He'd have to be up before daylight to get that little girl out of the upstairs window before anybody was up. Martin always got up almightily early, and so did that cussed Bess. It was nice and warm in the haymow. He knew. He'd spent the afternoon there, sleeping off the last of his hangover.

He hadn't dared to go to sleep at home, in case Oat Baker came down there after him. Willie'd be all right. He was shut in the shed with a dishpan full of water and them two dead coon carcasses to gnaw on. He wouldn't like staying in the shed, but it wouldn't hurt him not to get his own way for once in his life.

When Leafy had first waked up, he'd judged it was around lamplighting time, growing dusky in the hayloft. He'd felt too comfortable even to think of walking home. Wind was blowing like a fool. Be cold. He had burrowed into the hay, thinking that if Oat Baker got futzing around that shed where Willie was and opened the door, he'd get his leg tore off and serve the old sculpin right. From the shine on the hayloft window, Leafy had realized that lights were on in Martin's house.

I bet I could see right into them kitchen windows, he'd thought, and had hauled himself out of the hay.

Why, he could see the whole works of it! Mary and Bess in the kitchen and that little girl setting to the table, eating her supper. They'd got her all cleaned up and blue night clothes on, and wasn't she a sweetheart! Some pretty! You'd never believe it.

He'd watched Bess pick her up and carry her out of sight, and then lights had come on in their upstairs back room windows. He could see Bess putting her to bed.

That had been when he'd first got the idea of taking her with him when he lit out for the backwoods, upcountry, tomorrow. What good company she'd be, warm and cuddly. He already knew what room she was sleeping in, and downstairs in the barn was a ladder. A couple of boots in the ass would learn Willie to leave her alone.

It'd be one on old Bess if I done it. Let her know what Leafy Piper thinks of a woman who'd tell a man he stinks to his face and then shove him overboard.

When he'd waked up the second time, it was full dark, and he'd looked out the window again. And there sat Martin Hadley, eating his supper. Leafy's stomach had reared up and made a drum roll that the cow downstairs must've heard, because she'd moved in her stall.

I ain't et since breakfast, and what I did eat I lost. And oh, Geezus, look at them roasted ducks! And biscuits. And that, setting there, was a pie. And what I got to home? Two chawed-on dead coons.

Now he was back in the hayloft, with a roaring big bagful of vittles and a bottle of rum that had been out in plain sight on the kitchen counter. He ate roast duck till he couldn't eat any more, nearly all of a loaf of bread, and the rest of the pie. He finished off with a good, long swig of rum. That rum must be Martin's—he doubted if old Bess ever let a drop touch her ruby lips. He settled down in a warm cover of hay, humming a little tune— What *was* that? Oh, yes, a song about drinking liquor.

"No, no, no, never, never, never,
Will I bind myself with cords
So diff-eye-cult to sever."

Sometime in the night he was waked up by a dog, raving and scratching at the barn door. He rose up, fast.

That Willie! I left him shut up but he's bruk out, and if I don't get down there and tend to him, he'll roust out everybody on the place.

He hustled down out of the loft and opened the door. "Here I am, you damned old fool. So shut—"

Willie, it seemed, wasn't even looking for him. Willie blasted by him in a rush that almost knocked his feet out from under him and began to rant and roar at something back there in the building behind him. He worked his flashlight out of his pocket.

Sweet Geezus! Martin Hadley'd be out here in no time flat.

"Shut up, Willie, or I'll boot the living hell out of you!"

Willie couldn't have cared less. What he was after was in the woodbox, back there in Martin's workshop, seemed like. Couldn't be nothing but a rat.

Leafy pointed the flashlight beam through the slatted cover of the woodbox. A slow grin spread across his face. "So that's what they done with you, you cussed little varmint." He leaned down and belted Willie a good one across the nose with the flashlight, which went out. Leafy shook it, hearing a slight tinkle. Smashed the bulb, ding it! But he'd showed Willie what was what, he'd shut up.

"All right, you want him, I'll get him for ya, but one more peep outa you—" Grunting, he reached down into the box and scrabbled around, trying to get hold of the critter's scruff. A set of needlelike teeth found his thumb first and bit halfway through the thick of it. He swore and slatted his hand. The coon ran up his arm and jumped. Scuttled away somewhere. Not towards Willie, because Willie began to rave again and tear around. Probably gone up the wall into the rafters. No use to try to find him now.

Leafy made a quick grab, managed to get Willie by the collar, found that Willie was trailing his leash. God, that was one good thing. That flashlight he'd swiped out of Bess's kitchen drawer had had it, so he dropped it on the floor. The blasted red bow tie he'd bought up to Cousins's was around under his ear, choke a man to death. He yanked it off and dropped that, too.

And now, get out of here fast. There weren't any lights on in the house, not yet. Martin Hadley might not have heard anything on account of the wind, which had picked up into a turrible torrent, but with him, you never knew. He had an ear like a gimlet. He might be outside the barn, right now, sneaking around in the dark. Better go on home, dark or no dark, come back early enough in the morning to carry out the rest of his plan. Them groceries would be all right where they were.

He had to boot Willie to get him away from the place, but Willie, when he was on the way home, headed straight down the shortcut through the Hadleys' woodlot and went like a railroad train. It wasn't far, but it was rugged going and blacker than the inside of a crooked storekeeper's pants pocket. Leafy doubted if he could have made it home through the blowdowns if he hadn't had Willie to tow him.

PART FOUR

In the night, the wind blustered into a full gale. The Coast Guard watch at Wentworth Harbor, at 2:35 A.M., recorded from the Station's anemometer a gust of seventy knots an hour. Trees toppled in woodlots; power lines went down, leaving trails of darkness through the coast towns. A cat spruce, three feet at the butt, which had stood on the northerly jut of the Cove thirty feet back from Calvin Petersen's wharf, broke off halfway up; its top sailed with the wind onto the roof of his wharf building, which buckled and fell in, the old and rickety sides folding down around it. A pile of new lobster traps which Warren had just finished and stacked against the west wall of the building went un-damaged.

Two windows blew in in Leafy Piper's shack, and he, noting ominous creaks and shudders in its aged timbers, carried his kitchen table into the lee of the bank above his sand cove and made up a camp bed under it, in which he and Willie passed the remainder of the night. Albemarle Spicer, in his house on the Point, also lost windows. In the morning, he found a cattail from a nearby swamp on his parlor floor.

At Cross Island, Will McCarren got out of bed and

went from room to room, checking to be sure storm windows were tightly hooked, that no one was lying awake, scared by the wind. He found his children safe and warm; the ones he had left to him were all asleep.

Himself unable to sleep, to be quiet, to rest, Will dressed and went outside. He stood in the lee of the house, his back braced against its wall. He had gone around tonight seeing that all was well, as he had on other nights, comforting grief where grief needed to be comforted; but it had seemed to him almost as if another man, another father, had been doing that—someone with the body of Will McCarren, from which he, Will McCarren, had gone away.

The sky was blue-black behind a trillion stars, blown across by wind-ripped rags of cloud driven so fast that the stars themselves seemed to be moving, a vast procession rolling and tumbling in and out of darkness. Their dim light grew and faded, grew again; at times, he could make out the pale tan grass of the clearing, the tormented tops of trees. Above the roar and whistle of the wind, he could hear the thunder of surf on Cross Island Beach. Somewhere in the woods nearby, a tree snapped off and went down with a crash.

Recalling Rosie. Rosie, who once saw a big spruce flat in the woodlot and had said, "It's too bad. That was a good tree."

I've got to stop this, Will told himself. I've got to snap out of it. Get sensible about what to do. About supplies. We're running out. About a boat.

But how? When the horrors skittered around in his mind like dead leaves in a gutter, as they were doing now.

I'm to blame. I should never have brought them here. Amy said to get them away, and God, I got them away, all right.

I was a fool to think children could thrive in this lonesome place. An outland. A desert.

Shame at his foolishness. A load of black guilt. With a deadly wind blowing and a deadly cold ocean on all sides of him.

A yowling gust baffled around the corner, snatching his breath out of his mouth, shoving him sideways along the wall.

One thing, this house wouldn't blow down, he was sure of that; its builders had set up their walls against wind and storm. They had known about weather; they had had to know. Their house had stood here for more than a century and a half. Its stubborn gables had split gales worse than this one tonight; they had faced up to hurricanes and had not gone down. Three generations of old Jeremy Cross's family had lived here since his time. They had died here; here, too, they had lost children. There were five children's graves in the cemetery on the far side of the pond. Two of them, babies, one a boy of three. The others, older. Years back, all of them.

There are ghosts here, Will thought. And two of them belong to me.

It was no comfort to think that other men might have stood where he was standing, staring into a wild sky and grieving for lost children. He knew how they must have felt, that was all.

Or did he?

Did you curse this place? he asked the silent shade of Jeremy Cross. Call it a desert, an outland, a destroyer of your children?

Or had your people come here from a desert where a whore could be flogged through the streets at the tail of a cart, where men and women could be tried and burned for witches, where a starving child could be hanged for stealing a piece of bread? Was your desert better or worse than mine, where school grounds are rotten with dope, where a baby's brain can be crippled for life with a pep pill? Were you or your sons ready to run like hunted animals when the children died?

The answer to that was here for any man to know, in the tough walls behind him which had sheltered children for over a hundred and fifty years.

A wavering light appeared in one of the kitchen windows; someone was lighting a lamp. Bill, he saw, peering in. Bill was getting dressed, putting on outdoor gear.

Worried, Will thought. Coming to look for me. He opened the door and stepped inside. He said, "Quite a dust-up we're having. Couldn't you sleep?"

"Sarah woke me up." Bill began taking off his heavy jacket. "We got a little uptight about you, Poppa."

"I was just outside, taking a look at the weather. Stayed longer than I meant to. Everything's all right; we won't blow away. It's a stout-built house."

From behind the door where he was hanging up his jacket, Bill said, "We going to stay in it?"

"Do you want to?"

"Not if you don't."

"It would take some doing. Some figuring."

"Sure. I know. No boat. And me being here. If it gets around that we're alive and kicking, we'll get in the newspapers. Those town creeps will be back with the handcuffs. I've been thinking."

"I've been trying to," Will said quietly. "I want you with us, Bill. Don't make any mistake about that."

"No, I won't. Could we use a chain saw to cut lumber —boards, I mean—say, out of a blown-down tree?"

"We could try. It would be pretty rough lumber. Why?"

"I want to build up the bow on the punkinseed. Maybe put a deck on her—oh, you know, something like a kayak, so she won't ship so much water. Maybe row her ashore some calm night and locate our boat and bring her back."

"And then?"

"I don't feel I'm the one to say."

"You, as much as anybody. Would you like to take off, go somewhere else?"

Bill had been taking off his boots, looking down at them. Now he glanced at his father with a white-faced grin. "We've put a lot into this place. Sarah and I've been talking. She's got a batch of seeds to plant. She says what'll we do with them if we go—throw them in the ocean? I cut some teeth building the punkinseed. Now I want to build a skiff. Learn how, first, this time. Julian's got his windmill. We'd like to stick it here and tell those fat-assed constables to go to hell. You did it once, and it sure made our day. Only we want to be sure you can stand it here, because we lost . . . the . . . the kids . . ."

Sarah said from the doorway, "We said first it would be too tough to stay. But then we . . . we said, if we go back, if we give up after what we've started to do, it would be almost as if we'd lost them for nothing."

Will said, "Is it right for you here? No other friends? People? Don't you miss—"

"I don't miss anything," Bill said. "I feel stretched out, limbered up. As if something that was stuck and . . . and rusty had got cracked loose. Like that old pump I fixed. Or I did before . . . before . . . Sure, we said, it'll be rough to stay."

"But it would be rougher to go somewhere else and have to remember we left them alone here," Sarah said. She started to say more and couldn't, and Bill said, "If you could sleep some, Poppa . . . What you need now is sleep."

He did, Will realized. Suddenly he was dead for sleep and knew it, so worn out he could barely stand. Barely talk. But he managed to say something and he managed to smile. "We'll start tomorrow. See what we can do with the chain saw, Bill."

He collapsed into bed without bothering to pull up the

covers, and realized that the kids were doing it for him. It takes with one hand and gives back with the other, he thought, and on the edge of sleep, he got an answer from old Jeremy Cross—at least from somebody's ghost that did just as well.

What did you think we put into this place, into this house? Nothing?

❦

In his house at the Cove, Calvin Petersen, roused from his old man's sleep by the crash of the tree on the roof of his wharf building, got out of bed and went to the window. He could make out the stump of the tree, black against the tumbling sky.

Why, that goddamn old cat spruce! Cracked in two like a pepp'mint stick. Probably rotten with red heart halfway up the trunk, not that you'd know that to look at it. That was a big tree when I was a boy, been there more'n a hundred years. Wonder what it fell into that made more noise than a tree busting down.

He peered around, but there were too many clouds over the stars; he couldn't tell.

Well, the time of a tree is longer than the time of a man. I am going on for eighty-one years old and I ain't by a damnsight through yet, but if my time's coming, let'er come. I've been to the State Capitol and I've done all right in my business. I've fought the competition and the government taxes. Cheated some on them both, because, by the god, the way things was and still is, if a man don't shade a little bit here and a little bit there, he comes out the wrong end of the horn with turd on his head. I beat'em out and I had fun doing it.

Like I said to someone—who did I say that to? Some summer feller. It's a game you got to play, I told him, whoever 'twas. I played it and beat at it. I ain't rich but I'm comfortable at the age of eighty-one years. If you come out in one piece at that old and you've got enough out of it to live on till you die, you've beat it out and folks respect you, except you're older than God.

If you don't understand that, I told the feller, you're better off living on an island away from the world, because that's the way the world is to live in. And if you had any neighbors out there, you'd find that the same thing prevails. I know. I was born and brought up on one.

God, I can't remember what I had for dinner yesterday, but I can see pictures clear as a looking glass of the way things was there. It don't make any sense to say it was a heaven on earth, it was rugged going. And we had turd-heads and hoorers and folks cheat you as soon as look at you, same as anywhere now. I see Johnny Wilson and I remember Ferdy Oakes, same kind of a man, steal the meat out of your stew if your back was turned. But we had a plenty of good, honest, stiddy people, too.

I remember still mornings, go down through the pasture and leave dew tracks that a cow could follow, and the sun coming up like a piece of a wedding ring and the sound of the water and a sweet spring bird. In my herring weir—I had one, those days, never made any money out of it— in my weir, maybe some silver hake with the sun on their backs telling why they was called silver, or a school of mackerel, stripes like gold, under the water. Never made a cent out of mackerel, but they was a pretty fish and good eating. Or an old monkfish, had to get him out of there before he et up all the eating fish. I recall one I hooked under the chin with my gaff and towed him out through the weir gate and he puked. I ain't ever forgive myself for making that homely old objeck puke.

I recall down in my woodlot one day, I come on a batch of them bluebead lilies setting in the sun on a circle of green moss. Nothing had ever touched them, not a cow's foot or some goddamn fool picking the woods flowers to load into his car and wilt down, like I see all the time here. Them lilies was like they'd just been made on the first morning of God setting up the world to go where it was going to go.

Things smelt good and was good, as I look back, not all wovelled up like eels' holes in a pond. Where now what a man has got to do stinks, and the air stinks from a million cars going by his place every summer full of folks hunting whatever it is they think they're hunting, could be some peaceful place like an island. I reason to myself that an island was what I had when I was a boy and simple.

And we young fellers flew off of there like a flock of geese and never went back. If a man could hang onto his kids, with what kids want and God only knows what that is, he'd be all right for a time, living on an island.

Starlight, zigzagging out from behind a cloudy mass, suddenly showed Calvin that the familiar silhouette of his wharf building was gone.

For the godsake, that was where the top of that tree got flang to. No wonder it made hell's own racket. Folded her up like a blossom. Lit square in the middle of her, looks like.

Well, there was one more goddamned thing blowed down, smashed, lost. Next, might be me. But t'hell with that.

The jolt recalled Calvin sharply to the present, which happened these days more often than he realized. Or, perhaps, would admit. It was handy, sometimes, at home, to be deaf or not to take things in when Warren got hard to handle or Josie started 'ranguing.

Will McCarren, that's who I told all that to, one time he came into the wharf to buy lobsters for a feed for his kids, and if they et all he bought, I'll bet there was one helmonious plague of bellyaches. Did I tell him all that stuff? Yes, I guess I did, because he asked me what it was like to live on the islands in the old days. That poor devil. He never even held onto himself, let alone his kids, and not his fault, either. Not with Justin Bradley hounding him.

By the god, there's going to be justice done. What with Alby's telling, and with me putting out and around what I found out yesterday up to the County Court House, we can blast that gumshoeing son of a bitch right out through the roof of the Town Hall.

❦

The northwester, having wrecked everything it could get at, blew itself out to sea by morning. As was usual with such gales in the spring, it dried up mud- and potholes in the town road, so that repair trucks could get through. Following them, as early as possible after the road was cleared, came Otis Baker's car, with Otis himself and Dr. Fletcher, the County Medical Examiner.

Martin Hadley, lying on the kitchen couch with his sore feet propped up on cushions, was restless and cross. He hated to be laid up, and so far as Mary could remember, he never had been. He had got up early this morning, determined not to let a few barnacle cuts ruin his day's work, and found his feet swollen and so painful they would hardly bear his weight. It had taken some doing on Mary's part to keep him off of them. "Stay in bed," she'd said, but he wouldn't. He'd made it down to the kitchen couch. He lay there, looking out of the window, growling and grumbling.

"Look, I've got to get down and unlock that hatch for Otis. If I can get my boots on, I can walk all right."

"Your feet won't even go into your boots," Mary said. "Bess can take the key down to Otis when he gets here. He won't, right away. The power's off. Probably trees down across the road."

"Dammit, I don't want Bess or anyone else frigging around aboard my boat. I ought to go down there. Where is she, anyway?"

"Out feeding hens and the cow. Milking. Feeding her coon. You know where she is, honey."

He was silent for a while, commenting only when the power came on. "The power's on. What are you doing, making coffee in that old tin pot? Use the new one, why don't you?"

Mary had hoped that the power wouldn't come on until she'd got the coffee irrevocably started in Bess's old agate pot. The new one, electric, automatic, was a splendid object, exactly the kind of gadget Martin loved, but the coffee from it lately had begun to taste of the pot. She had boiled out the pot according to the directions which had come with it, but that hadn't seemed to make much difference. Looking over its insides, she had discovered on the bottom of the percolator unit a small circle of metal which looked as if it must jump up and down when heat forced the brew through it.

That's the trouble, she decided. There was no possible way to clean out under that. She'd tried, with cotton on a knitting needle, and no doubt had got it cleaner, but in doing so, she'd bent the thing. It no longer jumped. The pot wouldn't work.

Briefly, she told Martin so.

"That's supposed to be indestructable, that coffeepot. It's *guaranteed*," Martin said. "Let's look at it. Let's see what the hell you bent."

She brought the pot, set it upright on his stomach. "You fossick around inside it. You'll see."

"For godsake!" he said after a moment's silence. "You bent the flutter valve!"

"Yes, I did, didn't I."

"You'll have to use the old pot till I can get this fixed.

May have to get a new one, send this back to the factory. Now, look, Mary, that old pot of Bess's'll make good coffee if you do it right."

"What would you suggest?"

"Bess puts in coffee, a tablespoon to a cup, one for the pot. Got that?"

"Mm-hm."

"Then she takes an egg and—"

"What color? White or brown?"

"Oh, for the love of— Look, I'm only telling you. She holds the pot off, arm's length, like this—" He illustrated with the one he held in his hand. "And she heaves the egg into it, ker-slam, hard as she can, so it'll splatter around, mix with the coffee."

The back door opened, and Bess came in. The small coon, sliding between her feet, came in also. He sat up and looked around, seeing what everything was all about now.

Mary, with the egg poised, jumped a little at the sight of the coon, realized that her aim was spoiled, too late to hold back. The egg missed the coffeepot, skidded across a plateful of biscuits on the kitchen table, and, still unbroken, hit the coon in the middle of his soft stomach. He winced a little, dropped to all fours. Then, taking advantage of this serendipity, he bit open the egg and began to eat it.

Martin choked, threw back his head, and roared. "Jesus Christ, Mary," he gasped. "Could you do that again?"

Breakfast was good, and calming. Martin drank his coffee and said it was fine. Bess talked about the coon—the smart little duffer had somehow found out how to get out of the woodbox. She didn't see how, because the wooden button that held the screen cover down was on the outside.

"Coons," she said, "are always a mystery."

They were finishing breakfast when Warren Petersen arrived. "Thought I'd see how you weathered it," he said to Martin. "Glad to see you taking it easy today."

"Well, I don't need to," Martin grumbled. "Women-folks have got a headlock on me is all. I can get up anytime."

"No, you can't," Mary said. "So stuff it, dear heart. Coffee, Warren?"

Warren shook his head and grinned. "That's right, Mary, you make him rest. He took one awful pounding yesterday. Marty, if you'll let me have the key to the padlock on your hatch, I'll go aboard your boat and bring that . . . what Oat's here for ashore for him."

"All right," Martin said.

"Oat's just given me quite a reading on what the law is about unauthorized persons handling such things," Warren said. "Seems he's got to get all the statutes straight. Says you and I both have got to sign written statements."

"The hell we do!"

Warren shrugged. "Says he'll come by and see you later. He's down there now with Pretty Dick."

"Oh," Mary said. "Dr. Fletcher. Would you ask him to stop by here if he has time? I want him to look at Marty's cuts."

Martin let out a growl. "Don't bother him. I don't need him."

"Sure," Warren said. "You'll bust him one on the nose if he shows up, hey, Marty?" He took the key which Mary handed him from Martin's key ring, winked at her as he started for the door.

Mary, starting to clear away breakfast, lifted a hand at him. He would send Dr. Fletcher up, and she could take it from there. Meanwhile, she could plan lunch and dinner. There should be enough duck left for one meal anyway. But when she opened the refrigerator door to check, she didn't see any. The platter was there, with some scraps and congealed gravy, but the remains of both ducks were gone.

That was funny. Looked as though somebody had got up in the night and had a monumental mug-up. Not Martin, laid up with his sore feet. And Bess would never do such a thing. Rosie? Mary thought in bewilderment. Nonsense. No child could possibly eat that much.

Martin said from his couch, "Where's your refugee? She ought to be waking up pretty soon, hadn't she?"

"It's early yet. We thought we'd let her sleep as long as she would. She's awfully worn out, Marty. And we suspect Flo dosed her with something. Bess thinks, paregoric."

"The old wolf eel," Martin said. He lay quietly, from time to time glancing out the window.

"There's a mystery," Mary said. She had looked along shelves and opened cupboard doors, not that anyone with any sense would have put cooked duck anywhere but in the icebox. "We had a lot of duck left over from last night. It seems to have disappeared."

He answered absently. "Bess probably fed it to her coon, the fat little nuisance," he said, and let out a disgusted snort. "Look at that! Everybody in town, womenfolks and all, down there busting a gut to see what there is to see. What do they expect? A dance and a hootenanny?"

It was quite a crowd, down on the dock. Leaning to look past him, Mary saw that the crowd had parted to let Otis and the doctor come through. She could make out the small bundle, wrapped in yellow oilskin, which Otis was carrying to his car.

"Quite a sociable occasion," Martin said. "Oat ought to open that up, show it to all the slobs who hollered, 'Quack, quack,' at Will McCarren." He glanced at her. "I'm sorry, kid. I'll be all right in a minute."

She put out a hand to touch his cheek and carried his tray over to the sink. After a while, she heard him say, "Here they come. Hogfat and Handsome."

And that's a fact, she thought as she opened the door. Otis was certainly stout and Dr. Fletcher was handsome. He was known for it all over the district, was called "Pretty

Dick" by some who felt that a doctor to be any good ought to be rugged-looking and homely, and at least middle-aged. Dr. Winslow, who had died standing up in the midst of his practice, had been eighty-two and bulldog homely.

The protest against inevitable change hadn't bothered Dr. Fletcher. He had had excellent training, knew his business, and had brought off some cures thought miraculous, at least by the patients cured. Word had passed among the few who believed in such things that he was a faith healer, who used laying on of hands—look at old Miss Judy Friendly's cancer. What but some such of a thing could have cured that? Old Miss Friendly, eighty-five, had herself fully convinced that she was dying of cancer, and no one could talk her out of it. But she'd taken some pills prescribed by Dr. Fletcher, had "passed" her cancer, and was now seen at times riding around town on a bicycle.

If the ailment had been no more than simple stoppage, that was Dr. Fletcher's secret. He knew he was good-looking, broad-shouldered, and tall, with a wide, pleasant grin, and he rather liked his nickname. So did his wife and two children, who called him "Pretty Dick" to his face.

He came in briskly, said, "Hello, what have we got here?" and went to work at once on Martin's cuts.

Otis was solemn, a man whose job was serious and heavy on him. "Well, Martin. Warren tells me that was quite a job you done yesterday. Quite a undertaking. You git bad cut?"

"Barnacle scratches." Martin winced and jerked his foot away from the doctor. "What the hell . . .?"

"Sea urchin spines," Fletcher said. "Clobbered all over with iodine. What'd you do, soak your feet in it? Ought to've known better, open cuts like these."

Martin didn't say anything.

"Tch! Them whore's-eggs is awful things to step on,"

Otis said. "Work right up through a feller's foot. Like in my thumb. I got one of them spines in there, in the thick of my thumb, the fleshy part. Couldn't find it to get it out. Come right up through my knuckle. They'll do that every time if you don't get'em out." He cleared his throat nervously. "I see you've got that body all wrapped up. In bad shape, was it?"

"Yes. I told you over the phone."

"Boy or girl, you couldn't say. Couldn't tell nothing like that, hanh?"

"There's nothing to add to what I told you last night."

"H'm, painful for anybody to talk about. Thing is, I got a written statement from Warren. It's my duty to see that your story matches up with his. I know it ain't pleasant, but—"

Martin stared at him. "Any notion in your mind that one of us is fibbing?" he demanded. "For godsake, Oat, how legal can you get? We found the body on Cross Island Beach, got it, brought it in, called you. That's all. Here, give me Warren's statement, I'll sign it, too."

"Well, I d'know as—" Otis wilted a little. "I guess likely that'll do it."

"I guess likely it'll have to. Ouch, doc! You planning to take my foot with you when you go?"

"Hold still, dammit. I'm nearly through."

Otis produced a paper from his pocket, together with a pen. "Sign right there at the bottom, where my thumb is, right under Warren."

"I see the place. That the same thumb you got the whore's-egg in?"

This, obviously, wasn't worth answering. Looking hurt, Otis tucked away his paper and his pen. "There's one thing more, Martin. You know where Leafy Piper is?"

"No, if he isn't at home."

"You ain't got no idea where he is?"

"Why don't you lay off of him? What harm's he done?"

"Made a pass at the schoolteacher right in the face and eyes of Main Street. She's pressing charges. There's other ladies in town nervous and wrought up. Justin says we got to do something."

"Nuts! Hell with Justin. I can guess who the ladies are, too. Even Leafy wouldn't look twice."

"Well, I got to arrest him if I can catch up with him."

"You won't. He's likely gone into the woods, the way he does. Take a battalion of scouts to find him. Why don't you go back and say so? Let Justin and the ladies simmer down. Time they do, they'll find someone else to hassle and forget all about Leafy."

"I don't know. I just don't know. Toss it up, heads I lose, tails I lose. Either way." Otis spoke with a kind of hopeless patience—a man holding on, and barely that, not knowing where to turn. Justin's heavy hand was on him, and the heavier hand of his wife; and the hands of her friends, whose opinions, broadcast far and wide, had, in Otis's opinion, a great deal to do with the politics of the town. He fell silent.

"Okay, I'm done," Dr. Fletcher said. "Keep off those feet for a few days. Soak, plain soapsuds and hot boiled water, three times a day. Right? I'll want to see you again in a day or so."

Martin wasn't one to argue when somebody who actually knew had convinced him he'd been wrong. "Okay," he said. He glanced at Mary and grinned. "No iodine, kid."

Mary, who had been considering whether or not, now that the doctor was there, to ask him to look at Rosie, grinned back a little absently. Of course she couldn't mention Rosie in front of Otis, who was sitting there solidly, as if he meant to spend the day. If only Bess had come back

. . . but Bess hadn't. Better to see how Rosie was this morning. If she needed a doctor, Bess would have to cope.

The doctor snapped his bag shut and started for the door.

Martin said, "Hey, how much do I owe you?"

"Not a cent."

"Thanks, I appreciate it. Five dollars? Ten?"

"This business is something that involves us all, Mr. Hadley. I'm not charging you for what you did yesterday." Fletcher went out, shut the door firmly behind him.

Otis, too, got up to go. He stared out the window at the doctor, hustling down the path, his coattails fairly snapping with the breeze of his passage.

"Never give me a chance to answer that," Otis said. "I know what the whole town thinks, without him handing me a sideways snootful. A man, an officer of the law, has got to do his job. Ain't nobody realizes he ain't to blame for doing it." He was still stinging from the remarks he'd overheard down at the wharf when he was locking that body into his car.

"Who does he think he is?" somebody'd said. And somebody else: "Why, he's the hearse. Hang a bunch of carnations around his neck and he'd make a dandy."

All them people, blaming him. And the doctor. And he guessed Martin and Mary felt the same way, they weren't saying anything. Well, there was one more thing, and then he could go.

He made for the door, stopped with his hand on the knob, and cleared his throat. "I'll trade you Leafy for the Town Hall clock." Not only Flo but also Justin had got after him about bringing that clock back.

"You'll *what?*" Martin said.

"I'll lay off of Leafy if you'll let me have that clock back."

"What did you tell me just now you're an officer of?"

"Ayeh, I know." Otis opened the door and went.

"Why, the poor devil," Martin said. "Lord, there's a man on the end of a pin if I ever saw one."

Mary said as Bess came in, "Bess, did you do anything with the left-over duck? Martin says you fed your coon with it."

"He would. Isn't it in the icebox?"

"There's the platter, in the sink. Every bit gone."

Bess walked over to look. Somehow she had got her feet wet, they squelched as she moved.

"Fall overboard?" Martin asked.

Bess smiled at him. "Not like some," she said. "Went down to dump the water out of my punt. No barnacles on the float. There's quite a gathering down there. Mad as hornets, most of them. Having things over. Well, that's quite a conundrum, Mary. Where'd you suppose the duck went?"

"Got to be that coon," Martin said. He was sitting up, his feet on the floor, and he looked rested. "Sneaked in in the night and opened the icebox door."

"More like it was you, crawled downstairs on your hands and knees and cleaned up the works. I've known you to snabble onto the leftovers."

"Nope. If you didn't, that leaves Rosie?"

"Oh, sure. Is she still sleeping, Mary?"

Mary nodded. "I was just up there. All I could see was a little round lump under the bedclothes."

"She's slept long enough," Bess said. "I'll look in when I go up." She glanced thoughtfully at the empty platter. "Did either of you hear anything in the night besides the wind blowing?"

"I woke up once," Martin said. "Some dog barking. Other than that, wind was all I could hear. There's your solution, Mary—the wind blew the icebox open. You'll find your duck in the top of a tree somewhere."

"Oh, come on, shut up, you joker," Bess said. "If somebody got in in the night and raided the icebox, it doesn't scare me and Mary any more than it does you. There's only one I know about who'd be crazy enough to be out in that tommycane last night, and I expect he was hungry. He sure didn't bring any groceries home from the Harbor. That duck, or part of it, is probably down Willie's maw, and we're lucky we didn't lose more than leftovers."

Mary walked over and opened the supply closet door. "Oh, my!" she said a little breathlessly. "We have. We've lost about everything."

"Why, that light-fingered son of a gun!" Martin rose to his feet, furious, and found himself confronted by Bess, who sat him back down with a smart shove. "You stay where you are," she said grimly. "He isn't going to get very far, the load he's lugging, including a whole twenty-five-pound bag of flour. I'll catch up with him!"

"I'll bounce him up and down till he rattles . . ."

"Not with those feet you won't."

"But, Bess," Mary said, "he's taken the bottle of rum . . . What if he's drunk?"

"I'll see the day I'm scared of Leafy Piper, drunk or sober." Bess made for the stairs. "You stay where you are, you fireball!"

She'd have to change footgear—she couldn't make time down that shortcut sliding around in a pair of squelchy shoes.

She was putting on the second dry boot when she noticed the note on her desk. The paper was scrawled over, hardly readable, as if it had been written in the dark.

I didn't want him to steal your things.
Dad will pay for everything you lost.
Thank you.

Rosemary Chester McCarren

"Oh, my God!" Bess said aloud, to nobody but herself.

She raced along the hall to the spare room. There was indeed a round lump under the bedclothes, but it was a pillow.

Otis Baker was not only on the head of a pin, he was heartsick. For a week, he had been trying to tell himself he wasn't to blame for what had happened to the McCarrens, going over and over in his mind the reasons why he couldn't be. A Constable had to do hard things to people. If someone broke the law, he had to be chased down and arrested. A policeman made enemies; that had always bothered him. People took it the wrong way. No one stopped to think that it wasn't Otis Baker doing it on his own, but an appointed officer sworn to uphold the law and, with the McCarrens, told what to say by Justin, who was the head of the Board, who'd appointed him and who could fire him tomorrow.

Otis believed in the law, what he knew of it. He had to admit that he didn't know much, only the common things like drunk driving and malicious mischief, and so on. Anything out of the usual, he had to get his information from talk he heard around the County Court House, or at court trials. Sometimes he had to go ask some lawyer, who would know. Had to be careful how he asked, pry around sideways-like, so as not to let on what his trouble was—that he couldn't read nor write and was ashamed because he couldn't.

Oh, he could sign his name and do simple arithmetic, use a dial telephone, and he got away with his job as Tax Collector because Flo did the figuring. But he'd only got as far as the fourth grade in school and hadn't earned that. Teachers passed him along to get rid of him, because he was a heller on wheels. He'd been glad to get away from all those little kids' classes and go on a dragger, south, when he was fourteen and big for his age.

Easing his car over the potholes on the road back to town, Otis wished he'd never taken on this job as Constable. Wouldn't have if Justin hadn't got after him. Couldn't find anybody else, Justin'd said—not anybody who was a capable, strong man with the guts to do the job. Which Otis was, as everybody knew, Justin'd said. Made him feel pretty good, what Justin'd said.

Flo'd kept after him, too. What if he didn't know any law? she'd said. She'd read the statutes to him out of the state book. But her reading him the statutes hadn't been any use in the God's world. There were words in that book that he'd never heard of, didn't know the meaning of, never would. But when Flo got her hook into something, she'd come down on it like a hawk on a henpen.

She'd been after him about Will McCarren ever since that blasted old uncle of hers had gone back to Bullet Bay. So had Justin. Justin had hauled him over the coals more'n once, said he wasn't being tough enough. Said he hoped they hadn't made a mistake appointing him to the office of Constable. Hadn't sounded much like the way he had when he'd asked Otis to take the job.

On the boat going out to Cross Island, Justin'd told him what the school law was, told him what to say. And then hadn't let him say it; he had had to butt in.

I wisht I could've gone out there alone. That poor duffer could have been told in a decent way without making him ory-eyed mad and scaring his kids. Talk as rough as that to a man in front of his own children, that ain't a thing I would ever do, and I ain't going to be able to forget it for a long time, if ever.

That girl that run in there without much on, she only done it to grab the little feller out of there because he was scared and crying. I never mentioned that she slept with her father, and I never in the God's world would, even if I knew it to be so. Even if Justin had known it to be so, it wasn't nothing to tickle and titter about all over town.

A whole roomful of scared kids, he thought, his misery growing. Hell, I like kids, and most kids like me. I go to all the school times, not to be the law checking up on anybody's cussed actions but just to see all them little kids speaking pieces and singing, pretty as a row of nasturtiums. Used to visit school, too, when Bud and Isabel was going there.

Bud and Isabel. Gone away so long ago that he could hardly recall what they looked like. Gone, like as if to the far end of the world. Isabel in Oregon, far away as she could get without tumbling into the ocean, and Bud in the Navy, as if he *had* tumbled in. His own kids.

And that brought Otis straight back to McCarren and McCarren's kids, every last one of them dead. That little girl at his and Flo's, crazy she must've been to do what she done. Why, he'd hardly caught a sight of her, not to get acquainted any, been gone from daylight to dark hunting among the islands for the bodies of her folks, and her not up in the morning when he'd left and gone to bed before he'd got home at night. Hadn't had a chance to tell whether she was crazy or not. Chop up her dress with the hatchet and stick her head in that can of old roofing tar in the shed like Flo said she done was crazy-acting, all right, but that sugar bowl she flang at Justin . . . I wouldn't of blamed any one of Will McCarren's kids for heaving anything come to their hand at Justin Bradley. I don't think that was crazy. Me, I'd of give her a quarter for it.

That little girl was the last one of all them to be alive, and likely she'd never be found—that was a turrible swirl of tide went by Cousins's wharf. And that body he had in the back seat was the baby the girl had run in to comfort because he was scared to death and crying. If Flo had ever let me get handy to that little girl, I might of comforted her some, too. I don't know as Flo was a good one for the Selectmen to have put her out to board with. Flo ain't ever been overfond of children.

Otis shifted in his seat and let out a heavy breath, which in spite of him sounded like a groan.

Dr. Fletcher, beside him, glanced around. "You feeling all right, Mr. Baker?"

Stand him off. Man ain't spoke to me all the way up from the Cove, set there with a face like a meat ax to show what he thinks of me. What everybody else does, I guess. That I'm to blame for what's there in the back seat. He said, "I'm feeling all right, Dr. Fletcher."

When he had done all he had to do as law officer in charge of the case, Otis turned his car back down the road to the Cove. He didn't want to go home and have to talk to Flo about that poor little kid's remains; she'd already picked his brains out on that. And he didn't plan to show up empty-handed at the Town Hall today. What Justin wanted that blasted old clock for, God only knew, but he did want it, and he'd told Otis to bring it back along with Leafy Piper.

Hell, chances are I won't be able to turn up with either one, Otis told himself drearily. But I can show signs of where I've gone on a hunt for Leafy. I'll go check his shack.

The crowd down at the Cove still lingered, having things over. The main criticism was indeed of Otis Baker, his works and ways. Someone had brought up the fact that after he had put the body in his car, he'd gone around locking all the car doors. "What did he think—that anyone here's low-down enough to go nosing into that?"

"Just goes to show you what the high-diddles uptown

think of us down here on the Point . . ."

"As if we was a bunch of outlaws . . ."

"Oat Baker ain't any high-diddle. Them Bakers was always common as cow flops . . ."

". . . about as much good as Constable as an old poodle dog . . ."

A deep boom roared out, drowning all other voices. "You voted for the crooks that put him in there. And I'll say no more." That had been Calvin Petersen.

Warren, standing on the edge of the crowd, said, "Oh, wow! I guess I'd better go winkle Gramp out of there. Sounds as though he's opening up quite a can of worms." Warren began wriggling his way through the crowd and arrived too late. Albemarle Spicer was already facing up to Calvin with fire in his eye. His voice, of medium pitch, had had no chance, so far, against Calvin's.

"Republicans and Democrats," Calvin said. "For and aginst. One or t'other. Anyone would think that whoever you voted for was your own blood kin, no matter what kind of a hoss's ass he is. All he's got to be is on the same side your great-grandfather voted for seventy-five years ago."

He stopped for lack of breath, and Albemarle put in. "You any different? When in hell's name did you ever vote Republican, irregardless?"

"I don't know as I ever see one I'd vote for," Calvin said.

"Well, then. Don't shoot your mouth off. Anytime now I'd expect to hear you say it's the Republican Party that's responsible for blowing your building down."

The argument, turned against him in this unfair way, sat very ill with Calvin. He started at once to get his teeth into it. "You ever know anything, even the goddamned weather, to be something a man could live decent with when the Republicans is in?"

His voice broke into a squeak, and Warren laid an arm around his shoulders. "Come on home, Gramp," he began.

148

"I ain't coming! You go on home yourself or I'll take a stick to you. Sure enough, my wharf building's been blown down, whether by the mindless damn wind or by the mindless damn hot air of rotten politics, I ain't the one to say."

Calvin's breath played out again, but he wasn't through. He stood breathing deep, hoping that his face showed he wasn't. He had been a spellbinder in his time, a campaign speaker for candidates, the youngest and last of the men who had once lived on the Hill Road, when the Point had been top dog in the town. Now, in the middle of a speech, he found himself hounded by a lack of breath and a desperate need to pee when there wasn't a private place nearby which wasn't overrun with women. Nevertheless, he reached hard for what he had and came up with the old resonant boom which had always rocked the caucus.

"Sixty years ago I cast my first vote aginst crooked politicians, when these we got now wasn't nothing but tit-suckers, taking more milk from their own mothers than they was entitled to."

"Oh, come on, Calvin," Albermarle said. He had watched with some compunction Calvin's struggle for breath and Warren's concern. No argument living was worth having the old man get a stroke. Better cool things off, he thought. He said moderately, "Just because you don't like a man's politics don't make him crooked, does it?"

"Go ahead, back down if you want to," Calvin said. He eyed Albemarle, and his tone became silky. "You hear any talk about real estate values going up around here? Sounds foolish, don't it? Anybody owns an acre of land couldn't sell the hay off it to a goat, ain't that so? Take the offshore islands, ain't worth the powder to blow'em down to bedrock, now are they?"

Albemarle stared at him, puzzled. "What the hell, Calvin? What's that all about?"

"I'll leave you with the lovely thought of it," Calvin

said. "Warren, if you don't stop hugging me, people here'll think there's something terrible funny wrong with you. You go get your jeep and haul me home. I need a drink of water. That mackerel your ma canned last fall is salter'n Lot's wife." He stalked off the wharf.

Warren followed him, knowing from his stiff-legged gait what his problem was and guessing why he had let the argument drop. His grandfather dearly loved a fight, and this had started out to be a dandy. Calvin stopped behind the first substantial tree and Warren caught up with him. "You make it okay, Gramp?"

Calvin said pathetically, "Oh, ker-riced! Why does a feller have to get old?"

"You're in hard shape," Warren said. "You want me to bust out crying because you're so used up and decrepit?"

"You could show a little human feeling for an old wreck come as close as I did to pissing myself. All you'll likely do is tell me to button my fly."

"Sure. Button your fly, Gramp. You were being slick, there, about something. What was the idea, needling Alby about offshore island property and real estate values?"

"Why, we was talking about honest men in politics," Calvin said. His gaze, tranquil and innocent, met Warren's. "I believe that was what it was all about. Men of goodwill, like them told about in the Bible. You couldn't go along with them ones that would knock off a city, kill all the women and kids, and go through their houses, take what they had. But by and large, they had some good men in them times. Responsible in their civic duties, as old Judge Cameron, God rest his soul, used to say. I never mentioned names, not caring at the moment to lay my tongue to any, but I don't doubt Alby'll make something of it."

"What's that old Republican-Democrat battle got to do with real estate?"

"Your trouble is, none of you young fellers give a damn. Don't read the papers, don't take a look outside of your own affairs. If you did and put your mind to it, you might be able to mate two up with two. There's no question but what real estate's started to move, all them city people running round here looking for places where they can walk on Main Street without being hit over the head with a stockin'ful of rocks. I'm going home. You squat down here and mull it over." He started off without looking back.

"Don't you want me to get the jeep?" Warren called after him.

"What for?"

Warren caught up with him again as he was turning into the yard at his house. The old man looked at him and grinned. He sat down on the doorstep. Warren sat down beside him.

"If that feller McCarren was stealing lobsters," the old man said, "he was making a lifework out of eating them. There wasn't a week go by but he'd stop by the wharf and buy a dozen."

"I never believed he did haul traps," Warren said.

"I had plenty of chances to talk to him. I liked the bugger. He told me he was going to stay with us for good. Was interested in buying Cross Island. Ain't interested now. Ain't likely to be."

"No," Warren said. What the hell was all this? Gramp got pretty far out sometimes. Well, he was old. It was too bad.

"Now, Alby, he's putting it out and around that it was Oat Baker hounding him that drove McCarren off the island. Granted Oat's wife lugs him around in her placket-hole, he's a well-meaning and decent man. Who'd be likely to want to give Will McCarren the heave-ho off Cross Island? Him? Or someone whose ears was open like a hungry shark to catch the tunings of a voice divine?"

Warren said disgustedly, "Gramp, will you stop talking in tongues?"

"I ain't. First time I heard that was old Judge Cameron

lambasting the Legislature over a matter that was whiffling up the sacred halls. The old judge, times he could hit the nail on the head with nothing heavier than a piece of poetry." Calvin got up. "Oh, well, boy. What you want for your birthday? I got something. Good and damned expensive it was, too. If you don't want it, I do." He strode into the house and shut the door behind him.

Warren shook his head. Gosh, the poor old boy, off on cloud nine again. He couldn't think those binoculars he'd bought would be much of a birthday surprise. He'd been using them for days, sitting on the sun porch and focusing on anything that stuck up down in the Harbor. Kept telling what a pair of beauts they were. He wouldn't let Warren try them. That was to be the surprise.

Alby Spicer came up the road, walking with purpose. He gave Warren a nod, went up the steps, and opened the door wide enough to stick in his head. He said, "You want me to throw my hat in first?"

Calvin said, "Not unless I throw mine out first. Come on in, Alby. I thought you'd be by."

Later, when Warren went in, the two were sitting on the sun porch, their heads together—a couple of old cronies, having things over.

Hashing politics, Warren thought. Let'em. I don't know why Gramp thinks that rotten mess has got anything to do with me.

The way they were headed was into the woods back of the house, just a hubbly path, hard to walk on, with lots of blown-down trees you had to go out around. The sun was coming up, which made stones and roots easier to see now than when they'd started out. Rosie had felt better then, rested, and happy because she was going home. Now she wasn't so sure. To get to the island, you had to go to the shore, where there'd be a boat. After a while, when they didn't seem to be getting anywhere near a shore, she said, "Where are we going, Leafy?"

He didn't look around, just said, "You wait. You'll see. These is the woods. Ain't they nice?" and kept on walking so fast that she almost had to run to keep up. He had given her a big paper bag full of oranges to carry. The bottom had come out of the old dirty sack he had had over his shoulder and everything had fallen out of it. Now he had to hold it by both ends and there hadn't been room for the oranges to go back in. They got heavier as she went along. At last, she stumbled and fell down.

Leafy stopped and looked back. "You hurt yourself?"

All she could see of his face over the top of the bag was his nose and his little beady eyes looking at her from under his cap. She had bumped one of her sore knees and it hurt, but she wasn't going to say so. She shook her head, no.

"What's the matter, then?"

"This bag's too heavy. I keep stubbing my toe."

"Heb'm sake, if you're going along with me, you got to pull your oar in the boat. I got all *I* can lug. You come along; it ain't far now."

"Where are we going?"

But he just went along, not saying.

Rosie got up. All right. She'd pull her oar in the boat. But she wouldn't talk to him, not one word, unless he told her where they were going.

The warm lined boots that they in the house had left out in the room for her to wear were a little too big. They kept slipping up and down, making it hard not to turn ankles. There'd been other things there, jeans and a T-shirt and sweater and a heavy jacket with a hood to match. She'd put on everything because he'd said to, to keep warm. And she was warm all right, sweating hot, and everything so bulky she could hardly bend over. The new boots were already scuffed on the toes so they couldn't possibly be taken back to the store for a pair that would fit. Rosie fell farther and farther behind.

At last he stopped. "Well, come on, come on. We ain't got all day."

She just looked at him.

"What's the matter now? Don't you like the woods? You ain't scared of all them rustles and wiggles in the puckerbush, are you? Don't you know what them is, hanh?"

Rosie said nothing.

"Well, now. Them little noises is awful nice in the spring of the year. Any critter that's made it through the winter is coming out in the sun. S'pose you was a mouse, slept in a cold hole in the ground all that time, come out and felt the sun on your back?"

Rosie did feel it. All over. It was too hot.

"Warm on a mouse's back. Must feel awful good . . . God, you ain't going to turn sulky on me, are you?"

She didn't say.

Disgruntled, he started off again. That hadn't helped a mite. Left him jumpy as a rabbit. Oat Baker'd be down after him, sure as shooting today, no knowing when. First place Oat would look would be his shack, and there was Willie, tied to the table leg in plain sight under the lee of the bank. So Oat would know for sure Leafy'd be around there somewhere.

When he'd planned to run off with Rosie, he'd thought he'd had things fixed to run smooth as grease. And they would have, too, if Willie hadn't busted loose last night and spoilt everything.

If I could've started early from the haymow, the way I planned it, we'd be down home by now, all these vittles stowed in a backpack, me with my gun and shells, ready to start off for upcountry.

He'd had to find his way up this cussed shortcut before

daylight, without Willie—hadn't dared to bring him along, not with that coon in the barn for him to raise Cain about. It had taken him longer than he'd counted on. Then, after he'd got the ladder up to the window, he'd thought he'd never get that kid out onto it—not that she was scared, she wasn't, she'd flipped down hand over foot when she'd got ready to. Took her a while to get dressed, and then she'd gone somewheres else in the house—he'd thought he'd fidget right off the top of that ladder before she'd got back. Said she'd had to find a pencil.

Now, what in the living Lord's world had she wanted a pencil for? When he'd asked her, she'd said, "Oh, I might want to write something."

Things had gone wrong from the start of it. There she was now, hanging back and complaining, not helping one bit. And here he was, with this bag of stuff, weighed a ton, goweling his stomach off because he had to carry it in front, use both hands to hold the damn thing together, and him tired to death before he'd started. He almost wished he hadn't brought her along with him. For company, hanh? But *good* company and enjoyable, that was what he'd thought of, and she wasn't being. He didn't know as he wanted to take her with him if she was going to be twitchelly.

Martin's rum bottle had worked its way up in the bag; he could feel it nudgeling at his hand, trying to give him a message. He set the bag down, reached in for the bottle, took a good, hefty swallow. There, now. That was better.

She was staring at him, looking ugly at him.

"Ginger ale," Leafy said. "Good for the stomach. Makes a man feel like a holiday. Tell you what. We got all these vittles. Le's you and me go on one old slambanger of a picnic. How'd that be?" Ought to cheer her up. He never see a kid didn't like a picnic. He stuffed the bottle into a pocket and grinned at her.

A picnic? Rosie's uneasiness and worry changed into

pure rage. What she'd come with him for, he'd said he'd take her home. So now he was going on a picnic. He was just an old drunk who told big, fat fibs. Didn't he think she could read? Or smell? That wasn't ginger ale in that bottle.

"Well, come on," he said. "We'll never git where we're going." He bent to pick up the croker's-sack and froze, astounded. Rosie had given a great loud beller and heaved an orange at him. It bounced off his bottom and fairly straightened him right up, and she threw another one at his head. He ducked and it missed him, but he dropped the bag and that split wide open, scattered groceries all over the path. She didn't stop when he hollered, either. She kicked through the mess of paper bags and cans in front of him and skidded on the remains of the duck. Came right at him, bellering and plugging oranges as hard as she could plug. One of them caught him slam on the nose, made a *squelch* sound inside of his head, and started his nose to bleeding.

Leafy tried to fend off the flying oranges, but it was like trying to stop a windmill. Besides, it seemed as if what was left of his nose had splattered into his eyes—he couldn't see very well. He said, "Hey, now . . ." and flapped his hands. That bellering—they weren't far enough from town yet. Somebody'd hear it for sure and come nosing around to see what it was.

"I want to go home! You said . . . you promised. And we aren't going to the shore where a boat is. You told a lie! I hate you!" She kicked him on the kneecap, and it hurt like the devil.

No way to stop her unless he grabbed her and muffled her. He made a grab, but she was too quick for him. On the edge of the path was a leaner, a big cat spruce, half blown down. He jumped for it, scuttled up the trunk, and sat out of reach, peering down.

"Like I was going to say when you come at me," he began, and had to stop till she came to the end of a beller.

"My house is down the fur side of these woods, on the shore. I s'posed you'd have the sense to know if I lived on a cove I'd keep a boat there."

"Why didn't you say? I asked and asked you. Now I don't know if that's a big, fat lie, too!"

"You could've waited and seen. No need to kick a man's laig off."

Something in the woods not far off the path suddenly made a great thump and went crashing away through the undergrowth. Rosie's beller stopped in her throat. She started to run and couldn't make her legs move.

Leafy jumped, too, but then he began to grin, "Tch, Rosie! Look what you done, all that turrible racket!" and slipped down out of sight on the far side of the tree.

Where had he gone? Had he got scared and run away? What if some big thing, a wild animal, came out of the woods at her? She stood, staring around, trying to see where the path back to the house was, and couldn't find any opening that looked like it.

Leafy parted the bushes and looked out at her. He was mopping his nose with an old bandanna and grinning all over his face. He whispered, "Come see what's here, Rosie."

"What?" she asked, not moving. She'd thought she'd never be glad to see him again, but she was.

"Something awful pretty. You ain't seen nothing like it in your life. Prob'ly never will again, either."

Whatever it was had made him forget all about the fight. He wasn't even mad. He was happy as could be. He was crazy. Well, she wasn't. She wasn't going to move an inch. But as he drew back out of sight, she knew she'd rather go with him than stay here alone.

She thought at first that what he'd found was a brown rock with the sun on it. Then she saw it was a little speckled animal, lying so flat and still that it only looked like a rock.

"Come round here so the smell of you won't blow acrost

him. There. You've seen him, now come away. We mustn't stay here or his mother'll never come back to him."

Back on the path, he began picking up the groceries. He stuffed some into his pockets, scrabbled the rest back into the remains of his sack. "You never see a deer's lamb before, I bet," he said. "Ain't he cunning? Makes me raving hungry to look at him. Give him a chance to grow some, he's going to taste awful good next winter."

"You mean you'd kill him? *Eat* him?" Rosie's horror was in her voice, but he didn't seem to notice it.

He said, "Why, sure. That's what a deer's for. You got a lot to learn about the woods, Rosie." He went on, still stuffing away the groceries. "Danged if you didn't put your big flat foot onto this duck, but it ain't all spoilt. Why don't you help me pick up them oranges? You was the one throwed'em around."

She didn't move. She said, "I don't want to learn anything about the woods, and I'm not going to. They're horrid."

He had to pick up the oranges himself. He found most of them, he guessed, found the bag they'd been in, set it down on the path in front of her. "You'll have to lug it, Miss. I ain't going to."

Don't get nowheres near her, no knowing what she'll do next, he told himself. He gathered up his load, turned back-to her and walked off. She can come or stay there. I don't know as I care which.

There on the path was a goddamned orange, one he'd missed. To pick it up now, he'd have to set this cussed bag down. One more puzzlement was one more too many. He hauled back his foot and kicked it high over the trees, a yellow ball on the blue of the sky. Now wasn't that some old pretty, the yellow on the blue.

Behind him, Rosie said, "What did you do that for? That was a good orange."

The kick had proved to Leafy what he had been worried

about. He was going to have to limp on that leg—his kneecap had stiffened up. He said, "Ought to thought of that when you hove'em around." He went along.

That was the last straw. He could almost hear the flop as his plan fell apart. He'd thought they'd be friends, that he could take her to one of his still places back in the woods; keep her there till Oat Baker's hoo-ha died down. But she wasn't going to fit in, no way he could see. She had a temper like nothing on God's green earth—didn't get over it easy. That bellering would scare the bejeezus out of every wild critter there was. Try to hunt one, with them devilish actions going on. Like to broke his nose, must have took an inch of skin off'n his kneecap, and he was going to have to walk on that leg for miles, carry a heavy load.

The way the women has used me lately, why in God's name would I ever want one of them around?

They were coming out on the shore now, and she was right behind him. "Don't you go running out there on the ledges," he cautioned. "No knowing who's over there to my house."

Like as if she hadn't heard him, she was out there already. She said, "Is that your skiff, Leafy?"

Leafy stared at his skiff, anchored on a trip-line, off in the middle of the cove. I'd like to get into that and sail away from here for good and forever, he told himself. Aloud he said, "It's only big enough for me alone. Won't carry two very safe."

"Oh, when we go, I'll show you how to sit in the middle and not wiggle around. I can sail it, too. Dad showed me how when we had a skiff just like that, before somebody stole it. Let's go right now."

"We can't sail her unless the wind's right. She won't sail aginst the wind, no keel."

"I know. Skids sideways, like a Jesus bug. But you can row, can't you?"

"I don't know as I'll be able to row; my knee's killing me. And if the wind ain't right—"

"But it is! Don't you know how to tell? Stick your finger in your mouth and hold it up. The cold side's where the wind's coming from."

"Now, look. I'm tired out. I ain't had no breakfast and I got to find a bush. You set down here and scoot off the gulls if they come around these vittles. Mind, now." He started to walk away, but she came too, bearing down on him like a thundercloud. "You git on back. Fix us a picnic. Make some duck sandwiches."

"I don't want any duck. Yuck, I stepped on it. Has your skiff got a rudder to steer with, or do I have to use an oar? I know how to steer her with an oar."

"Maybe you do, but you don't know how to find Cross Island."

"I do, too! I can see it—right out there in front of us— four miles. I could find it after dark. You start with the light-house on the Point and line it up with the channel bell buoy. You'll fetch right into Cross Island Cove." Rosie, who had had McCarren's Survival course dinned into her, could repeat this part of it like a parrot.

Godfrey mighty, she's been back and forth numberless times with McCarren. I ain't going to be able to fool her, Leafy thought, and his brains felt wilted, as if the whole inside of his head had been frostbit. Likely they'd turned black and keeled over, the way a Indian pipe flower did when somebody that didn't know any better touched it. He said, "You quit coming after me; it ain't ladylike. You know so much, you ought to think what a man means when he says he's got to find a bush." He walked away from her, into the woods.

He didn't come back. Rosie waited. She fidgeted. She discovered she was hungry, and there were all kinds of things to eat. She ate a lot of bread and cheese and an orange. After a while, she went looking along the edge of the woods. He wasn't anywhere. He was gone.

All right. The big old fibber had run off so he wouldn't have to take her home—hadn't meant to in the first place. He'd lied and lied to get out of it. Now there wasn't anybody to help her. If she could sail Dad's skiff, she could sail Leafy's. She started to go, then she remembered what Dad had told everybody. "Don't ever go anywhere in any kind of a boat without a jug of water along."

There wasn't any jug, and no water. Rosie took along the bagful of oranges.

Leafy lay in a snug thicket a little way back from the shore. He had had a good long swig out of Martin's bottle. One had done him good, so he felt like another. And another. Now his insides felt soft and silky; his brains were smoothed out so he could think. If she walked around the shore to his house, she'd come across the road that led back to town. Thank the Lord, he'd be shed of her for good.

If I was to of told her that that bird off in the alders is a swamp robin singing, "Green tea, sweeten it, sweeten it," she wouldn't of cared one hoot. That deer's lamb, now, she didn't so much as give it a second look. City kid. Never tasted deer meat in her life. Never before seen one of the prettiest sights there was.

The sun striking down through the thicket speckled his pants and jacket—his good old woods-colored pants, his hunting jacket. Like the deer's lamb's skin, he thought. I'm some glad I took off them fancy duds I bought up to Cousins's dry goods, to go courting in. That red necktie, half-choke a man to death. Had the sense to change last night or here I'd be, looking like God's fool of the world.

His spring-of-the-year flood had ebbed. Thank God. He had his senses back again. Leafy flattened himself down and was still. Like the deer's lamb.

Down on the shore, a single sea gull circled a few times over the opened paper bags and the duck's carcass, dropped to the top of the ledge, smugly folded its wings. Two others, sitting on the water half a mile away, got the message, passed it along. One gull, two gulls; then out of nowhere, twenty gulls came screaming and coasted down on the groceries.

Bess, following occasional footprints down the swampy woods path, heard the gulls' tea party when she was some distance back from the shore. Footprints in the daffodil bed under the spare room window, unmistakably Rosie's and Leafy's, had led her across the still muddy kitchen garden to the edge of the hayfield. She had picked them up again where the shortcut entered the woods.

She hadn't told Mary or Martin that Rosie had gone. Leafy could not have had too much of a head start, and he wouldn't be able to travel like a bat, not with Rosie along and the load he had. Bess hoped to be back at the house before Martin began to raise Cain. Like as not, he'd phone around, get a search party going, regardless of consequences which would let the cat out of the bag about Rosie. In case of Willie, Bess took along a hayfork handle from the barn.

Coming out on the shore, breathless, she saw the fighting, squawking cartwheel of gulls and fell on it like an avenging fury.

That everlasting fool! Gone off somewhere and left all that food where the gulls could get at it! She threw a last furious rock at the fleeing gulls and surveyed the carnage. Nothing left unshat on but the canned goods, and them enough to turn your stomach.

Well, he hadn't taken off into the woods yet. He wouldn't go and leave his supplies behind. He must be over at his shack. Yes, he was. She could hear Willie barking over there somewhere.

She started along the top of the bank, pushing her way through the puckerbush, which had overgrown what path there was. Suddenly, from the woods in front of her, she heard a gun go off, followed by a child's high, shrill scream of pure terror.

Rosie had already met Willie. She had heard him barking as she had walked along the bank towards the place where Leafy's trip-line had been tied. There he was, a big black dog, chained up. What a funny thing to chain a dog to, the leg of a big, solid table. She wasn't scared of him. Dad always said, "Most dogs bark for the fun of it or to show his owner you're around. You just walk along by, don't let him see you're scared. But if it's a Doberman or an Alsatian, you freeze and wait till somebody comes." This was just a big black dog and he was chained up tight.

Rosie went down the bank past him. She had Leafy's skiff pulled into the edge of tide and the bag of oranges under the stern seat before she discovered that there were no oars or rowlocks and no mast and sail in the boat. Like Dad, Leafy probably put them away at night so they wouldn't get stolen. She went back up the bank. There was Leafy's house and a rickety old shed, not locked. The mast and sail, oars and rowlocks, all tied together, were in the shed, standing in a corner behind the door.

Otis Baker left his car at the entrance to the old road which led down to Leafy's cove. Once a town road, but now discontinued, it was half gravel, half mud. No use to try to get a car down there, Otis thought. He'd walk it, it wasn't far.

He looked through Leafy's shack, all one room of it and a loft. There it was, the bugger'd took off into the woods. No use to hunt for him now. Otis was glad of it. He could tell Justin—and Flo, too—that Leafy had gone where nobody could catch up with him. That would shut them both up till they forgot about it and dreamed up something else to drive a man crazy with. Them three-four females who raised all the touse about hooglums, sometimes he wished that Leafy, or some fellow a little better off in his equipment, would really have a go at them.

He was starting back up the road when he heard Willie begin to bark.

Blast it all, that meant Leafy was still around here somewhere. He'd better be. That dog ain't anything to fool with. If he comes at me and Leafy don't show in time to stop him, I may have to shoot the critter.

Otis unsnapped the holster on his hip and put his hand on the butt of his gun, hating the feel of it. Anything in the god's world he hated to do was to shoot anything living— he couldn't even go deer hunting, didn't want to. But he had always known that sometime he might have to if it was in the way of his duty.

He stood where he was, waiting. The dog wasn't coming any nearer. Otis walked over and peered around the corner of the shack. There was the dog, down under the bank, chained to a table. Of all the crazy things, did that nut eat his meals out there? Willie was up on his hind legs, yanking at the chain and raving and howling. The table jiggled up and down, but it was a stout table. He guessed the critter wouldn't haul the leg off of it.

Otis pulled back out of sight. He could still say he hadn't been able to find Leafy, and that was no lie. He was again starting to leave when he heard thumps and sounds coming from out back of the house.

That shed building! That must be where Leafy was hiding, and why hadn't he had the sense to keep quiet? In a minute or two, I'd been good and gone, wouldn't have heard a thing. It was too bad. Nothing else for it, now.

Otis considered. The minute Leafy sees he's caught up with, he's going to skeddaddle. I couldn't git within a mile of him in the woods, and I ain't about to try. One thing, he scares easy. Won't take much to help him on his way. Then when I'm gone, he can come back and turn his dog loose.

The shed door was half open. Otis took up a stand on doorstep and wiggled his gun out of its holster. He said loudly, "Come out of there, and come out with your hands up!"

There was a silence. Then the door slammed to. Something hard, like wood, crashed against it. He heard a scurry of feet. "I got a gun in my hand! Come on, give up, don't make no more trouble."

Since there was no answer, he put his shoulder against the door and pushed. It opened hard, blocked by something —a mess of sail canvas, oars, and what-all. The back of the shed was wide open to the weather, back wall blown flat off of it, probably by the wind last night. Through the opening, Otis saw a movement, bushes waving. Then the top of a tree in there began to shake.

What, is the darn fool climbing it? If he is, then, dammit, I *will* have to arrest him.

Otis pointed his gun straight up in the air and pulled the trigger. That ought to start him on his way.

The scream that followed stopped him in his tracks. A squawk like that could never in the god's world be Leafy!

It wasn't. He could see it wasn't. It was one of the school children. Wiggled halfway up that tree. Was scrouching part out of sight amongst the limbs of it.

Ain't I got enough on my plate this morning? But school's in session, and here's this scamp playing hooky, down here underrunning Leafy's shed, too.

Otis walked over to the tree. "What you think you're up to, skipping school, ranshackling around in somebody's building?" he demanded. "You come down here, right now."

He couldn't see the kid very well, only part of a windbreaker or something, but that didn't move. "You come

165

down or I'll shake you down like an apple," he said, and gave the tree a good solid shake.

Something whistled past his head and landed with a thud against the trunk of the tree.

That was a rock. Somebody had hove a rock at him. He spun around. "Who done that?"

"I did!" Bess Bowden was coming at him, making a bow wave through the puckerbush. "Gunning for little children now, are you?" she demanded between puffs. "That's real pretty, Otis. That's lawful."

"I ain't!" Otis said. He'd never been so shocked in his life. "That was far from my mind! I . . . You . . . You hove that rock straight at my head."

"If I'd fired it at your head, I'd have hit it. I'm an awful good shot with a rock." Bess called up the tree, "You stay right where you are, honey, till Otis Baker crawls back into his senses. He's drunk. No knowing what he's likely to do."

Outraged, Otis stared at her. "I am not drunk! That boy up there, he's one of the school children, run off from school. All I meant, all I'm doing, I was going to take him back there."

So that was who Otis thought it was. That was a relief. Maybe Otis had never seen Rosie without coal dust on her face.

"Seems like a grown man could do that without shooting at him," Bess said. "There's mothers around here won't think much of their kids not being safe in the woods from a pistol big as that one, law or no law. You wait till this gets around."

"Now, Bess. Seeing we're both mistaken . . . seeing I thought it was Leafy Piper I fired that shot for to keep him from running—"

"Leafy's done something he ought to be shot for? Folks are going to love that, Otis."

"Oh, God!" Otis said. Women! He had one pack of them swinging on his coattails already, and here'd be another lot. Mothers, this time, and mothers was the worst of all. He shoved his pistol back into his holster, turned and went off into the trees and up the road toward his car.

Leafy, in his thicket, woke up rested and refreshed. He reared up and peered through the bushes at the shore. Late afternoon, and Rosie was gone, sure enough, so that trouble was over and done with. Now to get packed up, fix a sandwich or two, get Willie and a can of matches out of his house, and light out for the woods.

He climbed over the ledges, glancing cautiously here and there. Nobody. Coast was clear. Then his eye fell on the place where he had left the groceries.

Why, them goddamn gulls! If they hadn't flewn in here and ripped the bejeezus out of everything.

He stood, eyeing the mess. Nothing left of the duck—cussed things had even et the bones. Not a scrap of bread left, only the glassy stuff it had been wrapped in. Give him any wild thing in the world but a gull. Eat anything. Worse'n a coon.

He turned over the pile, sorting out the canned goods, dumping the cans one by one into a nearby tide pool to rinse off the gull dung. He'd have enough to keep life till he could get set up back in the woods. It was early to go, be cold, but anytime of year was nice in the still places. Spring would come on. Fish would wake up out of the mud, birds' eggs be laid. His mouth watered.

He began swashing the cans around in the tide pool. All the labels came off, but what of it. He opened a can with his jackknife. Peaches. All to the good, he liked peaches. Wouldn't be able to tell whether he was opening peaches or beef stew. Willie'd know the difference, but he'd eat what there was. Every meal a surprise. Leafy speared out the peaches with the blade of his knife, drank the juice, and pitched the can into the puckerbush.

Later he and Willie set off by a way they knew and slept that night in the first of the shelters he had made on his last trip upcountry.

PART FIVE

Bill McCarren was putting the finishing touch on the punkinseed, which was decked over now, with a space left for a rower to sit. She looked like nothing on earth, and *Goony Bird* was a good name for her. She would float, and didn't seem to leak much except for a hole in the bottom where a knot had fallen out. Once that had been patched, she had had a good soaking in the pond.

Will had tried her out that morning, rowing her around in the pond. "She's a little crank," he'd said, coming ashore. "But she'll be all right. I'll have to get used to tholepins."

Since he had no rowlocks—the extra pair had gone with the big boat—he had had to bore holes for tholepins and had set in a stout pair.

"But she'll do," Will had said cheerfully. "I'll pick a good calm night, and it's only four miles." He had gone on to talk about his plans, and the kids had listened, their eyes on his thin face.

Julian said, "But, Dad, what if you get arrested? What if that fat fuzz sees you?" Julian wasn't crying, only almost.

"The fat fuzz won't know me. All this"—Will tweaked at his beard and grinned—"is going to be shaved off, and you can take turns giving me a short haircut. The way the weather looks today, I might be able to go tonight. I'll locate our boat. It may take me some time. I'll plan to shop at the supermarket late in the day, load up the boat after dark, and take off home with a flock of beefsteaks and fixings. How about that?"

"If the boat's here in the cove, everybody'll know we're here anyway," Bill said. "Lobster boats go by here every day. That Petersen fellow's got traps set right off the mouth of the cove."

"First things first, and the first thing is to keep from starving. After I get back with the boat and we all get a decent meal, I'll take off again. I'm going ashore in broad daylight and hunt up a lawyer. This situation's ridiculous. You'll have to handle things while I'm gone, Bill, and there's always the crawl space, if anyone makes trouble. Besides, I won't be away long." He had paused a moment. "We've run into a bad time and a few bad actors—small-time big shots, like the two who came out here and threw their weight around. But we know there're a lot of decent people in this town. Remember Bess? I'm going to let her know what's happened to us. We're going to get things straightened out. You've all let me know that you want to stay here, and I'm not knuckling under about staying."

After that, he had taken Hank and Julian, with casting rods, over to the eastern side of the island, to try for rock cod where the ledges made off into deep water.

Bill had done a lot of thinking since morning. He put a last dab of filler on the knothole patch, which Will said had been weeping a little, laid down his brush, and went to sit on a nearby stump.

If it wasn't for me being here, Dad wouldn't have to take a chance like that. He could hail a lobster boat anytime and get ferried ashore.

Someone had to do it. Supplies were nearly gone. They'd been living for three days on what the island provided. Clams. Mussels. A horrible jelly boiled out of a seaweed called dulse. They had tried a set line, baited for flounders, and cast off into the cove at low tide, in case any fish came in on the first of the flood, but they'd had no luck with that, and the crabs from Will's crab trap down in the ledges had been undersized and skinny. There was nothing to do about supplies until they had a boat that would float.

He stared at the *Goony Bird.* That filler he'd put over the knothole patch might set and it might not. It was scrapings from an old can of roofing tar, cast aside when they'd shingled the house last fall. Melted, the tar had at least stuck on. He got up to see if it was showing any signs of hardening.

Behind him, Sarah said, "Is it going to work?" She'd been helping earlier, but with the job nearly done, there hadn't been room for two. She'd hung around restlessly for a while and then had wandered off down the path to the cove.

She hadn't let on how she was feeling, but Bill knew. He felt that way himself. It still seemed as if Hal and Rosie had just walked off out of sight somewhere—were playing down on the beach or here by the pond. Places they'd gone to and had always before come back from. At times, before he stopped to think, he felt that he could almost see them in those places, not really believing they weren't there.

"I think so," Bill said, answering Sarah's question. "Who was that hauling traps off the cove? Your boy friend?"

Sarah smiled. "I almost went out on the beach and hollered to him. I just possibly didn't."

"You nearly had a thing going with him," Bill said.

"Not really. Just, he was nice. I liked him."

"And, oh, that boat of his!" Bill said. "Solid planks under your feet and an old lambaster of a diesel engine. Every time I see him go by, I feel like spreading wing and flying after him. This darned old *Goony Bird!*" He hauled back a foot.

"Don't kick her," Sarah said. "It'll go right through." She sat down on the stump, leaned her chin on her hands.

"Oh, no, she's okay now," Bill said quickly. "She'll make it ashore all right." He wished he hadn't said *"Goony Bird."* That had been Rosie's name for the punkinseed. He went over to sit on the stump with her. "Shove over."

As usual, she picked his thought out of the air. "I don't mind being reminded of Rosie. I am, anyway."

"Me, too. I guess Poppa's really going."

"He'll pick a calm night. He'll be all right."

Sarah shivered. It was a pretty day, warm in the sun. The bay, glimmering through the trees, was like glass. Not a ripple showed on the water as far as they could see, but looking at it, Sarah shivered. She had been managing fairly well, until this morning.

Bill glanced at her. "You really want to stick it out here?"

"I love it here. I wouldn't want to go back home. Would you?"

"I don't really have much choice. I won't go back to that hellhole I got away from."

Sarah stared past him at the sunlit bay, where a few cat's-paws were beginning to sparkle. "It's beautiful. But now . . . I keep watching."

Bill nodded. "Beautiful like a rattlesnake," he said, and was sorry he'd said it. "We'll get over it, kid. We've got to."

"I know. It was just that I was down watching Warren Petersen, his boat. I could've made him hear. I didn't care if he saw me. He's our friend; he'd help, I know he would. I don't want Dad to row ashore in that contraption . . . that *Goony Bird.*"

"I don't either." Listening to her, Bill had made his mind up. "Look, Sarah. Poppa isn't going to. I am."

"Bill, no! I'd worry as much about you. What if you got caught?"

172

"Now, wait, cool it. Nobody ashore knows me from Adam. None of them ever saw me. Listen, you remember that old crowbait who stopped here one time? Old sugar baby? Piper, he said his name was."

"Of course I do. What about him?"

"Remember the skiff he had? It was a dandy. And how when we were sailing out around the eastern shore we saw it anchored in a cove there? Well, what I'd do, I wouldn't go uptown. I'd row straight across to that cove, borrow that skiff, and bring it back here. Poppa could take it from there. He'd have a safe boat to row ashore in."

"*You* wouldn't have one." Sarah looked at him in anguish. "I won't let you do it. It's a foolish plan. Even if you didn't get arrested for stealing a skiff, Dad could be when he takes it back. Besides, what would you do with *Goony Bird?*"

"Who cares? Set her adrift. Leave her on Piper's haul-off for him to use while his skiff's away. He'd think the little green men had traded with him during the night. Come to think of it, if *Goony Bird* looks like anything, it might be a flying saucer."

Bill grinned. But Sarah didn't think it was funny.

"You don't learn," she said. "You still think if you want something it's all right to steal it."

"Oh, come on. It isn't just wanting. We *need* that skiff."

But she had got up and was going away.

She wouldn't tell Dad about his plan. She'd never told on anybody about anything. He could guess what she was going to do now. She was going to ask Poppa to hail Warren Petersen the next time his boat came by.

Bill sat and looked at *Goony Bird.* Of course I can row that thing ashore. If Dad goes, nine chances out of ten, he'll walk into something. Maybe nobody'd know him without his bush, but everybody'd spot a stranger. I can keep out of sight. I've done it, and I can wiggle into a smaller hole than he can. Whatever he runs into, he'll stick his chin out and say, "Yes, I'm Will McCarren, so what, go to hell." He's too honest to lie. Me, I'm not. At least, I've got the name of it. It's my fault, anyway, we're stuck like this. If he didn't have me hanging around his neck in the crawl space, he'd have a lot better chance of getting straightened out, with a lawyer to help him. Any lawyer'll tell him what to do about me.

So okay. He's not going. I am.

Behind him, Will said, "How's the patch coming?"

Bill jumped and turned, hoping he didn't look guilty. "I think I've sealed that knothole. Did you see Sarah? She went to find you."

"She must have missed us. We took a shortcut back through the swamp. The kids caught an old godwalloper of a codfish, they couldn't get back quick enough to start cooking. We're up there building a chowder."

"Chowder?" Bill's face showed what he thought of that. Fish, any kind of fish, yuck. Already he felt like more than half of a clam. What kind of a chowder could they make out of boiling up a plain old fish in water?

Will chuckled. "Sarah and I've got to admit we squirreled away the makings against the time we really starved. Two cans of milk, salt pork, potatoes, an onion. All in the kettle over an Injun fire of dry sticks, so no smoke."

Bill grinned back at him. "Give you time, Poppa, you'll come up with an apple pie."

"Maybe tomorrow. Maybe the day after. Depends. We'll have apple pie and coffee."

Sarah made her way down to the flat ledge where her father usually sat to cast for fish. It was in a hollow, surrounded by big slabs of granite. No one sitting there could be seen from the water. She kept her head down, as they had to over on this side of the island now, in case there might be a boat in sight. Warmer weather was coming, and fishermen were moving their traps in offshore. Boats came by here fairly often.

She saw that the rock was unoccupied. Dad and the kids must've moved along somewhere else. There were two or three good places. She raised up, cautiously peering over the tops of the ledges. No boats. Yes, there was one out by Lantern Island, a long way away, too far off to worry about. She guessed she could risk taking a look alongshore to see if she could spot the fishermen. She stood up.

It was good to stand straight again, look out over the water.

I thought when we came here this was the best place we'd ever lived in. I still do. But now we're hiding in it like wild animals. I'm not going to do it any longer. The man in that boat out there might be Warren Petersen. He's too far away to see me, but I don't care if he does.

I suppose we'll have to go away from here. Maybe back to town.

To that house that wasn't home anymore, with all those awful women, one after another, instead of Ma. Nosing into everything you were doing until you went crazy trying to keep something of your own. Back to school and what was there. The long hours of sitting, so bored you got goose bumps waiting for the last bell to ring. Where the in crowd was the dope crowd and if you didn't dope you weren't in. Didn't get asked to the parties you wanted to go to, didn't get dated by the boys you wanted to go with. Russel Gentry's crowd.

I died because I couldn't get in. It was fun to be popular again, when I did get in. To be Russel's girl, to go places with him.

Russel. Who didn't think anything was any good, so smash it. Rocks through the plate glass windows; stuff down off the shelves; bust it up. The old guy's going to get a surprise when he comes in in the morning.

I did it, too. I can remember how I felt, doing it. Smash something, no matter what. Not because you hated it, you weren't even sore. Once you got started, it was like being under a waterfall.

Russel said, "So we got busted, so what? Wait till the yobs get off our necks. They won't do anything to us. Cool it; you'll see."

And then . . . Hal . . . and what he'd been like before . . . That crazy girl.

And then, Ma died.

Sarah stood leaning against a tall jut of ledge, watching the boat out by Lantern Island. Another one had come into sight out there now. It was white. Maybe it was Warren's. The man out there, whoever he was, was safe in his boat. As Bill'd said, all those stout planks under him. The *Goony Bird* wasn't safe. Bill knew it, and if Bill did, then Dad must know it, too, with all he knew about boats.

Awful things could happen in boats. In a split second, you could be in the water, drowning.

I would rather have Bill in jail, and Dad, too, if he had to go there, than dead in the ocean.

I won't stand for it. I won't let either one of them do it.

Sarah stood straight up on the ledges and walked back into the woods.

Take a good look, whoever you are in the white boat. You may not know it's me but you can see somebody from out there.

Warren Petersen had nearly forgotten about the pale tan patch of something he had seen move in the bushes on the day he and Martin had taken the child's body off Cross

Island Beach. If he had thought about it at all, it had been in connection with the hunting season next fall. He'd certainly seen something, and if it had been a deer, a man might sneak out here come November and hunt without taking a chance on plugging Leafy Piper, who took it on himself to bug every hunting party he saw and try to scare all the deer out of the area, because he figured they were all there for him to shoot, the crazy kook. Hunting in the woods back of the Cove, sooner or later you either ran into Leafy futzing around or that blasted black dog barking his head off.

Then, after Warren had been past the Cross Island Cove a few times, he'd changed his mind. He guessed that, deer or no deer, he wouldn't be going ashore there ever, wouldn't want to set foot on the place.

He hadn't known the girl, Sarah, what he could call well, but enough to pass the time of day, up in town. He'd seen her put Finney Wilson to flight, one day on the dock at Wentworth Harbor—that slob, six inches taller and a foot wider than she'd been. She'd chased him with a gaff because he'd hollered, "Quack, quack," at her. Warren remembered how her curls flew out that day. She'd sure been one pretty girl.

All last fall he'd kept a couple of traps set off the mouth of the cove, because whenever she'd seen him hauling them she'd waved to him. She'd been on the beach almost every day. How could you believe that anyone as beautiful as that was dead?

This spring he'd set the traps again in the same place, and they were still there. Today he'd made up his mind to snake them out of there and set them somewhere else. He'd been getting over that heavy feeling, like grief, he'd had in his chest every time he'd looked into the cove. At first, everything in there had been so quiet . . . nobody on the beach, nothing moving but the wind in the trees. All he'd been able to think of was the little kid's body washing around in the surf . . . what Sarah's must be like now . . . gave a man cold chills all over. But the talk in the town about what could possibly have happened to the McCarrens had started up again, sizzling. Somehow it had got around that one of Justin Bradley's real estate deals was responsible for the whole rotten thing. And thinking about that, getting sweating mad over it, Warren found that he hadn't got over anything. He felt worse than he had in the beginning.

The next thing to murder—that's what it added up to. Somebody ought to do something. There must be laws to slap down an underhanded operator like that. If there weren't, there ought to be. Gramp ought to have some ideas about that, he sure knew a lot of law, when he bothered to remember it. Or could remember it. Bradley, of course, was who he'd been talking about that day he'd sounded off on the wharf, made Alby Spicer so mad. Alby'd got over it— he'd been up two or three times and had long talks with Gramp, according to Ma. She'd been about dead to know what they were talking about; hatching something, she'd said, but they'd gone out on the sun porch and shut the door on her. And with Warren, the old man had been vague as the devil. Wouldn't talk about Bradley or the law or anything else that made sense; he'd go off on some long rigmarole about his past, like, say, the first car he'd ever owned, a Model T that had brass lamps and drove like an angel with wings, for godsake!

Take yesterday, when Warren had got home from hauling. Gramp had been zeroed in on the binoculars, showing Josie how to use them. He hadn't even heard Warren come in.

"Right there, Josie, under the wharf. John Pray, see? You can even make out the bigod look on his face."

He fielded the binoculars neatly as she dropped them

with a squawk. "Calvin Petersen! You dirty old man! Shame on you!"

"You've got a female mind, Josie. All I told you was to look at his face." Deadpan, he focused again and grinned.

"Gramp, I want to talk to you," Warren said. "Look—"

"Shut up, I'm busy. Hey! Ain't there no secrets in this house? Here I go to all the trouble, send clear to New York for a birthday present for you, and in you come, snooping around to find out what it is. I'm a good mind not to give it to you." The old man had scrabbled the glasses into his chair and sat down on them. "Keep them myself, goddarned if I don't!"

"All right. Happy birthday to me." Warren had started off out, thinking he'd go and talk to Martin Hadley.

But Ma had chased him right out the back door. She'd still been spitting mad, and when she got mad all she could think of was chores—nine million things for him to do. By the time he'd got them done, it had been suppertime, and after supper he'd been too tired and sick at heart to talk to Martin or anybody, much less face all the questions: "Now, where you going? What for? It's too late to go calling on Susie tonight . . ."

He'd gone to bed early, waking to the morning of his nineteenth birthday, to be faced with the prospect of a birthday party planned for the evening and a long list of stuff to shop for at Wentworth Harbor after he'd got through selling his lobsters there. Stuff for the party. A list as long as his arm.

"Now, Warren, you quit hauling early enough to get home from the Harbor in time for me to get the cakes fixed. And don't you dare to forget the little colored tiddlebits for the frosting. I've got a great big crowd coming."

"Okay, Ma, *okay*. Don't bust a gusset."

"Don't you sarse your mother. Not in this house!" Calvin had begun spluttering and grumbling, and Warren had known why—Gramp didn't want to give up the binoculars.

He'd handed them over at breakfast, but it had been like pulling teeth.

"I s'pose you'll lug them off aboard your boat. Salt water'll rust out the metal. Turn your back, some lout'll swipe them."

Warren reflected that of course the only place he could use binoculars to any purpose would be aboard his boat, but to hell with it. He'd shoved Ma's list into his pocket, left the glasses on the table, and made for the door.

He'd been halfway down the walk when Ma'd caught up with him. She'd had the binoculars in their case and she'd flung the strap around his neck. "He's been peeking under that wharf and into every window in town, and I won't have it! So there! Now, Warren, don't you dare to be late, for heb'm sake! Susie Wentworth's called up, dear, and she's coming!"

You'd think it was the Second Coming. Susie Wentworth, for suh-weet ker-riced sake! Ma couldn't mention her without sounding like some teen-ager on the TV.

That had been the beginning of today.

Martin Hadley's dragger was gone—he'd left early, like always. His sore feet must be better. Maybe he could run into Martin somewhere out on the Shoals.

On the way out across the bay, Warren switched on his radiophone to see if anything interesting was going on, something that would take his mind off the whole dirty business. It was too good a day to have to think about a man as cussed mean as Justin Bradley. But nothing was coming in except Edie Bickford's morning concert. She was giving all she had to "The Farmer in the Dell," and Warren flicked the switch to "Off." "Damned old nuisance-puke," he muttered.

Warren was salvaging his second trap off Cross Island Cove when he saw the thing again—the quick movement in the bushes, the same tan patch—only it wasn't the same tan. It was lighter, almost white. It wasn't the color of a deer.

He stiffened and stared, the skin prickling on the back of his neck. The trap, still winding in, slammed against the barrel of his winch, tore loose from its warp, and splashed back into the water. Automatically he leaned to throw out the winch gear and stop his engine.

The patch, the movement, had gone. The place was like a tomb, some different from the day he and Martin had been there, when everything that could blow loose had been scaling through the air. Today there wasn't even a ripple on the beach. The kids' playhouse had sagged kitty-corner against the swamp maple tree. The silence was a soundless hum in his ears, a hum that almost spoke and said, "Silence." Something about it. As if the place was haunted.

Nuts to ghosts, but this was a weirdo. Nobody had landed here, or there'd be a boat in the cove. What the hell went on?

He grabbed his binoculars out of their case and swept the shore, north to south. Everything was the same as it had been, so near through the glasses he felt as if he could reach out and touch the trees. Nothing had changed. Yes, by gum! That rickety old punkinseed punt that had been on McCarren's boat cradle was gone.

It was this bit of reality that shook Warren loose from his jitters. Don't take the bastards long, he told himself with disgust. Leave something around, there's always some joker ready to rip it off.

Why anyone would want that punkinseed the Lord only knew. Martin had said it had bottom cracks a quarter of an inch wide. Still, it had been something left unguarded, to steal.

Warren ripped the tangled warp away from his winch, hurled it uncoiled into the stern of his boat. There was a good trap gone, but it wasn't the lost trap that made him mad.

What kind of a slob would you have to be to make off with a dead man's stuff? Before the guy was hardly cold.

He started his engine, went roaring wide open past the cove and headed for Lantern Island, where he had part of his string set along the shore.

I'll bet that same slob, whoever he is, has underrun the house, too. There must've been a lot of stuff left behind.

McCarren had lived on the island since last summer. That day he'd taken off in the gale, he couldn't have lugged anything with him—if he had, it would've been in the boat, though some light stuff might've washed overboard. Stoves —he'd had two—it had taken him a trip each to ferry them out to the island in his boat when he'd first bought them.

It was . . . dammit, it was pitiful. The man's house— Sarah's home—left like wide open, no one around to hand the thief a slam in the teeth. Someone like Johnny Wilson and that fat kid of his. You wouldn't put it past Johnny. Every time he hauled somebody's traps he put up a squawk about his own being hauled the same night. He might be one of the first to call around and see what Will McCarren had left in his house.

Warren's anger clotted in his throat. He found he had tears in his eyes and dashed them away.

There was Johnny Wilson now, just coming around Lantern Island Head. Hauling traps; he had traps set all over the place out here. So he wasn't ashore on Cross Island, not right now. Hey, wait! Looked like Johnny had a tender with him.

Warren reached for his binoculars again. Sure enough. Johnny was carrying a punt across the stern of his boat. Now what would a man hauling traps want of a tender to frig him up every time he put a trap overboard and circled to let the warp tail out astern to take the kinks out of it?

To land somewhere, of course.

Warren kept Johnny in focus until he made sure the man was alone aboard his boat. So where was fat Finney today? He always went hauling with his father.

"Gramp, old jackpot," Warren said aloud, "I'm sure making good use of my birthday present today."

It made sense. Nobody was going to leave a powerboat anchored in Cross Island Cove for all the world to see while he was ashore piling up loot in McCarren's house. He'd drop somebody, come back after dark and pick him up, with the stuff all packed and ready to roll.

I'll bet you that's where Finney is, and I'll bet a quarter that was who I saw ashore there just now. Would I ever like to get my hands on him!

No use to go in there now, without a tender. I could be back tonight, though, with one.

But, no, he couldn't. There was Ma's party. It would be hours before he could get away.

He glared furiously at Cross Island, a good way off across the water. And saw . . . what was it? As sure as God made little apples and crossed them with onions, someone in a whitish jacket was standing on the ledges. Finney, trying to contact his pa? Warren focused the glasses.

After a paralyzed moment, his jaw dropped. His hands shook so that he lost his focus. The figure was moving by the time he got it back. He said, "My God, it can't be."

But it was. Not Finney, nor anyone like him. And not anybody's ghost, that was for sure. Sarah McCarren, walking away, turned and glanced back just before she went out of sight among the trees.

"Well, I can't fathom you," Bess said to Rosie. "Every day you want to go down to Leafy's place and see if he's come back. Yesterday you even ran away to go down there. Scared Mary till she started down the old town road to find you, and there you were, coming up."

On yesterday, the day of Bess's regular trip to town,

she had left Rosie with Mary, as usual, even though Rosie had wanted to go. The youngster seemed to be crazy about sailing, though what she really wanted, Bess knew very well, was to be taken out to Cross Island.

What was the use to tell the child again that there wasn't anybody out there now? Bess had done this as gently as she could; Mary had done it. Neither of them had been believed. Bess supposed that someday she'd have to take Rosie out there and show her.

But I can't bear to do it now, not so soon.

Maybe it was a cruelty not to—Rosie was settling down so well, though; at least, she looked better. She was getting some color in her cheeks, showing the effects of sleep and Mary's cooking. Most of the time she seemed contented enough, played with the coon, whom she had named Roscoe, and acted like any normal child around the house. Then, the moment Bess or Mary took their eyes off her, she was off for the shore, hunting Leafy.

That scalawag, he'd promised to take her out to the island, and she was checking whenever she could to see whether he'd come back. Every day she wanted to go down to his cove.

Since it had got around town somehow—Bess hadn't said how—that the little girl staying with the Hadleys was Bess and Martin's cousin's youngster, visiting from downstate, it didn't matter if Rosie was seen out and around the village. Bess had several times walked with her to the top of the hill, where they could look down and see that Leafy's skiff was still anchored in the cove and hadn't been moved. They had warned her not ever to go all the way down there alone, because if Leafy had come back, his dog Willie would be running loose. "That's a mean dog. A biter," Bess had told her.

"He won't bite me. I like dogs and they like me." Rosie had already seen Willie. She didn't appear to be particularly scared of him. The warning hadn't made any impression. Yesterday, while Mary had been busy in the kitchen, Rosie had vanished and hadn't come back until nearly noon.

Bess, when she'd got back from town, had read a riot act. "Now, Rosie. You are not to go down to Leafy's again. He's gone, and there's no reason to think he'll be back for a month or two. It wasn't good for Mary, climbing that hill; she got tired and scared, and that was bad for the baby, too. We can't have it. If Leafy did happen to be there with that dog, you and she both could get bad hurt."

Rosie said in a muffled voice, "You just said you knew he would not be back for two months."

Well, that was neat. Bess had had to smile a little and to turn away, hiding it. "There's an easier way to find out without traipsing that hill every day. So I think what we'll do, we'll sail around there tomorrow, pick up that skiff of his, and tow her up into the harbor."

Rosie'd said, "Why isn't she all right where she is? He'll think someone's stolen her."

"You know some nuisance-puke's been bothering her. Hauled her up to high-water mark, where she'd ground out the minute the tide begun to ebb. Dry out her seams and chafe her bottom. That's why I shoved her back to the middle of the cove that day. But she's still trip-lined off and that same joker, whoever he is, could quite easy fool around with her again. So we'll just fetch her up here, where the menfolks can keep an eye on her. Then we'll all know when Leafy comes back, he'll come after her."

The look on Rosie's face had been the same one Bess had noticed when she'd asked her why she'd run away with Leafy—what had happened, why had he deserted her down there? Polite, of course, as if listening to every word. Watchful. Waiting. Eyes like little dark stones.

"Don't you want to go for a sail tomorrow?"

"If we could go out to the island, I'd want to."

"Oh, Rosie, lamb, why would we fib to you about such a thing?"

"We could just go out there and look at my home." It's the same old fib, Rosie thought. They all tell it. The ugly old woman told it first. When I *know* that Hal and I were the only ones in the boat.

"Well, tomorrow," Bess had said sadly, "when we pick up the skiff, we'll see what the weather is."

So we won't go. That's what Leafy said. None of them would go. They were nice enough people, but you couldn't trust them or believe a word they said. Not even Mary, who was the nicest.

Yesterday, after Bess had left for town, Mary had taken Rosie for a ride in the car, up to the top of the Hill Road, to see the new house being built.

"It's almost finished," Mary's said. "And after the baby comes, Martin and I are going to move into it. Would you like to come with us, or would you rather stay with Bess in her house?"

There it was. Rosie hadn't said a word, not then, but when they had gone all over the house and got up to the attic, where a window looked out over the ocean, there was Cross Island, four miles away. "That's my home, I can't get back to. Your husband's got a boat. Why can't he take me?"

And Mary had just put an arm around and hugged tight.

As if that ever did any good.

There had been whitecaps all over the water. She could see the bell buoy out in the channel, rolling and tipping like crazy. "He couldn't land there today. But couldn't he take me tomorrow?"

What a time for Mary to have to blow her nose and not answer. That was why, blow your nose and you can't answer and wipe out your eyes, too. And then say, as if your nose was stopped up, "Let's have something nice for lunch, Rosie. What do you like best?"

Stupid! Leafy'd said, "Let's have a picnic." Rosie had made believe to light up like a lamp. "Chocolate cake? With dark frosting in the middle and white on top?"

"We'll go straight back home and make one now."

"Oh, goody!"

Back at Bess's house, Rosie had waited till she could hear the hum of Mary's electric beater in the kitchen. That kind of a cake would keep her busy for a long time. Rosie was out of sight before the humming had stopped.

She'd been glad Hank and Julian hadn't been around to hear her say anything as silly as "Oh, goody!"

"Oh, goody, goody, goody! Kid stuff, Kid stuff, kid stuff," she'd snorted to herself while she'd made time down along the old town road to Leafy's place.

There, yesterday, she'd got everything ready to go. She'd brought from the shed his oars, his rowlocks, his mast and sail, his rudder. Three trips, back and forth, did it.

At the top of the beach, she'd unlashed the spritsail to make sure it worked the way her sail for her skiff had. It did. You set up the mast, poked the big end through a hole in the forward thwart, made sure it was solid in the step at the bottom. You hooked one end of a long skinny pole called the spreet into the peak of the sail, the other one into another loop tied to the mast. This spread the sail. Then you took the sheet back into the stern, held it in one hand and the tiller on the rudder with the other, sat back, and sailed.

Rosie went over the whole thing very carefully. She'd better, or she'd get a going-over from Dad when she got home. Then she hauled in the skiff, stowed everything aboard, checked the bag of oranges. Some of them felt soft, but they weren't spoiled yet. She ate one to make sure. It tasted fine.

She trip-lined the skiff off in the cove again, letting the wind push it out until it was as near as it could be to where it had been before. No one would know, now, that it had been fooled with.

Maybe tomorrow I can go. Too rough today. Whitecaps all over the water outside Leafy's cove.

She'd hurried, and it had been a good thing she had, because halfway up the road she'd met Mary coming down.

Not today, either, she thought now, listening to Bess's plan about the skiff. And not tomorrow, because that's when she's going to take it away. Tonight, after they're all asleep. Because when else could she ever get away from them? Every minute of the day they knew where she was. If she happened to be out of sight, one of them came to find her.

Warren Petersen stuffed his binoculars back into their case and stood bewildered. That had certainly been Sarah McCarren, alive and well. How could she have stayed alone on the island for so long without hollering for help, which would have been easy to do this morning or on any day when he'd been hauling traps off the cove? He thought with a lurch at his heart that she might be crazy, knowing her family were all drowned. But she hadn't looked it. She'd just walked quietly away into the woods.

Maybe she wasn't alone. Of course, all I found was the boat with one kid in it. Could have been there was somebody else left on the island.

But search parties had scoured the place and hadn't found a soul. Cross Island wasn't that big. He didn't see how they could have missed seeing anyone who might have been there, unless there'd been a cave to hide in or a secret hole in the cellars that nobody knew anything about. And why would they hide, anyway? McCarren . . . with two kids gone for sure and his boat gone, any man in that kind of a bind would've been desperate, wild to know whether the kids had been saved. If he's on the island now, he's got to have been there the day we picked the kid's body off the beach. Why didn't he make himself known? His own kid.

Whoever was there, they must be eating the bark off of trees by now.

Warren flung the toggle on his last trap overboard and sent the buoy spinning after it. The way the tide was now, he could get up into the cove close enough to heave ashore a mess of lobsters and holler good and loud, ask if anybody needed help.

He found the cove as deserted as it had been in the morning. Nobody came to the beach, and all he could hear was the echo of his voice bounced back from the trees.

Throw live lobsters onto the beach, all that'd happen they'd crawl back into the water. Damnedest thing he'd ever run into, and to hell with it. He was good and sore. She must've known it was him.

He reversed his engine, swung around, and roared out of the cove.

Since Calvin's building had collapsed, neighbors had helped to clear away the mess, and carpenters were already at work, but Calvin still had no facility for buying lobsters. Charley Franklin up at the Harbor was buying now from the Cove fishermen; he had told Warren that he was keeping account of what he bought, and as soon as the old man got going again, Charley would turn back not only the business but also a third of the profit to him. That was decent of Charley, but then he was a very decent guy.

Warren kept on up the coast. He sold his day's catch at the wharf and was just leaving when Charley called him back.

"Want to sign this, Warren? We'd like to get all the names we can on it." He indicated a paper on his desk.

"Sure," Warren said. "What is it?" He scribbled his name without looking, and Charley laughed.

"For all you know, it's a petition asking you to give your boat to the Dorcas Society to have picnics on. Why don't you read it?"

It was a letter to Justin Bradley, asking him to resign, already with a long tail of names, headed by Calvin's and Alby Spicer's.

So this was what Gramp had been coming at that day down at the wharf. The day he told me about half of it and then treated me like a kid. Asked me what I wanted for my birthday. Apparently everybody at the Cove had been asked to sign it; all the names were there.

"You folks down at the Cove kind of got the jump on us," Charley said. He began to chuckle. "On account of all your phones are on the same line. Old Calvin. I sure get a boot out of him."

"Gramp? Sure, I do, too. He's slipping some, though. Getting kind of vague—"

"The hell he is! He's got more on the ball right now than anyone I know of. He ain't saying so, but he's the one's got Justin pinned to the wall. So don't you know anything about this?"

"Oh, he don't tell me much. Thinks I'm too young to know anything, I guess."

Charley grinned at him. "Well, you do sign your name before you've found out what you've signed it to."

"Gramp bring that in here?" Warren, stinging a little, decided that if both Gramp and Charley felt that way about him, he was going to have as little as possible to do with the whole thing.

"No, Alby brought the petition. Told me anybody could go up to the records room at the Court House and find out the lowdown on Cross Island. So I was int'rested and I did. And the first thing the girl there said to me was, 'What gives with that island, anyway? Somebody find gold down there?' "

Warren perked up a little, and Charley, seeing his interest, went on.

"Seems I was the fourth person been in there asking about it." He held up four fingers and counted on them. "One, there was Will McCarren, he had the title searched. Two, Justin. She was well acquainted with him, because he'd been in and around the records room, asking to see deeds to offshore islands and shore property, including Cross Island. Number Three was an old man with a loud voice. Used it. Swore a lot."

"Uh-huh. Gramp," Warren said.

"And four, that was me. Now, I don't blame a man for taking care of his business, looking ahead, making money where he can. Long as Justin did that, it was his own affair and nobody else's. I came away from there kind of mad, but wondering just where the bug in the stump was. It was Alby's phone call to Jerry Cross in Singer, Oregon, that capped up the whole thing. That was when I got real mad. So did a lot of people. They're still mad."

"I thought everybody was anyway," Warren said. "There was talk enough about what Bradley did to McCarren."

"Sure. Talk. But no proof. No real lowdown. Calvin got hold of Jerry's address, off the deed, I guess. He and Alby foregathered one afternoon and got Ma Bell to hunt up his phone number for them. And Alby called Jerry up." Charley choked and started to laugh. "Them two coony old boys," he went on. "They did this in the afternoon, when all the ladies down to the Cove had got all the chores done up and didn't have a thing to do but listen to the phone calls on the line. When this one come along, it was a *toll call*, and there wasn't a receiver in the place that wasn't sizzling out steam. By the time Alby got through, all and sundry had the facts about the underhanded way Justin tried to buy Cross Island out from under Will McCarren. Added to what we already know about what took place out on that island, them facts ain't pretty. I ain't about to peddle them and get sued for slander. And Calvin and Alby ain't said a word around town. Haven't had to. It wasn't their fault if the ladies listened in on a private toll call. Funny you ain't heard more about it, Warren."

"I've heard some of it. Enough to make me blistering mad. Gramp could've told me, but I guess he thinks I'm still wet behind the ears."

Charley looked at him thoughtfully. "Not too," he said, and went on. "McCarren had an option, first refusal. He wrote Jerry that he'd about made up his mind and was having the title searched. Meantime, Jerry got two letters from Justin telling what a thief and a hoodlum McCarren was, all that, not to be trusted, and making Jerry an offer. Jerry wrote him he was waiting to hear McCarren's final word on it, and about that time he got Justin's third letter, saying McCarren was dead. That's about it, Warren. What Alby told me. Said to keep my mouth shut. Justin's a well-known sue-er."

"Sewer is right," Warren said. "Thanks, Charley. I appreciate it. Your telling me, I mean."

"So what with your grampop's brains, which you say he ain't got many left of, and which you show signs of, we've all got a nice fat pry, and our job now's to find someone to take Justin's place when he resigns. You got any ideas on who?"

Pleased to be asked, Warren said, "You'd be a good one."

"Fat chance. You crazy? I've got my hands full with my own business."

"Shoot, I don't know. Martin Hadley's the only one I can think of."

"H'm. I wonder . . ." Charley sat silent, thinking. "Now, I just wonder if we could get a Cove man elected. For once."

He didn't seem to have any more to say, and Warren glanced at his watch. Gee, he'd better get hopping. He'd spent more time here than he'd realized, and if he was late getting home, Ma'd tear his shirttail off. He said, "See ya, Charley," and went off out, headed for the supermarket.

He wandered up and down the aisles with Josie's list in his hand, ending up at the meat counter. Twenty pounds of spareribs—wow! Some party. His mouth watered as he dumped the spareribs into the shopping cart. Special birthday feed, something he liked best, next to steak. Ma could sure do a job on a barbecue sauce.

He paused, looking soberly along the succulent length of the meat counter.

If I'm this starved after a good stout breakfast, four roast beef sandwiches, pie, and coffee out of my lunch bucket, what would I feel like if I'd had to eat the bark off of trees? What did I have to be sore about? How dumb could a guy get?

Anyone marooned on Cross Island would be a sitting duck, especially Sarah, if she was alone. She'd be scared to death, and with reason, and the reason had to be Justin Bradley. Maybe she wouldn't feel she could trust anyone after the way that slob had tramped all over her father.

Warren bought steaks. A ten-pound bag of potatoes. Bread. Butter. Eggs and bacon. A box of chocolate bars. Sarah'd need other stuff probably, but nobody'd starve once he got this lot out to the island.

He'd have to go to the party. Ma'd been stretched out straight cooking for it. She had invited a big batch of people. He might have to take Susie Wentworth home; she'd be there with the bells on. Ma had it all set up between him and Susie, and he didn't doubt that Susie herself had a few ideas about it. He guessed she had reason to. But after that . . . it was a swell night for a moonlight ride out to Cross Island, and not with her, either.

Warren suddenly stopped dead in his tracks as he realized why. A lady coming along behind him, stepping spry with a shopping cart, bumped it hard into him, glared as she pulled back, and went by. "For heaven's sake, sonny! Blow your horn, can't you?" Warren didn't even hear her.

"For ker-riced sweet sake! I'm in love," he told himself with amazement. "I'm in love with Sarah McCarren!" Not realizing that he'd said it aloud.

The lady looked back and grinned. "Okay, I'll forgive you," she said. "But stick to shopping carts. Don't drive your car."

The party, with all of Josie's culinary clout behind it, was a tremendous success. She filled her guests so full of barbecue, raised rolls, salad, coffee, and birthday cake that nobody had any room for the second cake she'd made in case she ran out. A fabulous triple-layer caramel cake remained in untouched glory on the kitchen counter after the last guest had gone.

Warren found at the end that he didn't have to take Susie home after all. He'd given her some time during the early part of the evening, but when Martin Hadley turned up at the party, Warren buttonholed him and got him outside for a private talk.

"Let's go sit in the jeep," he told Martin. "She's around back."

"Something on your mind?" Martin said, settling down in the seat beside him.

"You weren't around the day Gramp sounded off down at the wharf."

"No. But I know about it."

"Sometimes when I make up my mind he's gone bananas, I find out he's still got a brain if he wants to use it."

"Don't make any mistake about that," Martin said.

"I guess he started something, in a kind of backhanded way."

"I'll say he did. There isn't a doubt now that Bradley saw a dollar getting away from him and used his authority as a town officer to shove Will McCarren off Cross Island." Martin's voice tightened. "Mary and Bess went to the McCarren youngster's funeral. I would have if I hadn't been laid up. People were pretty mad then. Now they know more, they're a lot madder. Justin's going to have to resign."

"You think he will?"

"Hard to say. Bradley's a tough customer. I don't suppose he thought McCarren would have lit out in that gale, and I'm not sure, myself, that he did it because he was scared of Bradley. He was quite a boy, McCarren. Could be, he had another reason for not wanting trouble. Didn't want publicity. Didn't want to be found. That accident was in the newspapers. If he'd had friends or relatives who knew where he was, it's funny none of them showed up here."

"Could be," Warren said. He hadn't thought of that. What he'd wanted to talk to Martin about had been Sarah. It had been on the tip of his tongue. Now he had to think twice about telling anyone.

I haven't any right to, until I know more. Maybe I'll see her tonight and she'll tell me, and I can help somehow.

"Hell and damnation!" Martin said. "What makes me mad is the way they lied to him. Take the school law—I got what that is out of Mary. Sure you wonder why a man doesn't make arrangements to send his kids to school. But if he lives in a place like Cross Island or, say, the backwoods, where he can't make daily trips to a schoolhouse, the law allows him to teach his kids himself if he's qualified. Which McCarren was. Bess told me he was a certified teacher. You had something you wanted to tell me, Warren."

Warren had to think fast. "Only . . . I heard talk

about Bradley resigning. Wondered if you'd have any ideas about who could take his place. Charley was asking me if I had."

"Lord, no. It's way out of my line of country. I know there'll have to be a special Town Meeting to elect a new Selectman, that's about all I know. Ask your grandfather. He and Alby are into it over their boot tops. They ought to be able to come up with somebody who isn't a crook. At least, a known crook."

"You wouldn't consider—"

"Me? Good God, no. Who put that notion into your head?"

"Well, I was talking with Charley—"

"Charley Franklin's a good one to talk. What the hell does he think he's doing, getting you to ask me? He's the logical one—ought to do it himself. Wentworth Harbor man, well liked—Hell, a Cove man hasn't held office since Moses Gwinn." Martin levered himself out of the jeep, putting his feet down carefully to make sure the ground was smooth where he stepped. "Feet still tender," he said, grinning back at Warren. "You get to be twenty-one, Warren, and you run for office. See ya, boy." He limped away toward his car, parked along the street.

Warren watched him go. Ought to be him, he thought. And he could do it, too. Easy, one hand.

The party was breaking up. Groups of people came out of the house, talking and laughing. Warren sat where he was until the last voice had died away.

Josie began as soon as he came in at the door. "Now, Warren, I can't see what got into you to act so standoffish with Susie."

"Well, I didn't. She gone? I was going to take her home."

"You know she's gone. Her feelings is real hurt." Josie sighed. "I'll just have to fix things up with the Wentworths tomorrow." She began to pack the leftover cake into a basket. "Snf! I think you're using that girl meager, and I don't care for it."

Calvin put in his two cents. "I ain't about to stand for you playing fast and loose with Jed Wentworth's girl," he roared.

"You two look here," Warren said. "I'm nineteen years old. If I want to go with a girl, I will. If I want to attend to some private business, anytime, I'm going to, without having to chew over what it was and where I've been."

Josie's jaw dropped. She turned and stared at him, amazed. Calvin stood where he was, not saying a word. Slowly his face broke into a wide grin.

"Now, Ma, and you, too, Grampop, tuck in your shirt-tails. You see that moon out there on the bay? You think I'm going to bed?"

Josie said in a fading voice, "Bed's the place for you this time of night." But it was an old tune and played out. She knew it.

"Didn't you ever go on a moonlight sail? Didn't you ever take a girl on one, even on your nineteenth birthday, Gramp? An old rauncher like you?"

Calvin let out a great hoot of laughter. "That's the stuff! That's the bigod way to talk! Josie, shut up and go to bed, let Warren be." He stumped off up the stairs.

To Josie, there was only one girl Warren could be taking out. "Warren, you beat all," she said, appeased. "You take the cake!"

By gum, Ma, I believe I will, Warren told her footsteps receding up the stairs. Cheerfully he scooped up the cake basket and let himself out the door into the street.

❧

Will McCarren announced at the supper table that tonight was the night, and grinned at the suddenly sobered row of faces.

"That young fellow who was down there in the cove hollering today smells a rat," he said. "Next time he comes, he might just be interested enough to bring a tender. I want to get things ashore rolling before the news of us gets out."

"It's a pretty good night, full moon and no wind to speak of," Bill said. "I guess somebody's got to go."

"Right. Can't tell what the weather'll do when the moon changes. If I start an hour before low tide, I won't have a strong tide to buck and I'll be across the channel before the flood tide makes."

Bill was silent. He was trying to figure out what time would be an hour before low tide, and didn't dare to ask for fear of giving himself away.

Sarah, too, said nothing. If I could only have got down to the beach when Warren hollered, she thought miserably. But at the time, she had been in the kitchen helping the boys to cut Dad's hair and whiskers and he'd told everyone to lie low. There'd been no way to get out without him knowing it. Warren must have spotted me this morning on the ledges. And all I did by that, I started Dad off sooner than he meant to go. Only Dad wasn't going. Bill was, and there was no way he could be stopped.

After dark, they all helped launch *Goony Bird*.

"See?" Will said "She floats. We ought to have a bottle of pop to bust across her bow."

Getting no answer, he glanced around at the faces of his silent children. In the moonlight, his own face looked white—strange without his beard. "I'll bring some back with me," he said.

Bill said, "Good. I could use one right now."

"That's on the agenda."

"What time'll you be leaving? Want me to stay up and

wake you in case you oversleep?" Bill had hoped, in this roundabout way, to find out what he wanted to know, but his father only said, "No need, I'll set the alarm. You get all the sleep you can. You'll need it to handle this wild crew till I get back. Good night, now, and don't worry."

He went off to bed, and they all tailed after him.

Bill was into the channel before he realized that the plan, whoever tried it, had been a mistake. Around Cross Island, the sea had been calm, glassy, with not much tide, so that he figured he hadn't been too wrong about that. But out in open water, in the channel, the tide was still running a good clip, with a small breeze pushing it, so that he had to buck both. The breeze had cuffed up a slight chop, and a slow small swell was running in from the open sea—nothing to notice in a decent boat, but *Goony Bird* wasn't a decent boat. She had brain damage.

She had no buoyancy. Instead of rising to the swells, she tried to plug her bow straight through them. He had to dig hard with his oars to lift her up and over each one as it came along. When he missed, icy water slid along her deck and down inside, with him. It was grueling work—the concentration on timing, the heavy pull on the oars, the slide down into the trough, and then all to do over again. And oh, those damn tholepins; watch every stroke or the oars would float right out of them.

After what seemed hours, he was not quite halfway across. He was coming up on the bell buoy that marked the center of the channel. He could hear its *clang* . . . and then *clang* again, slow strokes because the swells it rode were slow. He was dripping with sweat; his hands on the oars already felt numb. His breath wouldn't seem to go down over a sharp pain in his chest. He wasn't going to be able to row this darn monkey puzzle much longer, he knew that.

Clang! said the bell buoy, almost in his ear. He turned

his head to look. There it was, black against the translucent, pale water, little dribbles of moonlight sparking at its base. *Clang!* it said again, and he could see one of the ball hammers swing out to take its turn.

I'm crazy, but if I could get hitched up to that long enough to rest, take the strain off my arms, I might just make it ashore.

But how? *Goony Bird* had an anchor bent onto a rode. It was in the stern, in front of him—he could feel it with his foot. Since Will hadn't planned to anchor anywhere in open water, but intended to leave *Goony Bird* in a safe backwater somewhere, where a stern anchor would hold her until he could come back to get her, he hadn't bothered to rig a bow ringbolt, which would have been hard to do considering the kayak construction of Bill's new deck for'rad. The anchor rode was hitched to a ringbolt in the stern. It made difficulties for Bill now.

I'll have to get as close as I can, grab the anchor and throw it. Try to catch a fluke around one of those iron uprights.

It would have to be quick and it would have to be lucky, because, he told himself, if I move and change what little trim she's got, she'll dig her nose under for sure.

But it was that or nothing. It was all he could think of to do and it was plain nuts to try.

The bell buoy made up its mind first. Not stationary, but anchored at the end of a cable, it yee-yawed with the pressure of the wind and tide, swung one way as far as it would go, fetched up, swung back. It closed in faster than Bill had counted on. He didn't have time to grab the anchor. *Goony Bird* banged head on into the bell buoy's metal base and did what might have been expected of her. Thumped soundly on the nose, she stuck it underwater.

The bell buoy shuddered at the impact, but not much.

Both of its hammers clanged at once, and it kept on coming. The spidery structure towered over Bill, tipped toward him. He had a split second when he could jump before *Goony Bird* was overridden.

Bill caught an iron upright, clawed both hands around it, and hung on. For a moment, as his feet trailed between the buoy's base and the boat, he thought the thing was going over him like a bulldozer, almost with intent. Then it fetched up on its cable, the pressure eased. As it started back the other way, it freed *Goony Bird*. She made a last try—her bow came up under one of Bill's feet. The slight boost was enough to carry him nearly level with the solid iron platform. *Goony Bird* flinched away from his upward kick and with a slow, sodden heave, turned over.

He lay flat on the ice-cold, wet metal, hanging on for dear life. It seemed a long time before his breath stopped choking in his throat and the pain in his chest eased up. Then he realized he wasn't sliding off, that he could stay on the bell buoy in what light swell there was. He sat up.

The full moon was about where it had been. Its path still sparkled over Cross Island Shoals. Wide and glittering, it looked solid enough to walk on. He could see a long way —to the lighthouse on Packer's Point; to the dim notch in the shore that was Leafy Piper's cove; to the horizon out east, which was whitish and still. A flat, black, raftlike thing bobbing off there was certainly *Goony Bird*.

"Sister, did you blow it!" he told her bitterly. "Flat on your belly with your bottom up."

This was probably the last sight anyone would have of *Goony Bird*. He hoped so. But all that time and work gone for nothing. For a while she had been almost like a person to him. Next time, by glory, there would be a steam box to shape timbers, a design to give a boat what she needed against stress. The next boat would ride the water. Like

Leafy Piper's skiff. Like any boat built by a man who knew how to build boats.

He huddled down, trying one position after another, each one more uncomfortable than the last. If he sat up, with his back braced against an upright, water slopped against him; if he sat in the middle, there was nothing to hang onto. At last, he lay flat on his stomach, his feet braced, his hands clinging. And time went by.

After a while, he couldn't feel his hands. He realized all at once that he wasn't feeling wet and cold anymore—had to snatch himself back from going to sleep. Half-conscious, he thought, I've got to move, get up, flap my arms . . . or something. But if I let go with my hands, could I shut them again to hang on . . . to hang on?

The bell clanged over his head. From somewhere came a roaring sound. Thunder? A squall? If it is, I'm a goner. If it tips this thing more than it's doing.

He lifted his head and looked. No clouds, no more wind than there had been. The sea was calm, except for cat's-paws and a light swell. The roaring sound was the engine of a powerboat, wide open, passing the bell buoy not more than a hundred yards away.

Bill tried to jump up fast, but his knees wouldn't work. The yell he tried to give came out as a hoarse squawk he could hardly hear himself. He looked hopelessly after the boat, seeing its running lights diminish, hearing the sound of its passing fade. No use to holler, anyway, because that had been Warren Petersen, who couldn't have heard a gun go off over the racket his big diesel made, who, seeing the bell buoy almost every day of his life, probably wouldn't have given a second glance unless it wasn't there.

Bill clutched hard at his iron upright support and hung on, praying that the boat's bow wave wouldn't wash him off. He closed his eyes until it had humped on by.

If I'd only kept watch instead of falling in on myself like a fat lump of nothing!

It wasn't going to happen again. He flapped his arms around his body, one at a time, until he got feeling back into his hands. He pulled himself upright and bent his knees until his legs limbered up—not very much, but now he could stand up if he had to. He tried his voice, yelling until most of it sounded normal again.

After a lifetime, after the whole length of his life, he lifted his bleary eyes toward the mainland and caught the pale blink of a sail.

Warren Petersen, headed out for Cross Island, went past the bellbuoy without even thinking about it. As for the sound of its bell, he would have had to cut his engine to hear that. He did slow down as he neared the island. Off the mouth of the cove, he had his engine barely ticking over. Couldn't go blasting in there at this time of night. If Sarah was alone, he'd scare her half to death. She'd scoot and hide in whatever place she hid in. In case she did that before he had a chance to talk to her, he had a note ready, to leave with the groceries.

> Thought you might need a few steaks. If there's any other way I can help, I'll be off the cove tomorrow morning and you can hail me.
>
> Warren Petersen

He anchored in the cove, slid the punt which he carried across his boat's stern into the water, and rowed quietly ashore. He went with care along the path to the house, carrying his load, watching and feeling with his feet for roots or rocks he might stumble over and make a noise, but the path was smooth, beaten down with use—no sweat. The house was dark, stippled with moonlight, its windows blank.

One of them was open, the storm window hooked back, the only sign of life.

Warren tried the kitchen door. The latch clicked as he pushed, but the door was locked. He realized suddenly that he'd only thought his plan through this far. Seemed simple enough—take the stuff out to Sarah, tell her he'd help. Now, confronted by the sleeping house, all at once he couldn't figure out what would be best to do. Knock? Wake somebody up? But suppose Sarah wasn't alone. What if McCarren himself just happened to be there? Bothered at this time of night, what would he do? Suppose he thought that whoever he was hiding from—if he was hiding—had caught up with him? You had to know a man pretty well to come pussyfooting around his house in the dark if the man was scared of seeing anybody and, let's face it, just possibly might be crazy. Warren backed away from the kitchen door. That wasn't anything to fool with.

Leave the stuff on the doorstep, not bother to try to talk to Sarah? That would make him feel like a clunk, after all the happy thoughts he'd had about her, after what he'd looked forward to. No. He couldn't do that, because here was Ma's god-blasted cake basket. He'd have to get that back to her or she'd shoot fire till she found out where it was, and it wouldn't be at the Wentworths, oh, God; and besides, you couldn't leave a bare-naked cake on a doorstep all night for the skunks and coons—say there were any on Cross Island, he didn't know—but anyway, field mice and squirrels and ants. He had a horrid vision of this gorgeous cake covered with ants. Which, right now, he could sit down and eat every morsel of.

Warren stared at the open window. It would have to be that. He'd have to take a chance on that. Probably it wouldn't go up any farther without a screech to wake the dead. He have to unhook the storm window, tip it back at the bottom, squeeze between it and the sill. Pile the stuff inside on the floor. If he got his head knocked off doing it, Sarah'd at least know who'd been trying to help her.

He was surprised when the inside window went up without a sound. Good, that was one thing. He had to keep bending up and down for the packages of stuff, and each time the storm window flapped against him, making difficulties —what if it fell off its fixtures?—but he finally got things safely inside, dropped his note on the top of the pile, and stepped back with a sigh of relief. Now, hook the storm window back the way it was and— Oh, God, no. He'd forgotten the cake.

The lid of the basket squeaked as he opened it, but in his hurry to get done he hardly heard the sound. He'd have to lean way in there to set the cake on the floor—couldn't let that drop. Besides, it would make a noise. He was halfway in, bent at the hips, his toes barely touching the ground, the storm window bumping his stern, when he suddenly realized what it was that would make the noise if he'd dropped the cake on the floor. That cake was on a plate. One of Ma's fancy cake plates, it would have to be—fixed for the party.

Oh, ker-riced, what now? He hung, stopped cold.

A powerful flashlight beam blazed in his eyes and an icy hand shut to on the back of his neck. "All right, you! That's far enough. Who are you and what do you want?"

Warren squirmed like a worm. He tried, but he couldn't say a word. The beam shifted from his eyes, focused on the floor—on the pile of bundles, the note he'd dropped on top of it, on his agonized hands clutching the cake plate.

"Good Lord!" the voice said. "Don't drop it, son, that looks like one hell of a fine cake." The hand let go of Warren's neck and the fellow, whoever he was, burst out laughing. "Here, let me take that," he said. "You back out if you can without cracking in two. Come around to the kitchen door. I'll unbolt it."

McCarren himself, Warren thought. But when he went into the kitchen where a lamp was being lighted, he saw a stranger, with a face he'd never seen before in his life. He backed up, stammering. "W-who are you?"

"Will McCarren. You know me. Oh. Oh, sure. You've never seen me without my whiskers. How did you come to . . . to do this wonderful thing?"

Mary Hadley had said there was nothing in the woods to hurt you and Rosie had better believe it. But halfway down the old town road, where fields opened out on either side, she saw a big animal. The field, overgrown with dead grass, was sparkling with frost in the moonlight; against it, the big animal stood out dark. It wasn't looking at her. It had its head down, poking its nose into the grass. But as she stopped and stood, frozen scared, it lifted its head. Two big wide ears came up, listening right at her. Then the animal whirled and ran off in big jumps. A smaller one she hadn't noticed jumped, too, and raced after the first one. She saw the pale flashes of their tails as they went up and out of sight behind some bushes.

A deer. And, oh, it must be, the deer's lamb. They had been scareder of her than she'd been of them. Anyway, they'd run first. But maybe she'd better run, too. She did, and didn't stop until she came out by Leafy's house on the shore. The house was dark and lonesome. Foolish Leafy hadn't come back. She was glad of it.

There was his skiff off in the cove, with moonlight sparkling under its sides. In a minute, she would be aboard of it, and nothing could get at her there—no big animals, no ugly old woman, no people who all the time wanted to take her back to their house. The skiff was the safe place.

The tide was far out. She had to plow through clamflats,

which sucked at her boots, slowed her down. The anchor, tied to the trip-line, was fast in mud. She thought at first she wasn't going to be able to pull it out, but at last it came and the skiff came with it. She untied the trip-line, carried the anchor to the skiff, coiled the painter neatly under it in the bow. Her boots, heavy with flats mud and water, were slippery on the floorboards, so she took them off.

With only the moonlight to see by, she found that stepping the mast was harder than it would have been in daylight. It slid through the bow thwart all right, but it tried to fall over and she had trouble setting it into the step at the bottom. There wasn't much wind, but enough to flap the sail, so that for a while she couldn't locate the loops for the spreet. Her weight in the bow made the stern raise up high, where the wind pushed at it and kept turning the skiff sideways to the shore. Before she could get the rudder fixed on, she had to push off quite a long time with an oar.

Then, there she was, with the sheet in her hand, the sail taut and pulling, water making a whispery sound at the bow, and a sparkly wake out behind. Out aft, she corrected herself. She was tired to death and wished she could rest, but out there in front of her now was Cross Island with the moon shining on it.

After a time, she found she *was* rested. She was cold, but she was rested. The island was coming closer all the time. It was home. Now she was beginning to hear the bell buoy out in the channel, and that meant she was nearly halfway there.

But something was wrong with the bell buoy, the way it was ringing. It never rang a regular beat—it hiccuped even when the water was rough. On a calm night, like this one, it would say *clang*, and wait, or *clang-clang*, and wait, and once when she and Dad had been passing it in the boat, their wake had made it ring the first three notes of "Jingle Bells." This was funny, though, almost as if the bell buoy were trying to talk, and for a bell buoy that was crazy. Dad had taught them all how to signal with dahs and dits—you could bang on a board and say, "Come home to supper," or whatever; or if you were in trouble and needed help you could signal SOS.

And now, nearer, Rosie heard it.

Clang, clang, clang. Clang . . . clang . . . clang . . . Clang, clang, clang.

Bill had been ringing his call for help almost as soon as he'd spotted the sail coming off from the mainland shore. The wind, of course, was from the wrong direction, carrying the sound out to sea, but there wasn't much wind to begin with, and this bell buoy had authority. Except in a gale, it could nearly always be heard on the mainland, so this crazy fellow sailing around in the moonlight wasn't his only hope. There must be somebody ashore who'd know Morse code. He had stood up, grabbed a bell hammer in each hand, and rung three dits, three dahs, three dits, until he'd half-deafened himself and was almost warm again.

The fellow sailing the skiff, whoever it was, heard him, all right. He'd headed straight for the bell buoy. Then, as he came closer, he sheered off. Bill's hope dropped into his shoes. The guy must be nuts. He can see me. I can see him. And that, by golly, is Leafy's skiff. But Piper, all hunkered down in the stern, wasn't turning his head.

Bill clanged both hammers as hard as he could. The yell he produced came out first as a hoarse squeak, then, as he got breath behind it, a frantic baritone roar. "Piper! Here! On the bell buoy! Dammit, what's the matter with you?"

The skiff changed course again, but not quite in time to make a successful docking. She plunked bow on into the bell buoy, exactly as *Goony Bird* had done, but Leafy's boat was of a different breed. She bumped hard enough to knock Rosie off the stern thwart and dump the wind out of the sail, but being a workboat, she had tangled with tougher obstacles in her time. Her impact merely shoved the bell-buoy sideways. The sail flapped in Bill's face and did its best to push him overboard. He pushed back, jumped, and landed in a heap on the floorboards of the skiff. The bell buoy, left to itself, gave the boat a cordial tunk on the stern and clanged off on its other tack.

For a moment, Bill, paralyzed with exhaustion and relief, couldn't move. Then a dab of water hit him in the face and he realized that the sail was loose and flapping, doing its best to dip the end of the boom in the water, which was as good a way as any to tip over a skiff. He made a grab for the boom and steadied it, feeling along it for the end of the sheet. What ailed the fellow, just lying there, legs all scrambled up with his own? "Hey, get back aft and steer or we'll be—"

Bill had meant to say "over," but the beller that came out of who owned the legs stopped his voice in his throat and turned him cold—really cold, because there was only one beller in the world like that, a sound that he and every other member of his family had been familiar with for all of Rosie's years.

"Bill, Bill, Bill! I almost left you there. I'm so scared of all of them and I thought you were just another one . . ."

Bill heard about half of this. He had to hustle, scramble over her to the stern, get hold of the steering and the sheet, swing the skiff back before the wind. There was more chop than there had been; the flood tide was really rolling up the channel now. For a moment he was busy. Then, turning, he could see Rosie's face, the round hole of her mouth, with, coming out of it, Rosie's own beller.

My God. It can't be. She's dead.

But it was. No ghost, no weirdo come up out of the water or out of his own numbed and weary mind.

He tried to say how glad he was, and couldn't. Only a

croak came out of him. Presently she stopped bellering. She said, "Bill! You aren't sitting in the middle. You've got us all out of trim."

Rosie. Herself. Hadn't changed a bit.

Sarah had seen Bill off at the beach. *Goony Bird* had seemed to be all right—she'd got him out of sight around the western point of the cove.

Too worried and miserable to go back to bed, Sarah had got a flashlight from the kitchen and walked through the woods to the north end of the island, following a rough path which Bill and the kids had made a while back. The path was full of alder and sapling stumps; the walk took a long time, she had had to pick her way so slowly. When she had got out to the ledges, she couldn't see even a black dot on the water that might be *Goony Bird*.

He had to be all right. He had to be. What it was, she'd been so long crossing the island that he'd had time to row out of sight. Four miles of ice-cold water. Where was he? Was he all right?

The empty dark blue expanse sent back no message except silence, and then, softly flowing down from the northwest, a first, hardly perceptible breath of wind.

Back at the house, she'd thought of waking her father. But why do that? What could he do? Only worry, as she was doing. It would be only for her own comforting. Let him sleep. He needed sleep. She'd gone silently to bed.

How long till morning?

Sarah dozed and slept, and dreamed she heard a boat's engine down in the cove. After a while, voices in the kitchen snatched her wide awake. Bill? Had he come back so soon? No. Not Bill. That was a strange voice. Maybe it was somebody with news of Bill.

She tore out of bed, grabbing a robe as she made for the kitchen door. Warren! Oh, thank God! She said, "Warren, you came! I hoped you would. Is Bill . . . Did you see Bill?"

Will tensed. "Bill, Sarah? What about him?"

She snatched his heavy windbreaker and cap from their hooks, thrust them at him. "Oh, Dad, go after him. Hurry! He took *Goony Bird*. He's headed for Leafy Piper's cove after Leafy's skiff—he wanted to bring it back for you to go ashore in. Warren . . . Warren's boat. Oh, Warren, thank you!"

Warren said, "Oh. Yes, sure. Somebody . . . ?" What on earth was a goony bird and who was Bill? Some newcomer? Some guy, anyway, who didn't make any bones about stealing a skiff. Leafy was gone, and whoever took his skiff would have to steal it. What the hell . . . ?

But she had clasped his hand in both of hers, and her hands were sure sending a message. His arm was tingling up the whole length of it. Was she getting it, too?

She's sure tore out about this Bill, though, he thought. Could he be her boyfriend? Warren's heart sank into his boots. He said stiffly, "Yes, sure. Somebody needs help, we'll help him. So, come on."

He followed McCarren out of the door.

Will stood beside him in the big boat, which was roaring, wide open, toward the mainland. The running lights sloughed off red and green ribbons of color on the bow waves rolling past to port and starboard, split by the following wake of curdled foam. Warren hadn't said much, only, when they were coming aboard in the tender, "What do we look for, Mr. McCarren? Some kind of a punt, I take it," and Will had told him about the punkinseed. Now, over the racket of the diesel, no one could talk and be heard. Faced forward, intent, Warren was watching the water. Occasionally he flipped the switch of his searchlight, swung the beam from side to side.

The water, Will thought. The goddamned, beautiful, bleak, cold water. And the empty islands under the moon.

Think what you would about the offshore islands, love them as you must, they were still an enigma, a mystery. There they were, peaceful and lovely, the black trees with moonlight on them—places for a man to find his soul when he had lost it. But pitiless, silent, saying nothing back to warm flesh and blood. Sufficient to themselves; take them or leave them. People came; built houses; lived there; died; went away. The islands were . . . What were they? The meager answer, the only answer, totaled, which the entire universe of stars, moon, endless ocean ever sent back to any man?

I have brought my children, he thought, not into a desert but into a land of what it is all about, and what it is all about is too tough for me to face.

His kids. He had cursed from his heart the sick society which had done its best to destroy them. He had got them away from that, but at what a cost. They would be destroyed if they lost Bill. And so would he be. Bill, the wild, foolish, brave young devil. Reckless, stubborn, wrongheaded, but too good to be lost and for no reason other than that the world devoured its young. Its own ugly stresses and strains, piled onto a system which for many kids was grinding boredom, were responsible for the wild young cynics, whom society's laws punished, willy-nilly. Even a fool should know that what had been corrupted and lost was the sweetness, the goodness built into all children from their beginnings.

He could see Warren's back, his broad shoulders humped over the wheel. Warren had taken off his cap and thrown it aside. A strip of moonlight trembled across the dark head, the back of his neck, sturdy as a grown man's, but still with the tender, childlike look of boyhood.

This youngster, Will thought, with his goodwill, his compassion. Doing a thing he can do well, knowing he can do it well, and with honor. This is the kind of civilization I have been trying to hold out in both hands to my own . . .

Warren reached for the searchlight switch, flipped it on. The beam swung, suddenly focused. He slowed the engine and shook Will by the arm.

"There's a sail. Didn't Sarah say that . . . uh . . . Bill . . . went after Leafy Piper's skiff?"

Will's wild surge of hope choked any words he might have tried to say. He came alive, leaned out around the pilot shelter. There was the sail, not far away, near enough so that he could make out the outline of the skiff.

"Looks like he made it ashore," Warren said. "That's Leafy's skiff, all right. Two people in it." He opened his throttle partway. The boat closed in on the skiff.

The pale, calm water was different now. Flood tide, sluicing up the channel, had met the wind. The sea chop now was beginning to crest whitecaps.

Will let out a yell, "Bill! Is that you, Bill?" and heard across the closing gap Bill's hoarse, exultant roar.

"Hi, there! Everything's okay. I've found Rosie. I've got Rosie here."

"*What!*" Will had heard but couldn't believe.

"He says he's Bill and that he's got Rosie with him," Warren said matter-of-factly. He didn't know who Bill was and he hadn't an idea who Rosie might be, except her being there had sure knocked McCarren out. He was leaning, half doubled up, against the cheeserind, and Warren stretched a hand to grab the back of his jacket. "Take it easy, Mr. McCarren. You'll be overboard," he said.

Will straightened. "It's all right . . . I'm just . . . just . . ."

Well, there were things to do. Warren let his boat slide ahead slowly and called out, "Get your sail down and row up alongside. You'd better come aboard. I'll take the skiff in tow."

"Rosie," Will choked. He caught her as she climbed in over the rail and came plunging at him. "Rosie. Oh, my God, Rosie!" he said, feeling the wet, cold hands in his, the wet, cold cheek against his own.

She said, "Dad! You've cut off your whiskers! What did you do that for? They were good whiskers."

Be darned, Warren thought. That's his own kid. Called him Dad. Can't be the one I pulled out of the boat. That one's dead. The McCarrens. They were sure puzzlers.

Bill handed the skiff's anchor to Warren and jumped down into the cockpit. "Rosie, big as life," he croaked. "How I knew her, she bellered." His legs gave way, and he sat down hard on the platform. He doubled his knees and buried his head in his arms.

It was Rosie, no doubt of it. She spun around and addressed Bill loudly, through chattering teeth. "Bill, you tell it like it is! You did not find me. I found you!"

Back in the cove, Warren circled to pick up his punt, which he had left anchored off the beach. He dropped his boat anchor, pulled the skiff alongside, steadied her for his passengers to get in.

McCarren stayed where he was. He said, "Thanks, son. If there are any words to thank you. It isn't as if you haven't done enough, but I've got to ask you for one more favor. If I can go along with you tonight as far as Piper's cove, I can return this skiff before Piper has to worry about her being stolen."

"There's no hurry about getting her back tonight, Mr. McCarren," Warren said. "I can do it for you if you want me to, but Leafy's away, upcountry somewhere. He won't even know she's been borrowed."

"Thank you for calling it that. But that's not what most people would think. I expect you're wondering what this is all about. We've been pretty desperate, had it pull-devil, pull-baker, marooned here. What we were trying was for one of us to get ashore and locate my boat, if we can find where she is."

"I know where she is. I could tow her out here when I come by tomorrow. And I can drop Leafy's skiff back there tonight, if that's what you want."

"God bless you," Will said. "Not too much trouble?"

"No sweat. Glad to."

"I wouldn't ask you if I didn't have to," Will said. "We've been keeping out of sight. Had pretty good reasons for not letting anyone know we were still here. If that skiff were here in the cove in daylight, I expect we'd be having some callers. Unwelcome ones."

"No, you wouldn't. Not now," Warren said. "I know who you're talking about, and let me tell you, the whole town's been good and darn mad about the way those two clunks used you. If you have any callers, they'll be folks come to tell you how glad they are because you're all right. But I'll take the skiff back; just as well to. Get in. I'll row you."

The poor guy, he's all in for sure, Warren thought. For Will had flopped into the skiff and collapsed in a kind of heap.

Halfway to the beach, Bill let out a yell. "Hi, Sarah! *Goony Bird* blew it. But I've got Rosie back. This is old Rosie here."

Sarah. Warren could see her waiting on the beach. She must have been listening for the boat to come back. I've got a darn good excuse to come here tomorrow. Boyfriend or no boyfriend. I'm going to give old Bill a run for his money.

Rosie, too, yelled. "You just stop talking that way, Bill McCarren! I found you, and you're lucky I did. Who'd ever think it was their own brother sitting on the bell buoy like a fat sea gull?"

The skiff grounded.

"What in the world, Rosie?" Will said. "What is it?" He had started to get up, but she was down between his knees, scrabbling around under the stern seat. She came up with a soggy paper bag, which she plunked into his lap. "I found the boat and I found Bill, but I couldn't find any jug of water." She jumped ashore and raced up the beach to dive into Sarah's arms.

Will stood at the edge of the beach, holding the paper bag. He choked a little, and Warren guessed he was trying to say something, but nothing came out. The bag, which had had a wet journey in the stern of the skiff, disintegrated in Will's hands. Oranges cascaded down, caromed in all directions among the beach pebbles.

Will said, still dazed, "She brought us herself, and she found Bill, and a boat, and she brought us . . . My God, look at that. She brought us oranges!"

Warren stepped out of the skiff and began to pick up oranges. It gave him a reason for lingering a little in case Sarah came over to talk to him. He found he hadn't needed to worry about it.

She came, running. She said, "Warren . . . Warren . . ." and stopped, he guessed because she was crying. He put out his arms and she came into them. Her tears tasted salt. She said softly in his ear, "Will you come back?" and it took him two deep breaths before he could say darn right he would, what did she think?

The boat ripped through the water; the engine roared, a lovely sound. Alone in his pilot shelter, Warren sang. He couldn't hear a word of his song; he only knew he felt like a million dollars, he felt like singing.

Old Bill was her brother, wherever he'd dropped from. Rosie had to be the little girl he'd found in McCarren's drifting boat. He didn't see how she could be and the McCarrens were still a baffle-o, but so what? She didn't have a boyfriend, not old Bill, anyway.

Exultantly Warren tipped back his head and let go with

the full power of his lungs on Edie Bickford's morning tune,
which, it seemed, must have been rustling around somewhere
in the back of his head all night:

"Heigh-o the merry-o,
The farmer in the dell."

PART SIX

Mary nudged Martin awake, a good, hard poke, and he came to with a jump. "What? What is it? You all right?"

"I *would* do it to you in the middle of the night, Marty. I guess we miscalculated a little—I've had one or two thumping pains—"

"I'll get hold of Fletcher." Martin tore out of bed and made for downstairs and the telephone. He came back, breathless and sweating, to find Mary calmly getting dressed.

"What are you out of bed for? I told that joker to haul his tail down here. He said bring you up to the Harbor, he'd meet us at the hospital. Hell of a thing—"

"It's all right, honey. I know what to expect. I talked it over with him when I was in for my last checkup. First baby—it'll be a long time yet, maybe twenty-four hours. I'll be better off at the hospital."

"I'll get the car out, warm it up," Martin said. "Dammit, if I have to slam you around over those potholes in the town road, it'll be a lot less than twenty-four hours, I'll bet. What's the matter with him? He must be crazy. Meet us at the hospital, for godsake!"

"Call him again and see if he'll have a car meet us at the Wentworth Harbor dock. Then you drive me down to the wharf. You can get me to the Harbor in half an hour or so, and I'll be a lot happier aboard the boat."

Martin glanced out of the window. Light wind, northwest. Flood tide, he knew without thinking. Not enough chop on Packer's Pasture to hurt anything—nothing to compare with those potholes. His boat, opened up, would do close to fifteen knots. "Okay," he said. "I can get you there in twenty-four minutes. Put on the warmest clothes you've got. I'll tell Bess where we've gone."

He dressed, feverishly hauling on shirt and pants, fumbling with buttonholes as he hurried along to Bess's room. She didn't answer when he spoke to her, and he put on the light. She wasn't there. The bed had been slept in, covers thrown back. Maybe she'd gone in to comfort one of Rosie's nightmares. She did, sometimes.

She wasn't in Rosie's room and neither was Rosie.

Oh, hell! The blasted kid had run off again—this was about the third time, poor little devil. Well, as long as Bess knows it and has gone after her, she'll be all right. I can't do anything about it now.

No need to tell Mary, get her all hassled up. She had enough to handle already. But when he got downstairs, Mary didn't seem hassled up at all. She was talking quietly on the phone to Dr. Fletcher.

"He says it sounds like a false alarm but not to take a chance on it," she told him as she hung up the receiver. "He'll meet us himself at the Harbor dock. If I've hollered, 'Wolf, wolf,' I'll feel pretty silly, won't I? Anyway, we'll have a pretty moonlight sail. Look at the full moon—isn't it a nice one?"

Somewhat relieved that the emergency might not be as urgent as he'd thought it was, Martin grinned at her. "Thought you said it was the middle of the night."

The moon was already low in the west, and behind them, as they drove down the road to the wharf, daylight was showing above the trees on the Hill Road.

"Half an hour, and I'd have been up anyway," Martin said.

Mary smiled back at him and slipped her hand under his arm. "Half an hour, and you might have had your heir right in the bed with you," she said. "How was I to know? He might be like his father—gets an idea in his head and doesn't hang back for anything."

Two hours later, in the Wentworth Harbor Hospital, she had the baby quite efficiently. A natural birth, Dr. Fletcher said, and complimented her on her neatness.

Some time before, Bess had been waked up by sounds from downstairs—a solid *thump*, as if something had fallen off a shelf onto the floor; clinkings, rustlings. These were sounds she had come to be familiar with. They followed the investigations of Roscoe, who was very smart about getting into the house. Though how he'd got in tonight, she couldn't guess. Since Leafy's great rip-off, the doors had been kept locked. Roscoe had learned to turn the doorknob, but so far he hadn't figured out how to turn a key, though she wouldn't put it past him. She had locked that door herself. If Roscoe was in, someone surely had gone out and had left the door so he could open it.

She thought, Oh, Lord, not again! and went along the hall to Rosie's room.

How long had she been gone? And where to? Well, there was only one place. She couldn't have got away to check up on Leafy by daylight, so she's gone at night.

Roscoe had knocked a box of oatmeal off the shelf and was sitting happily eating it. "You come with me, you fat nuisance," she told him, and made a grab at his scruff, which Roscoe easily ducked. No use to try to catch him, she knew, unless she offered him something he liked better than raw oatmeal. She produced a piece of leftover meat from the refrigerator and tolled him back into the barn with it. She left him chewing, turned the wooden button on the outside of the barn door, and braced the door stoutly with an old hoe handle. "Let's see you get out by that," she said, and hurried off down the shortcut that led to Leafy's cove.

She didn't know about the fine hole—the drain that led from the cow's stall into the barnyard—but Roscoe did. He had found that long ago. He finished the meat, decided that there'd be more where that had come from, and when Bess entered the woods on the far side of the hayfield, he wasn't far behind her.

Some faint light from the westering moon filtered through the trees. She had to be careful on the path and through the blowdowns—Break a leg, like as not, she told herself—but when she came out on the bank by Leafy's cove, daylight was showing in the east.

Leafy was back. Not only was his skiff anchored in a different place, much closer to the edge of tide, but smoke was coming out of his chimney.

I thought so, she told herself grimly. He's done it again. He'll wish he hadn't.

She strode up to the back door and pounded on it. "Leafy! You come out here. I want words with you."

Inside, Willie started a screaming tumult. His body hit the rickety door with a slam. The latch didn't give, but the door buckled halfway up, enough so that Willie could get his head out at the bottom. Roscoe, standing on the step behind Bess, climbed her like a tree. Bess jumped and almost threw him off her shoulder before she realized what it was and reached up to steady him. He clawed into the collar of her jacket and hung on. She braced both feet against the bottom of the door, to keep it from opening wider.

"Leafy! You tie this critter up or I'll mash his head off."

She heard Leafy's feet hit the floor and his barefooted scurry as he crossed the room. "Let loose of him, you're choking him to death," he said. His hand came down, snapped a leash on Willie's collar. "That ain't no way to treat a poor dumb animal, for godsake! Let loose!"

"Dumb, my foot! At least, I've shut him up, except for a squeak or two. Hitch him to something before I have to stop him for good."

"Wait! Wait, now. 'N there! He's hitched."

Bess pulled back enough for Willie to get back inside. He had evidently had it, for there was no further sound from him. Leafy opened the door wide enough to stick his own head out.

"What'n hell's come over you?" he demanded. "Come ranting and raving round a man's house before it's hardly daylight and try to kill his dog. You gone crazy? Or have you been a widder too long?"

"Where's Rosie? I want her."

"That crazy young'un? She ain't here and ain't likely to be. I wouldn't touch her with a ten-foot pole."

"You did once," Bess said. "All right, Leafy. Where is she?"

"Once was enough. Maybe you want her, I sure don't. Not that devilish little—" He did a double take, thrust his skinny neck farther out through the door opening. "For the love of the long-tailed hangdowns! *What* is that hanging round the back of your neck? No wonder Willie went crazy! And you hurt him for it, too!"

"I'm sorry I had to. It's not his fault if you've trained him to rip up every helpless little animal he gets wind of."

"I got a good mind to let him loose, go for the both of you— Arrgh!" Leafy tried to pull back and found himself in the same fix as Willie had, head caught in the door. "You cut that out now, Bess! Honest to God, I ain't seen that kid—"

"You see how it is," Bess said. "It can get worse. I'd just as soon shove this door clean to."

"All right, all right. I'll tell ya." Tell her anything to get shed of her, he thought. "Slack up, so's I can talk. She's out to Cross Island. I took her there in my skiff last night."

"You left her out there? *Alone?* You crazy fool! You *worm!*" Horrified, Bess relaxed her grip a little. Leafy got a hand on the doorjamb, shoved, pulled his head in, and slammed the door.

"She came pestering around till I like to went nuts!" he yelled. "So I took her out there. You go see. You'll find her."

The pestering. That sounded like the truth, so far as Rosie was concerned. The rest of the tale, she wasn't so sure. She said, "You let me in there to look around. If you don't, I'll set this curiosity shop afire and burn it down over your head."

She would, too, the hefty bitch. Leafy said plaintively, "You want to see me in my shirttail?" When she didn't answer, he set the door ajar and got back into his bunk.

She had sure beat up on him and Willie. She'd shut that coon outside and closed the door or Willie might have raised some Cain, but neither one of them made a sound whilst she went over the place as if she owned it. Even looked up into the loft. He hoped the stepladder would bust whilst she was on it, but it didn't. Only creaked. "Didn't find nothing, did ya?" he said as she came down and started for the door. "Nothing there to find." Nothing for her to find out on Cross Island, either.

She said, "If I find you've lied to me, Leafy, I'll be back here with Oat Baker."

He got out of his bunk and watched her out of sight, up the road to town.

Now, wasn't that a hell of a thing for a tired man to come home to! It had been wet and uncomfortable up in the woods, and first thing, he'd caught a cold and a sore throat. If he'd been able to eat right, if them gulls hadn't got his groceries, he might've stivered it through. It hadn't helped things a bit to have her shut that door to on his craw.

224

What he'd planned to do was stay here a day or two, till he got rested and his cold let up, and then pack his things, some blankets and a frying pan, and set sail down east to another cove he knew about, where there was a shack nobody owned and wouldn't care if he lived in it. Might come back here someday, but no real reason to. No knowing when the hoot 'n' holler after him would let up. And when Bess Bowden didn't find that kid on Cross Island, she'd be back. She'd meant what she'd said about Oat Baker. So what he'd got to do, he'd have to light out right now, this morning. Wore out or no wore out.

Somebody had fooled around with his skiff whilst he'd been gone! She wasn't where he'd left her. She was a lot closer in, almost to the edge of tide, and she was off'n her trip-line, which was wound up into a whirligig, here on the shore. He'd have to wade out to reach her anchor. He took off everything but his boots—no sense to get his feet full of whore's-eggs—and had to wade in not only over his boots but up to his middle before he could reach. He splashed ashore shivering, towing the skiff and swearing at the hooglums who couldn't let a man's property alone when he wasn't there to take a shot at whoever done it.

One thing, just one midgeling thing, on my side. Wind was nor'west last night, but coming up sou'west now. Be more of it, too, later on, fair for the way he was going. So to hell with living any longer in a place where a man couldn't enjoy his comforts and his privacy.

Later on, the sun coming up warmed him. He spread his socks on the middle thwart to dry, turned his boots upside down. The triangle of his sail, tinted pink by sunrise, drew away from shore until, smaller than a fingernail, smaller than a pea, it vanished for good over the horizon.

Bess had hoped to catch Martin before he left the house to go out hauling. His big boat would hustle her out to Cross Island a lot faster than the *Daisy* could. But as she came out on the Hill Road and looked down at the Cove, she saw that she'd missed him as well as everybody else. Moorings were empty. She might have known. A nice morning like this, everybody would have started early. It would have to be the *Daisy*.

Home, in the kitchen, she bundled some bread and butter and sliced meat into a dinner bucket, stowed a carton of milk on top. Mary would be still asleep. No need to wake her, and she'll think Rosie's gone to town with me. We talked about that yesterday.

"Don't hang around me," she told Roscoe, tossing him a slice of bread. "Lord, I don't have any time at all. Mary'll feed you when she gets up. Maybe, with the brains you've got, you'd realize that chasing me all the time isn't such a good idea. You nigh got your comeuppance this morning."

Roscoe had realized it at the time. He had belted for home as fast as he could go. Bess had caught sight of him only twice on the road ahead of her, preceding, this time, instead of following. He, apparently, hadn't remembered any kind of lesson, though. She'd shut him back in the barn, knowing now that he'd found a way to get out of there, but she couldn't stop to hunt for his hole now. And he was down at the dock before she was.

Oh, Lord, she couldn't leave him loose around the wharf. There were two or three good-sized dogs who hung out there every day. Any one of them would make short work of him. Seeing it was her regular mail day, she'd planned to take the sacks with her to the island, make the trip to town on her way back. The mailbags were already on the dock, waiting. When she got them loaded into her punt, Roscoe was sitting cheerfully on top of them.

"All right," she told him. "Uncle Sam's mail's going to be late today. When we get to town, you can deliver it, take the blame."

He told her at once that he was starving—a slice of bread hadn't been any kind of breakfast for a growing coon, and what was the matter she didn't feed him—had she gone crazy?

"You can live off your fat for five minutes, you black butterball," she said.

Aboard the *Daisy*, she gave him a box half full of store cookies. He tore up the box, ate some of it and all of the cookies, and went to sleep on one of the bunks in the cuddy. Perhaps he'd help to comfort Rosie on the way back.

Cross Island Cove was quiet in the morning sun. The beach was deserted, but a thin drift of woodsmoke was lifting over the trees into the light southwest wind. Someone was here—that was chimney smoke. Rosie, please God. Alone, poor little thing, but at least she was keeping herself warm in the house.

Bess really hurried then. She anchored the *Daisy*, hauled alongside the punt she'd towed astern, and rowed ashore. She came out into the clearing and there was the house. Closed, abandoned—as it must have looked to Rosie when she came hopefully home.

"Rosie?" Bess called. "Are you here, Rosie? It's Bess. I've come to—" She stopped and stared. The kitchen door had opened, but it wasn't Rosie who stood there. It was a stranger, a man, who smiled at her and came toward her with open arms.

"Bess. My dear Bess," he said.

She knew at once who it was—she had recognized his voice—but try as she would hse couldn't find her own.

"I thought this bright morning who in all the world I would like to see," he said. "And here you are." He held her off a little and looked into her face. "You're crying. Don't do that. It's such a wonderful day to be happy in."

On the day when Warren had towed McCarren's boat in from the Shoals, he had beached it in the lee of Cousins's wharf in Wentworth Harbor. So far as he knew, it was still where he'd left it, but this morning when he went to get it for McCarren, he found it gone. He docked at the float and strode in on Old Man Cousins, who was sitting by himself in the warm cubicle at the head of the wharf.

"Where's the McCarren boat?" Warren demanded.

Mr. Cousins was resting his breakfast, which, though hefty, hadn't seemed quite to satisfy him. He was topping it off with bananas from a bagful brought down from his house. One of these, half-consumed, with the peel drooping around it, he held suspended before his open mouth while he blinked at Warren. After a moment, he closed his mouth, opened it, and said, "Hanh?"

"I asked you where McCarren's boat is? You know?"

"Nothing to do with me where it is. Was here on the beach for a time . . . for a time. Wait, now. Now, wait. I'm thinking." He took a bite, chewed, swallowed. "Come to me in a minute. Hah! Town fathers took it for salvage. Mr. Bradley come down."

"For ker-riced sweet sake! What right did he—"

"Come to that," Mr. Cousins said, "what right do you?" He grinned with all goodwill. "Have a banana."

Warren swallowed his fury. He wasn't getting anywhere this way, he could see. He said in a milder tone, "You know where Bradley took it?"

"Nope. I don't. Billy! You there? Who bought Quack McCarren's boat?"

His son, Billy, came in from the back shed, wiping his hands on a wad of cotton waste. A rich aroma of long-dead lobster bait accompanied him. "Hi, Warren," he said. "That last batch we got walks by itself, don't it? What you want to know about Quack's boat?"

"Where she is."

" 'N there, Pa. I told you if anybody had a claim on that boat, it'd be Warren. If you'd got here day before yesterday,

Warren, you might've been able to wrinch her away from
Justin Bradley. He said she belonged to the town. Town'd
have to sell her for what they could get out of her, pay for
the McCarren kid's funeral. I see Finney Wilson up 'n' down
by here in her, so I guess the town's already got the money
out of her."

"Okay," Warren said. "Thanks, Billy." He walked off
down the wharf, and Billy followed him.

"You going to make trouble about it, Warren? I wouldn't
blame you if you did. Salvage on her belongs to you."

"Could be," Warren said.

Charley Franklin, down-harbor, would know more about
this, Warren thought. Charley generally knew what was going on in the Harbor.

He found Charley in his office, sitting at his desk and
looking white around the mouth.

"Look, Charley," Warren said to him. "You know where
Will McCarren's boat is?"

"I wish to God I knew where she is now; there'd be
some fur flying."

"It's time some did," Warren said. "You look to be
about as mad as I am. That's as raw a deal as I ever saw
pulled."

"It's about as close to murder as murder can come,"
Charley said. "I'm waiting right now to hear how Joey
Folsom is. Fred said he'd call me from the hospital."

"What? We talking about the same thing? I just got
here."

"Oh. You ain't heard. Young Joey Folsom, Fred's kid,
got beat up last night, shoved overboard off of one of my
lobster cars. Poor little duffer like to drowneded getting
ashore, but he did. Made it to the head of the wharf and
passed out cold. Fred got worried when he didn't show up
home and started hunting. Found him around one this
morning."

Jolted, Warren said, "Fred know who did it? You know?"

"We know. Pretty Dick brought Joey to, enough so he could talk. Finney Wilson and two–three other of them smart-asses been raising particular hell around the Harbor ever since they got hold of McCarren's boat. Night before last, the great game was to sink punts. They tipped over three off the wharf here I know about. Joey was with them first off. Last night they stove out a window here, stole sixty-eight dollars out of my desk, raided one of my lobster cars. Took about fifty pound of lobsters. When they started in on my stuff, Joey quit on them, and they about beat the bejeezus out of him. Pretty Dick took him up to the hospital. He's hurt quite bad. Some fun."

"What about catching up with that bunch? Where'd they go? Didn't Joey know?"

"He talked all he could. Idea was, some kind of lobster feed out on one of the islands. Joey didn't know which one. Don't worry. Something'll hit the fan when we find'em. And we will. The State Police are out, and they've got a helicopter coming over from the Base. They'll spot the boat if it's in sight anywhere."

The phone rang, and Charley reached for it. "Fred? How's the boy? . . . That's good. I'm glad for ya, son. . . . Not so bad as it looked, hah? . . . God, that's a load off my mind. Well, you come on back down and we'll open up a can of . . . What? Oh. Sure, can of worms or whatever you say." He listened a moment longer. "The hell you say. Good for Martin. Tell him to give Mary my love."

He hung up and turned to Warren with a grin. "Well, at least there's some good news this merry morning. Joey's going to be okay, and on the way out of the hospital, Fred ran into Martin Hadley. Mary's had a seven-pound boy."

"Hey, that's okay, that's something!" Warren realized that when he'd come up the gangway, he'd seen Martin's boat tied up on the far side of the wharf and been so stirred up he hadn't given it a second thought. "Pretty Dick must've had a busy morning," he said.

"Starting early," Charley said. "Down here at one o'clock to pick up Joey, and Martin must've lit here poisonous early. His boat was here when I come down to work."

"I'm sure glad for Fred," Warren said. "He must've been half crazy over Joey."

"Fred's spitting fire and brimstone," Charley said. "He says he's going to plaster the Harbor with chunks of Johnny Wilson for buying that boat for Finney. Some punt owners'll be happy to help."

"Where'd Bradley get the idea he had a legal right to sell her, anyway?"

"I doubt if he had an idea in his head except about the seventy-five bucks he got for her."

"Seventy-five . . . ? Is that what he sold her for?"

"That's what the story is. Maybe what she's really worth would be a little too much for him to stick in his pocket without someone asking a question," Charley said. "Seventy-five, that's peanuts. Wouldn't be worth a man's time to put that in the Town Report."

"Oh, God!" Warren said disgustedly. "When are you Harbor people going to crack down on him for real?"

"Okay," Charley said. "I know what you're going to say."

"Well," Warren said, "it's your privy."

"Needs shoveling out, I'll agree. It'll get some. Bradley was on the phone a while ago. He's got wind of our petition. Quite a lot of names on it. Wants to come and talk things over with me." Charley grinned. "Can't think why."

"You can't?" Warren grinned back. "What'll you say to him?"

"Don't rightly know. Probably can't think fast enough to say much. Thought I might need help, so I called Calvin. He's on the way up from the Cove."

"Gramp? He is? With Alby?"

"Alby's out hauling. Calvin's coming in your jeep, he said."

"Lord, he'll drive that jeep up a tree!"

"You worry a lot about him," Charley said. "I don't believe you need to."

When Warren didn't show up with the boat, Will Mc-Carren decided to sail into Wentworth Harbor with Bess. He thought it might be sensible to check up on the boat before he brought her out to the island. After lying idle so long, the engine would need some overhauling for sure, and there was no way to tell how much of his gear would be left aboard her by this time. To go with Bess meant an undelayed trip to the Harbor, which was what he wanted now. He had made up his mind to come out in the open and to come out fighting, should fighting be necessary now.

Besides, he wanted some time with Bess. Throughout the agonized days, which, as he looked back, seemed to have lasted forever, he had thought of Bess—her serenity, her cheerful common sense, her goodwill. She had seemed the one steady rock he'd had left to build on. How much he had built on that rock he hadn't fully realized until she had walked into the clearing that morning. Seeing her, he knew now that he would never willingly be without her again.

Last night, holding Rosie on his lap, he had heard her story of her stay with "the ugly old woman." He had thanked God that Rosie had found sanctuary with Bess, but it was going to be a long time before Rosie trusted anybody again, outside of her own family. Rosie, his brash, confident child, was suspicious now of anybody she'd met on the mainland, even of Bess and the Hadleys. They had all helped to take Hal away; he wasn't here, so they still had him. She had got nearly to the end of the part about Leafy Piper before her voice had tailed off into a murmur and she'd gone to sleep. Sarah had lifted her out of his arms and had put her to bed.

Sarah had come back in tears. "She doesn't know about Hal, Dad."

"No. Apparently she doesn't remember. She'll have to be told, but we can't load on too much too soon. She's tired to death, and God knows what else. It's a wonder she isn't insane." He got up and began striding back and forth across the kitchen.

Sarah's tears had vanished. "She isn't."

"My God, Sarah! That crazy old sadist! What kind of people would leave a child with a woman like that?"

"We know what kind. Two of them were here."

"And Piper was here. The town idiot, or whatever he is. Who knows what he might have done to—"

"Listen, Dad. Our Rosie is a tough cookie. She fights back. She always has. She pasted oranges at Piper and drove him up a tree, not because he was trying to . . . to do anything to her but because he wouldn't bring her home. She bragged about that and laughed. She bragged about how she outfoxed him and stole his skiff. The little heroine, just as proud of herself as she can be. If he'd done anything to hurt her, she wouldn't not tell us. I wish you'd stop hopping around like that and sit down."

"I'm listening." Will had been sweating and had pulled out a handkerchief. "I wonder how sane *I* am, sometimes."

"You're tired to death," Sarah said. "Tomorrow, when you're rested, you'll see that Rosie's come back very much Rosie. Almost too much. She'll brag to Hank and Julian till they get sick of it and rock her back on her heels. And poor old Bill will have to clobber her before she lets up on him about the bell buoy. Our Rosie. Unbearable, sometimes. And, oh, lordy, Dad, are we glad to see her!"

"Yes." For a moment, Will had been unable to say more than that.

"Those two creeps who came here, and that crazy old

woman, they aren't everybody. There's Bess. You have to remember Rosie said Leafy Piper helped Bess get her away. The Hadleys helped take care of her. And Warren came."

"You like him, don't you?"

"I like him awfully. Don't you?"

"I do, and I don't care if you like him a lot, Sarah."

"So, if you look at our . . . our friends, it stacks up to more goodwill than spite and malice; you must see that."

"Yes. I do see that."

"We'll all help Rosie to . . . to bounce back when we have to tell her about Hal. The . . . the way we're all trying to. Let's get some rest, Dad. I'm going to bed right now. Good night."

"Good night, Sarah. Sleep well."

Spite and malice, he thought. And Sarah, child of civilization.

Out of the strong came forth sweetness.

The dead lion in the desert, the honey bees.

In the morning, on the trip across the bay in the *Daisy*, Bess relieved his mind about Leafy Piper.

"He's never been known to hurt anyone," she said. "He's a loudmouth and a blusterer, on account of he's lacking in his sex. He couldn't possibly have hurt Rosie, in the way you're anxious about. Poor soul has to make up for that, I guess, some ways, and hollering around is one way. He's an awful coward, really. Rosie told me how she put him to flight with a bag of oranges."

"Thank God," Will said. "I suppose I was working up a nightmare."

"And not to be blamed for that. I'm so glad you've got her back, Will. I want you to know that we'd have taken care of her, kept her with us, if things hadn't turned out lucky for us. I'm sorry about your little boy."

"I'm having to face it that I'm to blame for that, Bess."

"Blame is a foolish business," Bess said. "Most people have that to contend with when someone dies. They tell themselves, 'If I had done this, if I had only done that.' Whatever they did or didn't do might have made a difference or might not have, but who is ever able to look ahead and see?"

The *Daisy* bubbled along, tacking across the kind of breeze she liked on a sunny day. The bay crinkled with it, running a chop; behind them Cross Island stood out green and gold in a haze of sun.

"Hal was one of the reasons why I came here, why we lived the way we did . . . do," Will said. "Hal, my youngest, and Bill, my eldest, sons."

Bess had been aware of Bill for a long time; she had guessed that Will had six children instead of the five she knew. She hadn't asked questions before, and she didn't now.

"Bill is Sarah's twin. Seventeen, now. He ran away from a reform school work gang. He's hiding on the island, and I've helped him hide. I expect you could call us outlaws, breaking the law. But as for sending him back there, I have to say that I'll fight it every inch of the way and go to jail myself, if I have to, because I think that what I'm doing is right. Criminal? According to law, yes. Unethical? I'm not so sure. There are times when a man has to figure right and wrong for himself."

"Times, there's reason to," Bess said quietly.

"Where we lived, my kids, a lot of my neighbors' kids, were going to hell in a hand basket. My wife, Amy, and I took a long look at what we had there, what we were headed for. On the day she died, she said to me, 'Get them away.' I got them away."

Now that Will's story had started to come, it all came. The tragedy of Hal. The trouble with Potter at Bullet Bay and Bill's catching up with them there. The bad times; the good times. Sailing north among the islands. Cross Island, the clean and quiet place. "The kids liked it," Will said. "At first, I was mortally afraid they wouldn't."

"That surprises me, but not much," Bess said. "You'd think kids that age would miss their friends. Didn't they?"

"I don't believe so. They knew it was up to them whether we backtracked or not. None of them seemed to want to. We were busy, fixing the house—they were learning how to use tools, and I ran school, teaching them basic things they'd need to know. They read pretty well now, and handle a boat, they all know Morse code. Other things. With the boat, we'd go into town once a week, shopping, go to a movie, whatever. They always seemed glad to get back to the island."

"Anyone with the sense God gave a muskrat would say you're doing the right thing," Bess said. "What does Bill want to do?"

"Whether he surfaces or not is up to him. I won't force him, and he knows I'll fight for him if he does. What he wants to do now is work with boats. Study boat design. I can help him there."

"I wouldn't lambaste myself about that if I were you. He'll learn more from you than he would in reform school, I don't doubt."

"You don't call us outlaws, then? Many people would. And have."

"Not anymore."

"There seemed to be more venom in it than was called for," Will said. "Baker and Bradley astonished me."

"There's a reason. Not anything you did. Justin's in the real estate business. He wanted Cross Island. Some say he's got a customer for it. I don't know about that. Being a town officer, he can fling his weight around to get something he wants. Otis Baker's in his pocket. Justin appointed him."

"I see." He said under his breath, " 'A public office is a public trust.' As the man said. Using it for personal profit isn't unheard of, is it?" His voice was quiet, but ice-cold, and Bess, glancing at him, saw that he was sitting stiff and motionless in his seat.

"After what's happened, you'll have a hard time believing any good's come of it," Bess said. "People realize now what happened. The whole town was flattened out flat about you and your children. When people see you safe, you'll be welcomed." She sounded brisk and matter-of-fact, but Will, looking at her, saw that wasn't the way she felt.

He put his hand over hers, feeling it warm and steady. "Bess," he said. "Bess, how wonderful."

Warren's boat was tied up at the Wentworth Harbor dock, but he was nowhere in sight.

"Wonder where he is," Will said. "If you see him, will you tell him I came ashore with you and that I've gone up to the Town Hall?"

Halfway up the gangway, he met Fred Folsom coming down to help Bess with the mailbags, and stepped aside to let him pass. "Good morning, Mr. Folsom," he said.

Fred stared at him without recognition, answered, "Morning," and went on by. Down on the float he appeared to have second thoughts and did a double take. He said to Bess, "Who'n hell's *that?*"

"Will McCarren," Bess said, enjoying it. "Without his bush."

Speechless, Fred dropped the mailbag which she'd handed him and stood staring.

"Well, don't fall down," Bess said. "If you plan to help me, start wrassling mailbags."

But Fred was beyond that. He started on a dead run up the gangway. Too late to catch up with McCarren, who had already turned the corner, Fred stood at the end of the wharf buildings staring after him. Then he came back and hustled into Charley Franklin's office, the bearer of news.

The light was dim in the hall outside the town office. What light there was was behind the man who opened the office door and stood looking in at Florence Baker. He had on a nice dark suit with a white shirt and tie; she could make out that, but she couldn't tell who he was. She fumbled for her glasses.

Some outsider from away. Likely one of them government fellows from the State Capitol come down to hassle up the Selectmen with whatever new and foolish notion them numb-nuts in the Legislature had dreamt out to drive town officers crazy. Or, she thought, perking up, maybe it was that antique dealer Justin had wrote to about the Town Hall clock, come to offer a price for it. If so be it was and he offered five thousand dollars, Oat could certainly yank that clock away from Mary Hadley. After all, town prop'ty, and the law was the law.

Whoever he was, the fellow was letting the draught from the hall blow in here around her ankles. Polite, maybe, waiting for her to say come in. She said, "Don't stand there with the door open, we lose heat. Who are you and what do you want?"

"Will McCarren. I'd like to see Mr. Bradley."

"He ain't here— What! *Who?*"

He came in, and as he did, her heart gave a great bounce, made as if it might hop right out on the desk in front of her.

It was Quack McCarren. Them black hair and eyes, no matter if his whiskers had rotted off in the ocean. It was Quack McCarren, come back to hant people. His ghost. Like Uncle Nails said old Amadee Courvette done after he was dead. He could often be seen rampaging around the Bullet

Bay cemetery. Uncle Nails said he knew folks who'd seen him. And Quack McCarren was old Amadee's relative—them traits run in a family. She began rummaging in the desk drawer for the salt shaker that Oat kept there because he said she never put enough salt in his sandwiches. She found the shaker, shook out a dollop of salt, threw it over her left shoulder, closed her eyes.

The man said, "I want to see Mr. Baker, too. I'd like to pay the town for my son's funeral."

Flo opened one eye. If he could pay out money, he couldn't be a ghost. Unless it wasn't real money, not something that would fly in flames into the air, and him cackling. She would at least put out a hand to take it.

She said, "Oat ain't here, either. When he ain't, I c'lect."

"How much?"

Flo had to think. The town, of course, hadn't paid that undertaker's bill; the money had all been contributed by the townfolks. But who was likely to know, if Quack paid it, too, plus a charge for Otis's time and trouble? She named a sum.

He counted out the money, down to the last penny, laid it on the desk. She reached, but he kept his hand over it. He said, "I'd like a receipt, please."

She could certainly give him a receipt. Nobody'd know a thing about it if she tore the stub out of the book and put it in her pocket.

He took the receipt, looked for a chair, sat down. "I'll wait for Mr. Bradley," he said.

Florence was already putting on her outdoor gear. She wasn't going to sit in the same room with him. He was looking at her funny. Besides, she'd slid his money into her pocket along with the receipt stub and she wanted to get out of the office with it before Justin came nosing around. It was too bad she always had to share everything with Justin, he always took the lion's share. Like that old clock, he'd get three times what she would out of it when they sold it. Well, it was a thing she had to put up with. Without Justin, she wouldn't be able to keep her job, come election time. She said, "Mr. Bradley'll be here any minute now," and scurried away.

The ground swell of public opinion had reached Justin Bradley; he had been feeling it wash around him for some days now. He was planning to run for the Legislature in the fall, and loss of face in his home town might whittle away his chances, not that that would carry too much weight, overall. There'd always be some who'd fly over the house-tops at the idea of somebody they knew—a man from their own town—headed for the State Capitol. He could count on their votes, anyway, but a smart politician didn't gain anything by ignoring the fringes. So far, he hadn't made any public announcement about running for the Legislature—hadn't planned to until he'd found out how the mop was going to flop here in town. He'd been thinking, this morning, that now might be the time to do it. The place, of course, would be Charley Franklin's wharf, where the action was. Most of the fishermen would be out hauling, but they'd hear the news when they came in to sell their catch. Justin had phoned Charley, earlier, and had said he might drop by.

Martin Hadley and Warren Petersen were in Charley's office when Justin got there, and he was surprised and pleased to see old Calvin there as well. Old Calvin knew the ropes about running for state office—handle him right, he might let a man pick his brains.

Martin, it seemed, had just come down from the hospital, where his wife had had a baby. Warren and he were talking about it, and Justin chimed in heartily.

"Good for you, son, and congratulations! Your wife come through all right?"

"Thanks. Yes, she's fine," Martin said, and didn't go on.

Calvin and Charley, deep in conversation, glanced up, but no one said anything in reply to Justin's greeting. He made a note of that.

"Sure, you'll take it," Charley was saying. "Shoot, you'd do the same for me if I had the bad luck to have my building blow down. I'm keeping a third and handing over two-thirds, and I'll do darn well out of it. So shut your trap, you stubborn old son of a gun."

"Great balls of fire, boy, you ·think I'll take it? You've looked after my business for me, bought the lobsters and fish, gone to all that trouble, and now you're handing back what's got to be your profit. The favor's enough. I say God bless you and thanks, and let that be the end of it. Your father's boy calling *me* stubborn, for godsake?"

Justin figured it was about time to make his presence felt. "Thing like that warms my cockles, Calvin. That's just like Charley, he's all heart, every inch of him. How are you, anyway? Mighty good to see you out."

"Why in hell wouldn't I be out?"

"No reason not to, no reason at all. You must've come up with Warren for an outing today?"

"I drove up in Warren's jeep. A jeep's about all that'll make it until you tightwads grab loose of some of the Cove's tax money and put some blacktop on that road."

Well, that hadn't got him anywhere. Justin let it go. He thought, Maybe this isn't quite the right time, after all. But wait. Just wait, something'll come up.

What came up was Quack McCarren, alive and kicking and all dressed up. Not that anyone recognized him without his whiskers as he walked past the wharf building windows, but in came Fred Folsom, with his jaw hanging down to his tonsils, and said:

"McCarren alive, huh?" That'd do the trick. Justin hid his satisfaction under a look of interest and concern, listening while Warren told what actually had happened. After everybody had exclaimed and commented and asked questions, Justin spoke his piece.

"Well, boys, I guess we know how we all feel about this. It's sure mighty good news to me. If McCarren isn't dead and all his kids are safe, except for the poor little duffer who went adrift *by accident,* I don't see how anyone can blame Otis and me for murdering them, looks like. There's been some talk about me resigning."

"There still is." Charley picked up the petition, with its long tail of names, and handed it over.

Justin read it through, glanced at the signed names, and burst out laughing. "Darned if I don't get the message," he said. "Hell, if you want me to resign . . . I can't speak for Oat, but I came in to say I'm resigning pretty soon, anyway, to work up a head of steam running for the Legislature this fall. I've been asked to, and I've accepted. I'd just as soon resign here and now. Kind of thought I'd be useful to the town if I stuck around till you boys got a special Town Meeting set up and a man chose to take my place. Hope you'll think about that and let me know." He folded the petition carefully and tucked it in his wallet. "Guess I'll have this framed. It'll make a nice memory to look back on, time to come."

Nobody said anything.

Justin started for the door, but had to step aside for Calvin, who was also leaving and who would have run over him if he didn't. The old man was climbing into his jeep when Justin caught up with him.

"Calvin, my friend, you've had a lot of experience with elections. Can I count on your advice?"

"Justin, old tadpole, you don't need advice from anybody." Calvin started the motor, set it roaring. His voice boomed out, loud and clear, over the racket. "With that head of hair, you can go about anyplace you want to in politics."

242

Justin went off to his own car. Sore's a boil, he thought. Old Cal. He'll get over it. If he doesn't drop dead first.

Justin himself wasn't sore. Things happened. You didn't get mad. You patched holes in the fence. If you got mad, you had to cool off before you could do that. So first things first.

He ran Johnny Wilson to earth in the warm cubicle at the head of Cousins's wharf. Billy Cousins was there, and the old man; they were all jabbering over McCarren's rise from the dead. The news had traveled.

Good! Justin told himself. There wasn't a more fruitful center of gossip in town than Old Man Cousins's wharf, unless it was his son Floyd's dry goods store.

"Well, fry me!" the old man said. "If it ain't Justin. What you want, Justin? A kiss?" He cackled, and looked around at the others.

A while ago, none of these numb-nuts would've spoken to him like that. Justin said cheerfully, "Well, I could kiss somebody, might's well be you. I see you've heard the news about Will McCarren. Best thing I've about ever heard in thirteen years of running this town. His kids, too—all safe, except the poor little tyke we had to bury. I take it you've heard how that accident happened."

"Heard McCarren didn't shove over," Old Man Cousins said. "You git Cross Island away from him, Justin?"

"Good Lord, no. Wouldn't want to. Cross Island's only one of the islands I inquired about, now that they've turned into real estate instead of old-time garbage dumps. Shoot, you've been in business all your life. You think a man ought to be blamed for running his business for profit, as best he can?"

Old Mr. Cousins looked flabbergasted. He began to chew on that, his underjaw working up and down.

Got him right where he lives, Justin thought. He turned

away to hide a grin and started in on Johnny Wilson. "Johnny, it looks like the town didn't own that boat we sold you. We're prepared to give you your money back. Seventy-five bucks. Okay?"

Johnny glanced at him sourly. "I ain't about to sell her back for that money. She's worth more'n that."

"Oh, no, you don't! Wouldn't want you to get your tail in a crack over that boat on account of me, Johnny."

"She's my business and nobody else's."

Justin's friendly voice became smooth as silk. "Where is she now, Johnny?"

"Finney's out in her somewhere. I d'know."

"You know the State Police are out and the Coast Guard's got a helicopter looking for him?"

"What t'hell you talking about?" Johnny reared up and spun around. "My boy Finney's been home all night. His ma and I'll say so."

"Better not. Your boy Finney's been raising seven different kinds of hell in that boat ever since you got her for him. If I was you, I'd pipe down. Take this seventy-five and pay Charley Franklin for damage to his property and stolen lobsters. Give some of it to Fred Folsom, to help him pay young Joey's hospital bill."

"By godfrey, Joey Folsom's in with that gang just as much as Finney is!"

"You don't say. Now, I'm not speaking for myself; every fisherman in the Harbor is square-toed behind what I've got to say. Any more trouble of any kind, neither you nor Finney'll ever set another trap or trawl in these waters without having it cut off."

"That's a criminal crime! Cut off a man's gear!"

"No worse than hauling it nights, wouldn't you say? A man who does that would be a fool not to realize how many people are onto him."

"You naming me? By the god, I'll—"

244

"I didn't name a name before witnesses. What I am doing, before witnesses, is handing you seventy-five dollars for that boat. She's going back to McCarren, and if you or Finney hassle him about it, I'll personally see that you go to jail."

Justin chuckled to himself as he got back into his car. The way he'd just cut the ground out from under Johnny Wilson would fly out of Cousins's place on the wings of birds and be known all over town before dark. Old Justin's stock would rise with the fishermen, that was for sure. And so far as the rest of the town was concerned, old Justin's resignation would be in the next issue of the local paper, with the reason why. If he did get nominated to run for the Legislature, he could count on a nice fat block of votes anyway from the loyal boys who'd vote the Party ticket irregardless of who ran for office. Any gossip or lies about old Justin would be put down to the opposition's dirty pool.

He went back to his Town Hall office, found McCarren waiting for him, and wrung him cordially by the hand. "Nobody could be happier than I am to see you here in health, Mr. McCarren. There's been a good deal of misunderstanding about your case."

"So it would seem," Will said.

"We've had a lot of trouble with trespassers on wild land," Justin went on. "We watchdogs for the people have to be careful. Damage to private property, fires in the woods and on the islands, and so on. If we made a mistake, we're sorry. No hard feelings. Right?"

Will looked at him, saying nothing.

"They say our people here don't welcome outsiders," Justin said. "That's poppycock. Anyone from anywhere who wants to settle, buy property, pay honest taxes, is welcome as the flowers in May. We are hard on the criminal element, the delinquent kids and the hippie crowd, as a right-thinking man like yourself can see we have to be."

Justin sat in his swivel chair behind his desk, tilting slightly back and forth, so that the chair squawked under his weight. Will stared at him. The jovial, stout man, whose plump, rosy cheeks and clear blue eyes gave out friendly goodwill—a warmth that fairly seemed to heat the air around him. Even the mass of fatherly snow-white curls which rippled handsomely over his ears and down the back of his neck said steadfast honesty and an almost boyish innocence.

But here, Will thought, is the enemy of the world. Here is a rotten cornerstone of the world I ran away from. The man who would agree with you loudly and with all his heart if you mentioned that tax money is the people's money, that a town office is a public trust. And then, election after election, handclaps and cheers for the known crook. He said, "I have a few words to say to you, Mr. Bradley."

Justin lifted a hand. "About your boat. I can guess. Laid there on the beach, seams drying up, kids playing in her, going to rack and ruin. We tried, but we couldn't locate any relatives of yours in Bullet Bay, where you were said to've come from. I figured it was only right to sell your boat to pay for your little boy's funeral. I'm some blazing sorry about that, Mr. McCarren. A tragedy. A terrible tragedy."

Will stood up. "I'll have my boat back," he said between his teeth. "Since I haven't sold her, I don't take any responsibility for the word of anyone who has. I've just paid Mrs. Baker for my son's funeral expenses."

He didn't miss the sudden narrowing of Bradley's bright eyes.

"How much?" Justin said. "How much did you pay her?"

"We are not trespassing," Will said. "I am closing the deal to buy Cross Island. I have always paid the owner rent as he asked for. We do not interfere with the fishermen's gear. The law allows me, if I am capable of it, which I am, to teach my own children. If either you or Baker sets foot on my property again, I'll take you to court."

He walked out, closing the door quietly behind him.

Hey, hey, there's one fancy-pants sorehead. Those kind you might just as well write off. Outsider. Wouldn't carry much clout anyhow.

Still, a vote was a vote. That money Quack paid Flo for his boy's funeral. Take that, enclose it with a pleasant letter to him, saying Flo made a mistake, that the townspeople, out of goodwill, had collected money for all bills concerned and there had been none outstanding. Wonder if Flo gave him a receipt. She'd have been a fool to, but then, she was a fool. He went to check and discovered that a receipt was gone from the book, torn-out stub and all. That figured. She'd gone off with the money. He'd better go clamp down before she got any more notions.

Flo was at home. Justin knew it because the doors were locked—which they seldom were—and she wouldn't answer his knock. He didn't waste any time waiting. He pulled out his jackknife and knocked with it, unopened, on one of the glass lights of the back door. "Flo! Come on, open up! I want it." There was no answer. He knocked again, and a section of the glass fell out. Too bad. Oat would have to fix it. Give him something to do with his time. "You want the whole town to know how you diddled McCarren?" he called through the opening. "You want Otis to lose his job? We could fire him tomorrow."

She was coming. He could hear a shuffling inside there. The door opened a crack and Flo's hand, full of bills, thrust out. Justin took the bills. "Not my share this time, Flo. I want all of it. I know how much it is."

The hand thrust out again with another roll. He pocketed the money, gave the hand a cordial shake. "Thanks, dearie," he said, and went on his way whistling.

Finney Wilson and three friends had had a fine time camping out on Lantern Island. They hadn't been able to eat fifty pounds of lobsters, but they'd had a mighty feed, which had caused disturbed dreams, so that in the morning no one felt like ever looking at a lobster again. The remaining ones were dumped out and left to die and rot in the sun. They agreed that they all felt lousy, but a little pill-popping helped the bellyaches, and when they left the sand cove on the back side of Lantern Island, they were high enough to be regardless of consequences. What if they did get caught? Old Fin owned the boat; there weren't any stolen lobsters aboard, or proof that there had been any. The cash stolen from Charley Franklin's office had been shared out among them. Who was to say it wasn't their own hard-earned money?

The only touble was, they were low on gas. They had jigged around the bay quite a lot yesterday and last night, and the boy who'd been told to swipe a can of gas and put it aboard had forgotten to. So what? They'd go into the Cove and buy some at old Calvin's fish wharf—he had gas pumps. Then they could do what they'd planned for today, which was jig around the bay some more. But passing Cross Island, Finney had a great idea.

"Hey, I betcha old Quack McCarren kept a drum full of gas in there," he said. "Le's go look. Might be some other stuff around the place worth taking a look at, too." His father'd be sore as a boil—he'd had it all set up to go out there some night and see what Quack had left—but the way Finney felt right now, he didn't know as he gave a damn who was sore.

"I d'know," one boy said. "What about old Jeremy's ghost?"

"Shoot, it's broad daylight. Nobody hants nothing in the daytime. I'll bet we could find us a shotgun. Darn good one, too. That bugger was richer'n God."

Another boy said, "He couldn't take it with him, that's for sure."

"Hey, look, there's a chopper off there to the west'ard. Geezus, would I like to have a ride in that!"

"You enlist," Finney said. "Maybe you could get to fly one."

"Ain't old enough. You are, though. Why don't you?"

"Me? T'hell with that. I got a trick kneecap, anyway."

They watched, lazily, the helicopter drift along, far away, close to the horizon, and forgot about it as Finney steered the boat up into Cross Island Cove.

Bill McCarren saw the chopper, and he, too, thought little about it. It belonged to the Wentworth Harbor Base and occasionally flew over the bay or across the Shoals on one errand or another, a not unusual sight. The only thing, if it ever seemed to be coming over the island, you got everybody under cover.

With his father away, he'd thought he'd be as jumpy as a cat, but he hadn't been. So when Hank and Julian had wanted to go over to their brush camp in the woods on the far side of the island, he'd told them to go along but to keep an eye out. He and Sarah had felt pretty relieved after Bess Bowden had told them what a mess of foolishness all this chase after them had been. He himself, of course, had to be careful still, and he'd promised his father to get everybody into the crawl space, anyway, if strangers came visiting.

He heard the sound of the engine in Will's boat and recognized it. Dad must have come back sooner than he'd planned to. Bill started for the beach, then as he peered out through the underbrush, he ducked down. It was the boat, all right, but not Will. Four boys were aboard—Finney Wilson and a part of that gang of his—Sarah had pointed Finney out one day when he was hauling traps with his father off the cove, and she'd told him about the day she'd got mad

249

and chased the slob off the Wentworth Harbor dock. She'd also told him about Finney's gang. "Like ours," she'd said wryly.

Bill didn't stop to do any guessing as to how they'd got the boat. He took off, back up the path at a dead run.

Sarah and Rosie were in the kitchen. Also there was Roscoe, left on the island to comfort Rosie when she hadn't been allowed to go with her father to the mainland that morning.

He hustled the two girls into the crawl space, pushed the ladder up to Sarah, made sure the hatch was tightly closed. He didn't dare to go into the crawl space himself. Somebody had to be out and around to see what the visitors had in mind, and to warn Hank and Julian in case they came back. He scooted Roscoe out of the back door and tried to scare him out of sight, into the woods, but Roscoe took that as a game. He merely went dodging just out of reach around the yard. Bill gave it up.

He went back into the kitchen for a last look around. The fire was out and the stove was cold. Sarah had got the dishes cleaned up and put away. The perishable groceries were in the food locker in the cool cellar. The place didn't look too much as though people were living there, but if these jokers ransacked around too much, they'd see signs.

Bill didn't suppose he could do much defending, outnumbered as he was—that Finney was a big brute, too—but he might be able to throw a scare into them. He took down his father's shotgun from the rack, filled up his pockets from the drawer where the shells for it were kept. Then he went along the path to the tree his father had used, climbed it, and lay stretched out face down on one of the heavy branches. He had the gun loaded and ready to his hand when he heard the "ki-yi-ing" coming up from the beach.

Sounds like they're stoned, he thought with a sinking heart, recognizing some signs he had once known well.

There wasn't much doubt as to what their intentions were. They were after gas and they meant to underrun the house. He heard the talk as they went by on the path under his tree.

The Lord help me if I point this gun at anybody, he told himself. Come on, jail . . . That's assault. Oh, wow! But a few shots fired into the air might send them scooting.

"Hey, look, there's a damn coon," one of them said. "Le's get up there and get hold of old Quack's shotgun, give him something to think about."

They wouldn't find any gun, but Roscoe was as tame as a house cat. Any one of them could clobber Roscoe with a rock or a club. They could sure get close enough to him. I'll have to start shooting right away, Bill thought, watching them go out of sight around a corner of the house. He sat up to do it, and paused, because Roscoe knew an enemy when he saw one. He came pounding down the path, sensed the whereabouts of a friend, climbed the tree, and sat down companionably on Bill's shoulder. From the kitchen, Bill began to hear various thumps and bumps as things fell or were thrown down.

I won't stand for it. They're thieves on private property. They're going to get bounced out of there at gunpoint, and if they holler assault or battery or whatever it is, I've got a story to tell too. He gathered himself up to start down the tree.

A banshee wail came from the house, rising and falling, ending in loud and agonized sobs. Bill froze, knowing Rosie's beller for what it was. He almost dropped the gun, and caught it with a desperate grab. Roscoe fled to the top of the tree.

The four raiders came piling out of the house. They belted down the path, shedding odds and ends of loot as they ran. One of them skidded on the path, somersaulted head over heels, picked himself up, and fled on. A pair of lined mittens, Julian's property, fell out of his pocket. He didn't stop to pick them up.

Bill watched them go. He was not completely out of sight now—his feet could have been seen dangling—but nobody looked up. He could hear frenzied splashings as they ran into the water, apparently in too much of a hurry to climb aboard dry-shod and push the boat off with the oars. Presently the engine started. He climbed down, walked along the path to where he could see the beach through the bushes. He saw the boat making out of the cove. Her anchor, with painter trailing, was on the beach, still tied to Will's tripline. They'd used the tripline to anchor her off and had hauled her in with it, but they hadn't stopped to untie it; they'd cut the painter off the bow.

Some fun. To quote Rosie, it's too bad—that was a good painter. Anyway, we've at least got the anchor back. Half-witted hoodlums!

He was tempted to let go with both barrels of the shotgun, scare them some more, then pulled himself up short as something occurred to him.

That guy back home. The one who owned the store we got busted for. What he'd said. "If you don't want your damned kids shot, you better keep them away from me."

Bill unloaded the gun. He walked soberly back to the house.

Sarah and Rosie had heard the boat depart; they were already down out of the crawl space. Sarah was picking up the pile of loot heaped up by the door. "You know Dad always said watch Rosie or she'd spit down through a knothole on somebody's head," she said.

Rosie, still showing signs of tears, went at once to war. "I *did not* spit! I bellered. They said they'd find Dad's gun and shoot Roscoe, and I didn't know you had it or I wouldn't have."

"Darn good thing you did," Bill said. "Just a gang of crazy kids, Rosie, and you scared the livers out of them. You ought to have seen them hop it." He hung the gun on the rack, began to shed shells out of his pocket, back into the drawer they had come from.

"That's all they were," Sarah said. "Just happy-go-luckies, having fun."

He didn't need to look at her to guess what she was thinking. "They dropped some stuff on the path," he said. "I'll go get it."

Roscoe fumbled at the doorknob, turned it, and came in. Rosie reached for him with a moan of delight. "Poor Roscoe! He's had an *awful* time. What can he have, Sarah?"

"His cookies," Sarah said. "Bess left a boxful. It's there on the floor."

She followed Bill outside, saw him on the path with Julian's mittens in his hand.

"Okay, I got the message," he said. "You needn't come after me."

"Are you sore?"

"I don't know what I am. Boiling mad. Uptight. Whatever you call it. I know I don't like this much when it happens to me."

"It took you a while."

"Okay, it did. But it took me," Bill said.

Hank and Julian came bursting out through the bushes. They were bubbling with excitement. "We saw them running and we hid. Wow! Did they chuck all that stuff out of the house? Look, Julian, there's your mittens!"

"I see 'em," Julian said glumly. "Who was it? Looked like that Wilson clunk."

"It was," Bill said.

"Oh, he scares easy," Hank said. "Sarah chased him once with a gaff. Hey, there was a chopper out there over the water and a big Coast Guard boat heading in from Lantern Island. They must be after somebody. I hope it isn't us."

"Not now," Sarah said. "Nobody's after us now."

The helicopter spotted McCarren's boat before it reached the mainland, and Finney and his friends were almost glad when the Coast Guard boat took them in tow. There was something safe and sane about the chopper hovering overhead, escorting them into the Harbor.

There'd always been talk about old Jeremy Cross's ghost haunting Cross Island. Nobody really believed it. Nobody had ever seen him. But there'd certainly been *something* in that old farmhouse. They'd heard it, every last one of them. It wasn't as if only one had heard it, or had lied to the others to scare them. And it hadn't been any old, old man's ghost that'd made that awful scream. It was a little child, screeching and sobbing, like somebody dead and come back, and it couldn't have been anything in the world but one of Quack McCarren's drowneded kids.

PART SEVEN

The news of Justin Bradley's resignation bounced back and forth across Wentworth Harbor. Some people found it hard to believe at first, but then the local paper confirmed it. Its repercussions were many, some foreseeable, some not. At the Harbor, in places where people were accustomed to see one another daily—the Post Office, the drugstore, Floyd Cousins's dry goods, the diner—arguments started quickly, quickly split in two as sides were taken.

Justin's reason for resigning carried weight with some, who pointed out that it wouldn't hurt the town any to have one of their own neighbors in the Legislature.

Others disagreed. It depended on the neighbor, they said.

A letter signed by the faithful was sent to Justin, expressing confidence, thanking him for his years of fine service to the town. Quite a bloc of voters refused to sign it.

Josie Petersen, at the Cove, out of the goodness of her heart and because she thought Justin might be unhappy, baked him a cake. It was one of her best efforts, a replica of the State Capitol in pure and gleaming white to represent marble and with Justin's name and the dates of his first and last years in the town office in pink frosting on the side. She wasn't too happy with it when it was finished. She had had to make her own mold, copied from a picture, and the best she could do it had slipped a little. The building, made out of hard-candy frosting, certainly looked like the State Capitol, but it also looked somewhat like a cemetery monument with the name and dates.

Calvin, however, reassured her. The dates, he said, weren't death or birth dates, and Justin would, of course, take it as meant. It was a work of art, he said, something beautiful. He volunteered to run it up to the Harbor in Warren's jeep and present it. He even helped her find something to put it in when she couldn't find her best cake basket. It was a hatbox from the attic which for years had sheltered an old beaver hat—not what she would have liked for one of her gift cakes, but it seemed to be all there was. He was roaring laughing when he left with it, and she wondered why.

Down at Charley Franklin's wharf in the afternoon, the fishermen coming in from hauling usually stopped by his office for talk and gossip over what was new. Today, since the town's machinery was moving into action to set up a special Town Meeting to elect Justin's successor, quite a quorum had gathered, the main topic being who was going to run. Warren and Martin were there, and Albemarle Spicer, along with several other Cove men and men from the Harbor itself. Calvin, who wasn't missing a thing these days, had come in early with Josie's cake. It now sat on Charley's desk in all naked splendor—chocolate tiddlebits, artistic curlicues, snowy-white Capitol and Justin's name and dates. Charley had taken one look at it and had completely broken up.

"My God, Calvin! Did you put Josie up to that?"

Calvin said, deadpan, "Why, no, Charley. It was Josie's own idea." He had been appreciating comments as each man had come in.

"That a cake? Geezus, looks like a tombstone. Who's dead?"

"Justin God Bradley! Must be a going-away party."

"Who in hell wants to give him a party?"

"Why not? Thirteen years he's worked for the town. That's what them dates mean, you clunk!"

"Thirteen, hanh? That's a good number to wish him luck with, if you ask me!"

"Sure like to see anyone here do as good a job's he's done."

"Done good? He has? Why that old monkfish has *et up* the town!"

"You think you could do better? Why don't you run?"

"Christ, no! Nothing to do with me."

Not a man, though, who didn't drool, looking at Josie's masterpiece.

"Don't believe that would taste like a marble memorial, do you?"

"If anyone was to offer me a junk of it, I'd be glad to eat up one-thirteenth of all them years, if that wouldn't be more than my share."

"And be done with him, once and for all."

"Who's got a clean knife?"

"Come on, le's bury him."

Charley lifted an inquiring eyebrow at Calvin, who said, "Well, I was supposed to take it to Justin. But if he sees the same thing in it you fellers do, might hurt his feelings some. I can guarantee it's a good cake, boys."

"Okay, if you say so," Charley said. "You could take him the tombstone part, Cal. Don't look as though it'll cut too easy with what I got here." He fished out his jacknife, wiped it on his handkerchief, and counted heads.

The partisans agreed it was a good cake, one thing. Quite amicably they settled down to a discussion of who was to run for Justin's job. A number of names had been suggested, talked over, and rejected before pressure was brought on Charley, who said flatly no, he wouldn't be caught dead.

Alby Spicer said, "Why not, Charley? You'd do fine."

"Don't doubt I would. Be good as most, I guess."

"Then why don't you?"

Charley flapped an impatient hand. "Dammit, you know. I'm a lobster dealer. I do business with you boys all the time. I've got to keep your goodwill."

"Sure. So what? We're all your friends."

"You are now. If I was to run, likely I'd win, hands down. But the first time some town business came up that there was a difference of opinion on and I had to vote yea or nay, I'd lose half my trade, and you know it."

"Oh, come on!"

"Why don't you lay off me? There's plenty of smarter men than I am around town. Go talk to one of them. It's no use to talk to me."

Calvin, who, so far, had been listening, said, "You boys're all too young to remember Moses Gwinn, I guess."

"I recall him," Alby said. "Ran the town for years."

But Alby was the only one who spoke up.

"Yes," Calvin said. "Got his fun out of sticking to his guns instead of knuckling under. I remember one time, some feller with a wild hair came roaring into his office. Said, 'I'll never trade with you as long as I live, I'll take my custom elsewhere.' And Moses grinned at him and says, 'So you do, dear. I'll have to get by without you.'"

It could be noticed that Charley was feeling considerable strain. He thought a lot of Calvin and of Calvin's opinion, and was beginning to glare around. "Getting by them days was a damnsight easier than it is now," he said, "with all a man in business has to contend with. What's the matter with one of you boys running? Time one of you did your share, took a crack at it, anyway."

This was passed over, left unanswered as foolish. They were all interested, they had over endlessly the politics and the affairs of the town; some of them went to vote if they remembered it in time, but nobody wanted to run for office. It wasn't up to them.

258

"Uh-huh," Charley said. "About what I expected. Not a peep out of a one of you."

"When the capable men ain't interested, don't care what happens to their tax money, only to cuss and rave because their taxes go up, you'll likely see a monkfish or two swimming round amongst the eating fish," Calvin said. "Moses Gwinn used to say a town official was a setting duck, shot at by every sorehead in town. The Lord knows *he* was."

"Moses Gwinn!" Charley said bitterly. "Talk, talk, talk, and who do you come up with? Moses Gwinn, dead and gone years ago. You think so much of him, why don't you get after Martin, here? Moses Gwinn was his wife's grandfather. A little of that good old-time honesty could've rubbed off on him."

Martin grinned at him. He hated to see Charley hassled, and he could see that Charley was feeling it. Nobody but him was taking the hassle seriously—everybody knew that Charley wouldn't run, and they could all see the reason why. What it was, it was fun to back somebody into a corner, as Charley was certainly being backed, getting madder every minute. "You know a Cove man can't get elected, Charley," Martin said.

"Didn't take you long to come up with an excuse, did it?" Charley said. "Like everyone else. You could try it, you're one of the old-time Hadleys. Oh, hell!" He banged his fist on the desk in front of him. "I'll tell you what I'll do. I'll draw straws on it with Martin. Short straw's got to run. How about it, Martin?"

Martin gulped. Oh, brother! How did I get into this? he thought. But there it was; he was into it up to his neck. Still, he knew he couldn't get elected. So did Charley, who was trying a fifty-fifty chance to get out of the knot he was in. "Okay," Martin said.

Charley reached into a corner for his office broom. Anyone could tell he was good and mad, the way he twitched out a straw and threw the broom down. He turned back-to for a moment, then held out his fist, two straws showing. "Take one," he invited Martin.

"Now, Charley," Calvin said. He reached and drew, not one but both straws out of Charley's hand. They were both short, exactly the same length, and Calvin shook his head. "Them straws is well known to be older'n creation. Only an amateur would try that. You hand me another broomstraw. I'll fix'em and hold'em."

He turned his back, fished in his pocket for his jack-knife, cut the straw Charley handed him. "Take one," he said amiably. "Who's first?"

Charley was nearer. The straw he pulled was the short-est straw in the world, scarcely an inch long. He stared at it, dropped it on the floor, and stamped on it. He said, "God-dammit to hell!"

Martin and Warren walked out of the office with Calvin between them. The old man was chuckling to himself, feel-ing fine on a good day. At the edge of the wharf, he opened his fist, let the second straw float down to the water, where a slight current of tide twirled it out of sight under the pilings. It also was the shortest straw in the world, exactly the same length as the first one, and Warren stared at it, flabbergasted. "For ker-riced sweet sake, Grampop!" he said.

Calvin grinned. "Sometimes you have to take steps. Do what you can with what you have. Now, Martin, here, couldn't beat anyone Justin's crowd had a mind to set up. But Charley can, and Charley's a good boy." He waved a hand. "Two short straws," he said. "I seen'em work before, when the politics gets dirty."

Mary Hadley had been home from the hospital for a week. Since she had had a not too difficult time with young Walter—Walter, named for Martin's father—she was up and around, feeling fine, enjoying not only the baby but also Martin's reaction to him, which Bess said was a caution.

"For a rough and tough veteran of the Marine Corps, you're certainly smushy about Walter," she told him. "Baby talk, for heaven's sake."

"No, it isn't," Martin said. "I'm just talking to him in his own language."

"Seems he isn't an English-speaking baby," Mary said, smiling at him.

"Of course he isn't. He's a work of art. You don't talk English to a work of art, do you? You go 'oo' and 'ah' and 'mumble-mumble.' I do that and he likes it. He grins."

"Gas," Bess said.

"Gas, nothing!" Martin remained cocky and unashamed, and went off with his chest out.

He was going that morning to drive Will McCarren to Waterford, where Will had business with the Waterford Bank in the final closing of his purchase of Cross Island. Will had stopped by the house yesterday afternoon to ask if he could leave his three youngest with Mary and Bess while he made his trip to Waterford. He didn't like to leave them on the island while he'd be away, he said.

"I've got quite a pile of business at the bank," he'd told Mary. "I'll be better off without my comet tail—if it's not too much to ask of you."

"Of course it isn't," Mary said. "Bess'll be in town tomorrow, but I'd love to have them."

"It's mostly on account of Rosie. She doesn't seem to want me out of her sight, and I thought where she was here with you before—"

"We love Rosie," Mary said. "And I'll be glad to meet the others. We'll have fun."

"Rosie's having a bad time," Will said. "She knows about Hal now. To tell you the truth, I hate to leave her. But I do have all this business and, among other things, I want to talk to the Chairman of the School Board about not sending the kids to regular school."

Mary nodded. "Mr. Duncan," she said. "You know, I think I may have paved the way a little for you there. I know him quite well—now and then I do a little work for the school when they're in a bind. I phoned him the other day about Rosie. Bess and I were talking about your problem, and I thought I might be able to help. I said I hadn't met your other children, but Rosie could skip a grade right now if she wanted to, and if she's any indication, the others probably could too."

Will's sober face lightened. "Why, bless you," he said. "And how do I thank you for that, Mrs. Hadley?"

"Mary," she said, smiling at him. "And I expect, from what Bess tells me, I'd better begin calling you Will. Bring the kids tomorrow. I'll be happy to see them."

He brought not only the children but also Roscoe, who had had a fine time on the island, everyone said. They were all crazy about him, but Roscoe was definitely Rosie's now.

"I didn't want to leave him alone on the island," she said.

She seemed quiet, for Rosie, but her brothers were good for her, Mary could see. They were rambunctious boys who teased her a lot. It was good-tempered teasing, though, and healthy, and Rosie had no trouble holding her own with them.

"We've got to whittle her down to size," Hank said. "She thinks she's something because she sailed out to the island alone in a skiff. Pooh! Anybody could do that."

"Don't be so pompous," Rosie told him. "Maybe you could, but you didn't. I did."

They all sat down to a lavish breakfast. A second breakfast, for everyone including Walter, who woke up and demanded his in no uncertain terms.

"Why's he crying?" Hank was fascinated. He hung over

the bassinet. "See his fingers. Aren't they little alongside of mine!" He offered one of his own, which Walter gripped, stopped yelling and tried at once to eat. Not succeeding, he opened his eyes and gave Hank a long, sober look. "See his eyes. Aren't they blue, though! He wants my finger. Is he hungry?"

"He says he is," Mary said. "He's a big bluffer. But it's a party today, so I'll feed him. Does anyone want more bacon and eggs? There's toast in the oven."

"I do," Julian said promptly. "Could I fry them while you feed the baby? He's going to yell again. Do you have to fix something?"

Mary laughed. "His breakfast is built in," she said. "Yes, go ahead, Julian. You know how?"

"Sure do." Expertly he began separating the bacon slices. "You kids are making pigs of yourselves."

"Says who?" Hank said. "We can't get used to having lots of eats around, Mrs. Hadley. We ate crabs and dulse out on the island. Did you ever eat crabs and dulse? Yuck!"

"It sounds dreadful," Mary said. And dreadful, she thought, it must have been.

"Oh, they were just surviving," Rosie said. "Dad showed them how." Her eyes watered suddenly, but the tears didn't roll down. She blinked them resolutely away. "When will he be back?"

"This afternoon," Julian said, "He's buying the island today. It'll be ours then. Nobody'll bother us there anymore. Want some more bacon?"

"Yes," Rosie said. "And another egg. Maybe two." But she didn't make much effort to eat when he slid them onto her plate.

"We're sure surviving now," Hank said. "Eat what there is or you don't. I'll have the same, please, Julian. Look, Rosie. Walter's surviving, too." He broke down into a fit of giggles and gave Rosie a friendly poke.

"Walter's gone to sleep," Mary said. She, too, was having trouble with held-back tears, which she managed to keep from showing. "Could everyone please be quiet so as not to wake him up?"

They cleaned up the bacon, and Mary didn't try to count the eggs. When they offered to clean up the dishes, she shooed them all outdoors. "See where Roscoe is," she suggested, and produced a plateful of leftovers from the icebox. "He ought to get in on the banquet, too."

They're wonderful children, she thought. The way they comforted Rosie, without seeming to . . . They did much better than Bess and I did.

For a while, she could hear their voices out in the yard. They sounded subdued—no whooping and yelling and racing around, such as you might expect. She had the dishes washed and was putting them away when she realized that all sound from the yard had stopped.

Oh, dear, she thought, opening the door into dead silence. I hope they haven't gone off somewhere.

They hadn't. The two youngest came racing in past her, Roscoe after them. It was a panic over something, she could see. Rosie had her hands full of rocks. The coon skittered into his usual place behind the stove and ducked down out of sight. Julian came in, closed the door, and put his back against it.

"For goodness' sake! What's the matter?" Mary asked. "And, Rosie, what on earth have you got those rocks for?"

"I've got them to throw at him if he comes in here after us," Rosie said. She was white-faced and a little blue around the mouth.

"Why, who? Who's out there?"

"It's the fuzz. The old fat one." Hank, too, was pale and scared.

Julian said, "Put the rocks down, Rosie. He can't get us here."

"Nobody can hurt you here," Mary said.

She saw the stout figure came past the kitchen window, and for a moment didn't recognize Otis Baker because he hadn't got his uniform on, but was dressed in neat gray—his Sunday suit.

"Oh, now," Mary said. "That's only Otis Baker. He isn't even being a policeman today. Nobody needs to be afraid of him."

Julian said, tight-lipped, "Don't let him in."

This is wild, Mary thought. Knowing what she knew, she didn't blame the children, but surely Will McCarren must have explained to them that they had nothing to fear from Otis Baker now. She put a hand on Julian's shoulder, feeling his tenseness through the thin T-shirt.

"Don't worry, Julian. I know he hasn't come after you. He's got no reason to, and never did have one, and he knows that now. He's probably come to see Martin about something. I'll have to talk to him; it's only manners."

"Manners!" Julian said in a half-whisper. "Does he know what they are?" But he moved away from the door. "You two sit still. Don't either one of you so much as peep." He himself sat down, pulled a paperback out of his pocket, and seemed to read.

Otis came right in. He stood for a moment, his eyes roving around the room. "Well, Mary. Didn't know you had company. Entertaining relatives?"

"No," Mary said. "No relation, Otis."

"Well, whosomever they be, I don't know as I recall seeing a handsomer batch of children," Otis said. "That little girl's pretty's a Valentine. How do, kids?"

The two boys stared, not saying anything. The little girl stuck her tongue out at him.

Oh, well, Otis thought drearily. They likely belong to somebody I've had to run in, time past. Wonder who it was. They looked someways familiar, but as far as he could tell, he'd never laid eyes on them before. He didn't like to leave things like that, though, them all looking at him ugly, as if they'd like to do him harm. He felt too bad today, anyway, to go off, leave town, with any such of a taste in his mouth. He tried again.

"Reading a book, I see," he said. "Always like to see a boy reading a book. What you reading, son?"

"Plato," Julian said in a voice of ice.

It wasn't any such thing, Mary knew. It was his book on windmills. She could read the title from where she stood.

"That so?" Otis said. "Only feller I ever knew named Plato was a Greek. Run a rest'runt."

"This Plato was a Greek philosopher," Julian said.

Oh, Julian, don't be a little snob, Mary thought. Not now. Because she could tell by Otis's face, by his eyes, which —now he stood in full light from the kitchen window— showed traces of tears, that something very bad had happened to him, and not long ago. This joviality, put on for the children, was a sham. Otis, from the look of him, was a very unhappy man. It was time somebody put a stop to it. Perhaps he knew these children and was trying in his awkward way to make some kind of amends, but she didn't believe he did. Otis wasn't that stupid—he would have known from the beginning that it would be useless to try.

She said, "These are Will McCarren's children, Otis." She said their names, ending with Rosie's. "Rosie's the one who spent some time at your house." She wondered why she'd thought that would help very much.

"Oh," Otis said. "I see. I wouldn't have known it was the same little girl."

There was a slight flurry from the chair where Rosie sat between Hank and Julian. She had started to jump up, and the two boys had bounced her back into her seat. A few rocks fell out of her lap and rolled on the floor.

"I guess likely them rocks is for me," Otis said. "You can

heave them if you want to. I s'pose you won't believe that I didn't know what was going on at my house until it was too late to do anything about it. I know I saw you all out on the island, but not your faces. I was too shamed to look anybody in the face that day. But even if I'd known you was Will McCarren's kids in here, I'd of come in just the same to tell you fellers that I'm sorry for what took place and that I wasn't all to blame for it."

He stopped and stared at the stony faces. After a moment, he cleared his throat nervously. "I wouldn't be a one, anyway, to tell you you ought to go to school. I ain't never told a soul in this town about it, but me, myself, I can't neither read nor write. Never learnt to."

That was amends, in plenty. Probably these youngsters didn't realize it, perhaps wouldn't even when they were older, but the apology which he had just made to them was magnificent. And it had come hard. Mary, looking at him, could see that it had. It had been the best he could do, and it had left his pride, his self-respect, hanging in shreds around him.

He said, "I see Martin ain't here, Mary. Hoped he would be. I thought he might have Jerry Cross's telephone number in Oregon. I'd kind of like to have it."

"Alby has it," Mary said. "He can give it to you, Otis. I . . . I'm sorry."

"Thanks. I'll go ask him."

Otis didn't say good-by. He closed the door behind him and plodded past the windows. In a moment, she heard his car engine start.

Roscoe came out from behind the woodbox, and the children shot out of their chairs to watch out of sight from the windows the man who couldn't read or write.

Hank, peering, said, "How did he get to be a cop, then?"

* * *

Albemarle Spicer said, "Sure thing, Otis," and handed over the address and telephone number. "Long ways away, ain't it?"

"No long ways is too far," Otis said.

"You going out there?"

"I stood up to Justin today and flang his job in his face," Otis said. "I got a full tank of gas, and when I run out of that, I'm going to sell my car and buy a bus ticket."

Alby stared. "Flo going?"

"Flo's all right. She's got every cent I ever earnt and a stockin'ful of money that I didn't. I'm going to see my girl Isabel and I ain't coming back."

"Sweet godalmighty, man, a bus! I never heard of such foolishness." Alby reached his wallet out of his hip pocket and produced a fat roll of bills. "Here. For godsake, take it."

Otis took it and the goodwill that went with it. "I'll see you get it back, Alby," he said, and wrung Alby's hand.

Florence Baker, when Otis didn't turn up at dinnertime, swore she'd have the skin off of him when he did come. She ate, and put the food away in the refrigerator. Let him eat cold, serve him right. Then, passing through the hall, she saw his belt, with holstered gun and handcuffs hanging on the telephone.

"Why, you careless old fool!" she said, aloud, to him. "S'pose that pistol had worked loose from there, fell off, and killed me!" She took the horrible thing upstairs, hid it in a closet. He was going to do some begging before she ever gave it back to him.

And then she spotted through the bedroom door what seemed to be him, lying on the bed in the place where he always slept next to her. She strode in there, words ready on her tongue. But it was only his empty policeman's uniform, stretched out, with his officer's cap on the pillow. She'd never in her life seen anything that looked so indecent.

"Otis Baker!" she said to it. "Have you gone stark, staring crazy?"

Frank McCarren, Will's brother, sat at his office desk, reading a letter from his nephew Bill. It was a long letter and he had already read it twice. After a while, he put it down and stared at the air in front of him.

That wild kid, he told himself, astonished. I didn't know he had that much decency in him. Well, if it's there, it's about time some of it showed up.

Time had been when Frank McCarren would have been pleased to see young Bill take a thrashing as well as a spell in reform school. Neither, in Frank's opinion, would have done any good. He had blamed Bill bitterly, both before and after Amy's death. The selfish young hophead had driven his father half-crazy at a time when Will had had trouble too heavy for one man to handle—first, Hal, then Amy. In the end, Frank was sure Bill had been responsible for Will's going away and leaving no tracks behind him. Frank didn't discount his own anxiety when, for over a year, he had had no news of Will. He had guessed the reason when police had come around with the news that Bill had run away. Skedaddled to his father, Frank told himself then, and no one knows where. He had been murderously angry.

There were many reasons why he needed to get into touch with Will. The business was doing well; Will's share of profits had mounted up. Meticulously Frank had deposited them, together with the rent from his house, in Will's account. But the main reason was that Frank loved his brother and missed him. That hopeless young skunk wasn't worth anyone's trouble, let alone Will's. Will, a man of courage, honest as sunlight—and our family, the McCarrens, a decent one always.

But here was this letter. Frank picked it up and read again the part that had puzzled him.

> I would like you to see the Judge for me and tell him this. That I'll come back and serve out the rest of my term if it won't get Dad into trouble. That I've been off dope of any kind for more than a year. That I'm studying boat building and design and would like to stay here and go on with it because that's what I want to do with my life, if I have any life left after reform school. I've worked. I haven't been in any trouble. If the Judge can parole me again, I'll try hard not to get into any.

That kid. When he left school here, he was the next thing to illiterate. He couldn't have written a letter like this —not at least what anyone could read. Sharp and to the point, too—said what he had to say, came to the end, and stopped.

Frank liked this. That's one thing that shows up here, he told himself. I could show the Judge that.

The rest of the letter was the news about Will that Frank had longed for.

So that's what he's been up to, what he vanished to. Much as I hated to see him go, I guess I believe that he did right. That it seems to have paid off.

The house. The Survival course. Julian's windmill. How Rosie picked Bill off the bell buoy.

They lost Hal. It had flattened them out.

But Hal was dead before he died, Frank thought. Poor little devil, I guess nobody but Will had any hope for him. I know I didn't.

For a long time, Frank sat, staring at the telephone. Then, thoughtfully, he pulled it toward him and took the receiver off the hook.

❦

"So that's the way it was," Sarah said. "Bill said he'd go back. We didn't want him to. I . . . we love Bill, we want him with us. Uncle Frank wrote that the Judge down home wanted confirmation of Bill's letter, so Dad's lawyer took the whole story to the Judge in Waterford, along with a letter backing him up, signed by—oh, a lot of our friends, Charley Franklin and your grandfather, and Bess and Martin Hadley. And they sent everything, and the Judge down there gave Bill a parole."

"Nice going," Warren said. "So they should have. Bill's quite a boy."

They sat on the sand beach at Lantern Island, where they'd stopped for lunch. She had gone out hauling with him that morning, and lunch was over. There were a few more sandwiches, but they had forgotten them.

"It was horrid, where we lived," Sarah went on. "We ran with a crowd and did our thing, which was what I told you. We got caught. The only difference between Bill and me is that he got caught twice. If you want to look straight at it, there's no difference between us and Finney Wilson."

"There's one," Warren said. He reached for her hand. "I wouldn't ask Finney to marry me."

"I hope you've listened."

"Sure, I listened. Kids'll do anything when they're on dope. There was plenty of it being pushed in the Wentworth Harbor High before I quit there and went to Vocational School, so I know. Some get over it. Some don't. So forget it."

"I will. But you had to know what I had to tell you."

"Okay, so you've told me. There's been some changes made. What you want now is to marry me. And what Bill wants is to build boats, learn how to handle them. Well, look. Anyone who'll try what Bill did in that poison *Goony Bird* is all right with me. If I had a sternman, I could handle twice the traps I do now. If he wants a paid job, he's welcome to go with me. I'd be tickled to have him, and he could learn a lot from me about handling a boat."

"I think if my mother were living, she'd love you for that," Sarah said. "I wish she were. I'd like her to know you. To see us together." Her voice shook a little, and Warren put his arms around her.

"It's . . . kind of nice, families getting to know each other," he said soberly.

"M'm," she said, leaning against him. "I liked meeting yours, the day we took the cake basket back." She felt Warren heave a little as he started to laugh. "What's funny? I liked your grandfather. I think he liked me. Your mother— I wasn't quite sure she did."

"Oh, she did, all right." He spoke through his chuckle. "Ma's a slow picker-upper of events is all. She's been zeroed in on that cake basket and plate ever since the night I swiped them. Asked all over town who had 'em. I think you'd been there for five minutes or so before she realized you weren't Susie Wentworth, and when she did, the rest of it was flabbergast."

"And *who* is Susie Wentworth?"

"Nobody you'll ever hear of again," he said, and stopped her mouth with his.

On the day the carpenters and plumbers packed their tools and went home, Martin drove Mary and Walter up to see the finished house. They walked slowly through the spacious rooms, which still smelt of fresh wallpaper and paint; the old house had taken well to its remodeling.

"It was a nice old house to begin with," Mary said. "I always liked the old-timers."

"They're hell 'n' all to heat in the wintertime," Martin

said. "We can close off the upstairs in cold weather, though, if we want to." With some pride, he showed her the ingenious plywood hatch, designed to fit neatly over the stairwell. "Keep the heat downstairs, where it belongs. Take it off and stick it in the barn in warm weather. We'll be moving in before you can spit. Furniture'll be down the end of the week."

"I almost hate to have any furniture put in here," Mary said, glancing around the clean, bare room which was to be their living room. "It's beautiful, just as it is."

Martin grinned. "That'd be pretty Oriental. I'll get you some Japanese mats. You can fold them up at night and roller-skate all day. Okay, Walter? That would suit you, wouldn't it?" He joggled Walter, who smiled. "See? He likes the idea."

"I'll put up with ordinary beds and tables, thank you," Mary said. "And I'll be really glad to see some of your mother's old things back here again. They always looked as though they belonged."

"Well, they're ancestral, all right," Martin said. "I only hope that old stuff hangs together in the truck on the way down. Maybe I ought to have run for Selectman after all. That old town road is something real, this spring. I could at least have mentioned putting some blacktop on it."

Surprised, she looked at him. "Did you really think of running? I didn't know you were interested."

"Darned if I'd ever want to, but I was almost hornswoggled into it. Hadn't been for old Calvin, I'd have had my tail in a crack. Not that it wouldn't have been anything but a waste of my time—I couldn't get elected in a hundred years." Chuckling, he went on to tell her about the short straws.

"Why, you big frauds!" Mary said. "Somebody ought to go and tell Charley Franklin just what you did to him."

"No need to," Martin said comfortably. "My trouble is, I'm an honest man. I don't steal clocks or kidnap children. I did tell Charley, and I offered to hold the drawing all over again if he wanted to. But he said he'd heard enough about short straws to last him a lifetime. He said he guessed it would take that long to live it down, seeing he did it first and got caught. I said the only difference was Calvin didn't get caught. So we flipped a quarter. Charley took tails, and three out of three it came up heads."

"Whose quarter was it? Yours? Heads on both sides?"

"Nope," he said, grinning. "Tails on that quarter was an American eagle, baby."

Roscoe stood poised on a flat rock, watching the kids unload a catch of flounders for Julian to dress. Cast-off morsels came to him. His belly grew round and rounder. Bess and Will, coming down the path together, stopped to watch.

"Now he's really sitting in a butter tub," Bess said. "No dogs, no hunters with guns, no big black cars tearing down the highway to mash a little critter flat."

"And he can go wild or stay tame, it's up to him," Will said. "Like my kids."

Rosie yelled and held up a big flounder, the one *she* had caught, and Will flapped a hand at her to show that he saw and admired.

"You know, Will," Bess said, "sooner or later, you'll have to let them go. They'll need friends . . . neighbors . . ."

"Of course," Will said. "I know they'll go. But when they do, my hope is . . . that is, my hope is they'll have something built in to help them survive in . . . in whatever wilderness . . ." He stopped and turned to her, smiling. "A smart coon knows there isn't, not really, a safe and quiet place. I know that now, too. Except, with you, I have one. We might even consider moving into the Cove, winters; that's for the kids to say. Why, here in this cove, you know there isn't a place to keep the *Daisy*."